# When Solomon Sings

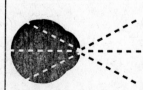

This Large Print Book carries the
Seal of Approval of N.A.V.H.

# WHEN SOLOMON SINGS

## KENDRA NORMAN-BELLAMY

**THORNDIKE PRESS**
*A part of Gale, Cengage Learning*

Detroit • New York • San Francisco • New Haven, Conn • Waterville, Maine • London

LIBRARY OF CONGRESS CATALOGING-IN-PUBLICATION DATA

Norman-Bellamy, Kendra.
  When Solomon sings / by Kendra Norman-Bellamy. — Large print ed.
    p. cm. — (Thorndike Press large print African-American)
  ISBN-13: 978-1-4104-4799-9 (hardcover)
  ISBN-10: 1-4104-4799-5 (hardcover)
    1. African Americans—Fiction. 2. Widows—Fiction. 3. African American singers—Fiction. 4. Christian life. 5. Large type books. I. Title.
PS3614.O765W44 2012
813'.6—dc23                                    2012009268

Published in 2012 by arrangement with Urban Books, LLC and Kensington Publishing Corporation.

Printed in Mexico
1 2 3 4 5 6 7 16 15 14 13 12

**To the Ministry of Melvin Williams
and the memory of Bobbie Smith**

**Melvin** . . . I've long ago stopped trying to justify or defend my heart connection to you. It is what it is, and people's opinions no longer matter to me. I can't expect them to understand. They weren't there on that April evening in 1996, during what was the absolute darkest time of my life, when God used you to breathe life back into my dying spirit. In the prelude of my favorite Melvin Williams album (*Never Seen Your Face*) you said, "Singing, for me, is a ministry. It's about giving people hope, faith, love, and encouragement. And I feel like if I accomplish that, my singing is not in vain." I am a witness to the fact that God has used your ministry to do just that. You are an amazing man with an anointed voice, and I count you among my angels and my heroes. I will always be your greatest admirer, and you will forever be my all-time favorite gospel legend. Don't ever stop singing.

**Bobbie** . . . It's hard to believe that a year has passed since I received the news of your transition on January 25, 2011. You were a remarkable woman who was like family to me long before we ever met in person. Thank you for being one of my greatest cheerleaders and most dedicated supporters. Even in our last conversation, during your time of grave illness, you never once complained. Instead you were still encouraging me to keep writing and publishing great stories of faith. You made my heart sing, and I will miss you always.

# ACKNOWLEDGMENTS

In everything give thanks for this is the will of God concerning you.
(I Thessalonians 5:18)

**My Father, my God!** I can't begin to thank you enough for all that you have done and continue to do for and through me. Regardless of how high I am allowed to be elevated in this journey, you alone, Lord, will forever get the glory. This is my promise to you.

To my home base foundation, **Jonathan, Brittney,** and **Crystal:** Thank you for your ongoing support of my writing ministry. Every writer can't say that they have the endorsement of their family, so I count myself especially blessed.

To **Daddy** and **Mama** (**Bishop Harold & Mrs. Francine Norman**): I love you dearly. Thank you for loving me to life! I am truly blessed to have you as my parents. **Crystal, Harold Jr., Cynthia,** and **Kim-**

7

**berly:** Birth made us siblings, but hearts make us friends. I love you guys!

**Jimmy** (1968-1995): Thanks for being my guardian angel. You are forever missed.

To **Terrance:** What would I do without you, cuz? Thanks for everything!

**Aunt Joyce** and **Uncle Irvin**: Thank you for being the best godparents in the world.

**Carlton:** Thanks for your legal representation. You are so appreciated.

To the dynamic design duo, **Lisa** and **April** (a.k.a. Papered Wonders, Inc.): For nine years, you have made me look fabulous on paper. Thank you for your endless creative genius.

To my sorors of **Iota Phi Lambda Sorority, Inc. (IΦΛ)** and especially to the dynamic divine divas of the **Delta Chapter:** Turtle hugs and White Rose kisses go out to each of you for being my support system, my safety net, and my sister friends for life. I-PHIIIIIII!!!!!

To the awesome women of the other outstanding organizations that have enhanced my life — **Bossettes,** the **Daughters of Christ Sorority, Inc.,** and the **National Council of Negro Women:** Thank you for the wonderful connections, experiences, and memories that will surely last a lifetime.

To all of those who have partnered with me in the ministries of **KNB Publications LLC, The I.S.L.A.N.D. Movement, Cruisin' For Christ, Pages of Grace Book Club, Gospel Girls Group,** and **M-PACT Writers:** Thank you for sharing in the vision.

To **Bishop Johnathan & Dr. Toni Alvarado:** Words can't express how blessed I feel to be connected to the vine that is **Total Grace Christian Center.** Thank you for my spiritual home away from home.

A special shout-out to **Shawneda Marks,** for permitting me to use one of her crazy one-liners in this story. Thanks, girl (you so crazy)!

Last, but never least, to those who provided the music and melody that streamed through my speakers and kept me motivated as I wrote this novel — **Melvin Williams, VaShawn Mitchell, Brian McKnight, Antonio Allen, Vanessa Bell Armstrong, Fred Hammond, The Williams Brothers, Maxwell, Wes Morgan, Lowell Pye,** and **Isaac Caree:** Thank you all! And a special thank you goes to Oprah's Karaoke Challenge winner, **Abraham McDonald,** for actually taking the time to call me and sing "Happy Birthday" to me over the phone. Told ya I was gonna give you a shout-out, Abe! ☺

# PROLOGUE

Cloud nine. This had to be what being on it felt like. Officially, Valentine's Day was over, but what a perfect one it had been! In fact, everything about the past three days had been perfect. The time was nearing one o'clock in the morning when Neil walked — rather *floated* — through his front door and into the warmth of his home. The anticipation of it all had only allowed him two hours of sleep last night, but there wasn't a tired bone in his body. And there was a great deal of irony in that because though there was no fatigue, he felt as if he were sound asleep and having the dream of his life.

*She said yes!* Neil pumped his fist victoriously as the thought filtered through his head.

Shaylynn Ford had obviously not expected his proposal. Shucks . . . he had barely expected it himself. The young single mother of one was visibly shaking from the moment Neil sank to his knee and took her hand in his. But as unsuspecting as she had been, Neil had barely gotten the heartfelt words out of his mouth before Shaylynn tearfully agreed to be his bride. It was just too easy. Neil had sweated for weeks . . . *months.* They had been an exclusive couple for just over a year, but he had known from day one that he wanted to make Shaylynn the next (and last) Mrs. Neil Solomon Taylor. He would have proposed on day two had he known it would be so simple. Now he felt ridiculous for holding on to the ring for three solid months before taking the plunge.

Neil stood with his back against the door for a long while, still trying to digest it all. It was hard to believe he was the same man who had avowed himself to lifelong bachelorhood after the painful dissolution of his first marriage fifteen years ago. And it was equally as mindboggling that Shaylynn had been the same woman who, in the not-too-distant past, was still wearing the ring of her first husband, a man who had now been deceased for more than eight years. When Neil first met Shaylynn, her heart had been so committed to the man who'd left her widowed that, seven years after burying him, she was still insisting that people refer to her as *Mrs.* Ford. As much as Neil prayed to God that she'd give him a chance, he wasn't at all sure of how his and Shaylynn's story would end. But here they were, and their ending was on the threshold of a fairytale.

*Thank you, Jesus.* The praise had been silently repeating itself in Neil's mind ever since it all became official, from the second that he slipped that impressive stone on Shaylynn's finger. Two hours had passed since then, but Neil's heart was still doing somersaults. He had almost not done it. As much as he wanted to propose, and despite all of the rehearsing, the prayers, and the spiritual counsel, Neil had come frighteningly close to changing his mind. It wouldn't have been the first time he'd chickened out.

The night had gone without a hitch. It was apparent that Neil had made good choices for celebrating the day set aside for lovers. First he treated Shaylynn to a special Valentine's Day old-school R&B concert at the Atlanta Civic Center. Using a broker, Neil managed to secure tickets that placed them in first-row-center seats, right behind the orchestra pit. He wondered if Shaylynn, as a woman of only thirty-two years, would be able to appreciate the music, but all doubts dissipated in short-order fashion.

The stage featured a wealth of talent and definitely catered to the ladies. Natalie Cole was the only female to perform on the four-artist ticket. The others were Jeffrey Osborne, Peabo Bryson, and James Ingram. Shaylynn seemed to enjoy them all, but when James took the mic, she got so captivated that Neil felt a twinge of jealousy. And he couldn't believe that Negro had the nerve to step down from the stage while singing his hit song, "Baby, Come to Me," and single out Shaylynn. Neil struggled to hold on to his counterfeit smile when James kissed the petals of a long-stem red rose before handing it to Shaylynn. For years, the smooth vocalist had been, and would probably always be, one of Neil's favorite artists, but at that moment he wanted to knock the shine off of James's Grammy Award–winning bald head. Until then, Neil didn't even know that he was capable of that level of jealousy. Never before had he felt the desire to physically fight another man over a woman. But how could he not be a little insecure? I mean, this was James Ingram, and Neil was living proof that Shaylynn didn't discriminate against well-kept older men. Reminding himself that James was a married man helped out a little, and all residual doubt was erased when, at the close of the concert, Shaylynn turned to Neil, cupped his cheeks, kissed his lips, and thanked him for bringing her to the show. Then she linked her arm through his and held on tight as they left the auditorium together.

During dinner that followed at Canoe, a romantic restaurant at which they hadn't dined since their first official date, she only had eyes for Neil. All the while, a little black box was nestled inside the pocket of his suit, but no time seemed like the right time to present it. There was that one moment — when they were holding hands across the table at dinner and looking into each other's eyes — that he was right on the verge of going for it, but then Shaylynn said something about how Emmett probably would have loved the dessert, and that dampened the mood and changed Neil's mind. It had been weeks since she'd brought up her former husband's name. *Was she ever going to just let that man die?* There was no way Neil would ask her to marry him when she had *the great Emmett Ford* on the brain. If she turned him down — no matter how gently she may have done it — it would have been far too humiliating. So Neil surmised that he'd ask for her hand later; maybe on her birthday.

Neil's mother was playing the role of babysitter tonight, so Shaylynn's eight-year-old son, Chase, was one of two children Ella was keeping overnight. After leaving the restaurant, Neil drove Shaylynn home and sat with her for a short while before deciding that it was time to leave. But as he and Shaylynn stood at her front door, sharing a long kiss good night, something welled in him. It was that same overwhelming love and passion that Neil felt every time he was alone with her . . . and standing that close to her. That feeling that assured him that he couldn't keep waiting. He wanted Shaylynn in more ways than one. Neil hated saying good-bye and good night to her. His soul desired to stay. He wanted to share his love with her; his life with her, his bed with her, and there was only one way that he could make that happen. That's when he decided to do it.

*And she said yes!*

Neil couldn't recall a time ever in his forty-six years that he'd been so happy. It was too early in the morning to call his best friend or his mother to share the news, but when his alarm sounded five hours from now for him to rise for work, Neil would begin spreading the joy.

*Am I too happy?* he questioned himself.

That new thought slowed Neil's movements as he peeled off his jacket and draped it on the arm of the sofa nearest him. The black wool Kenneth Cole design was a gift from Shaylynn. She'd presented it to him last Christmas. They were so in sync. Without even consulting each other, she'd bought him a coat, and he'd done the same for her: a black-and-white wool Worthington skirted peacoat that hugged her waist and draped her hips with perfection. Neil removed his driving cap and carefully placed it on top of his jacket and released a sigh, but he failed in his effort to shoo away the new notion that had forced its way into his head.

*Was* he, in fact, too happy?

Family history — especially history among the male population in Neil's bloodline — had taught him not to get prematurely keyed up about anything. Twenty-three years ago, Neil's dad was excited about finishing the new roof on his family's home, because he knew it was something that his sweetheart of forty years was looking forward to. His dad lived to make his beloved Ella Mae happy. But days before completion, the man they all called Pop was killed instantly in a freak automobile accident en

17

route back to the house after purchasing the material needed to finish the job. And then there was Dwayne, Neil's best friend and older brother. Next month would be nineteen years since the family had buried him, and Neil still missed him like it was yesterday. Dwayne had been battling a rare lung ailment for some time, but was doing well and was excited about performing the lead solo for a choir function when he suddenly collapsed and died of what was determined to be acute cardiorespiratory arrest. And then there was the time his uncle . . .

Neil chuckled as he sat on the sofa and leaned back against the cushions. What was he doing? He didn't believe in bad omens. Never had, never would. So why was he becoming his own party pooper? The woman he loved had just agreed to spend a lifetime loving him back, and here he was allowing Satan to steal his joy with all of these foolish, unfounded doubts. He wasn't going to die just because he had found a new level of happiness. Die before he had a chance to marry the love of his life? Die before the honeymoon that every fiber of his being was looking forward to? Absolutely not! Neil's closest friend and pastor, Charles Loather Jr., better known as CJ, had preached about that very thing — allowing the enemy to sap the joy that God gives — just two months ago. Neil's soft chuckle turned into an all-out guffaw. It was one of those loud laughs that seemed to fill the room and free his mind of all of its reservations, but it came to a sudden end at the sound of the doorbell.

Who would be coming to his door at this hour? Neil sat in the quiet darkness for a moment, wondering if he was hearing things. A second chime verified the obvious, and Neil stood and flicked the wall switch that brought light to his living room. There was no sense in pretending no one was home. Whoever was at his door had surely heard him laughing just moments earlier. Neil looked at the watch on his wrist. The little hand was grazing the edge of the one, and the big hand was on the ten. It was probably CJ. It had to be. He was the one person who knew Neil's Valentine's Day plans, and he probably couldn't wait to hear the results. Neil couldn't wait to tell him either. No doubt, CJ had told Theresa by now, and more likely than not, she was the one who had shooed her husband to his house to get the juicy details.

A smile twisted his lips, and he reached for the doorknob. But just to be sure, he asked, "Yes? Who is it?"

19

"Sean Thomas."

An automatic reaction snatched Neil's hand away from the door. *Sean Thomas?* One moment, the name sounded vaguely familiar, and the next, it was very familiar. This was the mystery man who had called his office twice over the past two months, but had never left a detailed message with Neil's assistant. Neil knew the name, but he didn't know the man. Whoever this Sean Thomas character was, Neil wasn't about to let him in his house at ten minutes before one in the morning.

"Who are you looking for?" Maybe the gentleman was confused. Neil Taylor was a pretty common name. Maybe it was a different Neil Taylor he was searching for. Maybe —

"Neil Taylor, son of Ernest and Eloise Taylor," the voice replied.

Okay . . . maybe not. Only a few people in Atlanta knew his mother by her given name of Eloise, and even fewer knew his father by anything other than Pop, so this person must have known Neil from his youthful days in Mississippi. But he still wasn't ready to identify himself as the person being sought. He wasn't exactly fearful, but he could hear his heart pounding in his own ears. Neil had no idea who Sean Thomas was or what he wanted, but for some reason, his gut feeling told him that his ride on cloud nine was over.

# ONE

"Hi, there. Back again, I see."

At the sound of the familiar accented voice, Neil glanced up from the glass counter and into the face of the same handsome, grey-haired gentleman who had waited on him the last time he'd stopped by the store. And the time before that . . . and the time before that. "Hi." Neil was already looking down again by the time he returned the greeting.

"Dr. Neil Taylor, correct?" the salesman said.

Neil brought his attention back to the man and accepted the friendly hand that was extended toward him. "Yes. Rabbi Ezra Bernstein, right?" He was glad that he could recall the Jewish community leader's name as readily as the rabbi had done his.

"Right. Very good." Ezra seemed pleasantly surprised, but he shouldn't have been so impressed. It was Neil's fourth visit to

23

his store in the last six weeks. "I see that you keep gravitating back to this same spot," the man observed. He pulled a copper-colored key from his pocket and unlocked the door to the glass casing before carefully sliding it open. "You like *this* one, don't you?"

Neil's eyes followed the direction of Ezra's hand as it navigated toward the two-carat, emerald-cut diamond set in white gold. It also came in yellow gold, but for some reason, the clearness of the flawless white solitaire against the silver of the brilliant white gold looked more breathtaking. It defined *her.* "Yes." Neil's fingers tingled, but his hand was steady as he took the ring from the jeweler's grasp and studied it carefully. It was his first time holding it, and it felt good. It felt right. "This one catches the light perfectly."

"Yes, it does," Ezra agreed. He hesitated for a brief moment, adjusted the white yarmulke that partially covered his graying hair, and then said, "Am I correct in assuming that you're not quite sure about this one yet?"

"No, it's not that," Neil assured him. "The ring is extraordinary. I love it, I just —"

"No, no." Ezra's voice stopped him. "I don't mean the ring. I mean the woman.

You're not sure about her just yet."

Neil's posture straightened, and he shook his head from side to side. "That's not it at all, Rabbi. She's the one. Shay — that's her name — she's the one; no doubt about it. I'm just . . ." Neil clamped his lips shut. Why on earth was he about to spill his guts to a practical stranger? This man didn't need to know about his insecurities. "I'm just a careful shopper," he concluded. And he was. So it wasn't a total lie.

"So it would seem." Ezra reached forward and reclaimed the jewelry before gently setting it back in its place in the display. "It's always a good practice to shop with care; especially when you're shopping for something as precious as a diamond." He closed the door of the glass casing, locked it, and then looked across the counter at Neil. "But we do have a thirty-day return policy, you know. If for any reason you're not satisfied, you can return it as long as it's still in the same condition as it was when purchased. That means if the bride-to-be doesn't look at this ring and immediately embrace it, you are at liberty to return it and even bring her in with you and let her pick out something else that better suits her taste."

That wasn't it either. Ezra was totally missing the mark, but Neil didn't want to tell the man that it wasn't the jewelry that he feared Shaylynn might reject. His reluctance to make the expensive investment had nothing to do with the ring. "That's good to know," he opted to say. "I'll definitely keep that in mind. Thank you, Rabbi. I suppose I should be getting back to work. My lunch break will be over soon." Fridays were particularly busy days at Kingdom Builders Academy, the private Christian school where Neil served as director.

"Yes." The store owner reached for his hand once more. "And I suppose I can look forward to seeing you again in the next week or so?"

Embarrassment heated Neil's face. If he weren't a black man, he would have turned candy apple red. Neil accepted the handshake, but determined in his mind that whenever or *if* ever he decided to ring shop any further, he'd go to a different store. In light of the rabbi's comment, he would just be too self-conscious to return to Menorah Jewelers . . . especially if he still wasn't ready to make a purchase. "Have a good day." Neil figured it was best not to give the man's question a direct answer since he had no plans to return.

Technically, it wasn't even winter yet, but cold temperatures had arrived in metropolitan Atlanta on an early flight. With the wind chill factor, the temperatures had been in single digits for three consecutive days, and even wearing a coat, hat, gloves, and scarf, Neil felt chilled to the bones as he climbed in the driver's seat of his SUV. The black Toyota Highlander had served him exceptionally well for seven years. After turning the key in the ignition, Neil sat behind the wheel and listened for the engine to idle down. While he waited, a photo caught his eye, and he slowly picked it up. It was a picture of Shaylynn and Chase. Shaylynn had given it to him just yesterday. During the Thanksgiving holiday break, she and her son had taken Christmas photos at Stonecrest Mall, and she had given Neil one eight-by-ten that he'd immediately framed and hung on his bedroom wall, and another that was so small that she'd presented it to him in a thermoplastic frame that dangled from a keychain. Neil had placed the frame in the built-in cup holder beside his driver's seat.

"That ring would be a great Christmas gift." He whispered the words while brushing his thumb over Shaylynn's image. "I wish I were sure of where your head is . . . and *who* your heart is truly with."

Neil didn't doubt Shaylynn's love for him.

Every time she looked at him, he could see the love in her eyes. But as strong as her feelings were for him, he knew they were stronger for someone else. Emmett Ford still owned her heart, or at least the better part of it. The flowers that Emmett had presented to her on the day he proposed were as dead as he was, but eight years after his passing, she still had them. Just the thought of it made Neil subconsciously shake his head. He tried to avoid looking at them whenever he visited Shaylynn, but with them sitting on the mantel of her fireplace, those annoying, dried, pressed violets were like the centerpiece of her entire house. They were like some bizarre kind of urn of Emmett's ashes, and to Neil they served as a painful, constant reminder that he'd never be Shaylynn's one and only.

Would she accept a marriage proposal from him? The inward battle continued as Neil placed the frame back in the cup holder, shifted gears, and began backing from his parking space. Accepting would mean permanently wearing his ring on the same finger from which she'd only recently been able to remove Emmett's. Was Shaylynn ready for that? Being Neil's steady was one thing, but would she be willing to be his *permanent?* Only when the sound of a horn resonated in the air did Neil realize that he was mindlessly holding up traffic at a green light.

The ride back to Kingdom Builders Academy took twenty minutes. Neil walked through the front doors just as lunchtime was ending, and the children were walking in straight lines on their way back to their classrooms. The enthusiastic reception he received made him forget his troubles. Temporarily anyway.

"High five, Dr. Taylor!"

Neil laughed out loud as he went down the line, slapping the hands that were attached to the chorus of voices that had given him his orders. The children, and especially the boys, loved it when he high-fived them, and Neil loved doing it. Twenty years from now, when he retired from this job he held so dear, Neil was sure that it would be the thing for which he'd be most remembered. Not all of the late hours that he'd put in without pay. Not the many times he'd gone beyond the call of duty and visited the homes of the students to check on their wellbeing. Not even for the incident last year where he used the Heimlich maneuver to save the life of an eight-year-old student who began choking while eating her lunch. He was honored by the school and the church for his quick reaction in the crisis situation, and the *Atlanta Weekly Chronicles,* the city's most popular newspaper, even printed a feature article about it. But it wouldn't be what the teachers or students would remember most. The high fives would be Neil's legacy, and truthfully, it would probably be what he would miss the most.

"Where've you been, Dr. Taylor? What did you have to do . . . go slaughter the cow before making the burger? And why didn't you answer your phone? I tried to call you twice."

Missing his mother hen of a secretary would probably run a close second. Margaret Dasher was a sixty-year-old who swore that she would die working. The word *retirement* wasn't in her vocabulary. Although she was somewhat hearing impaired, Margaret was an amazing-looking woman who easily looked ten years younger than she was. She had been talking loud all day long, and that was a clear sign that she'd chosen not to wear her hearing aid today. She adamantly denied her constant need for it. Neil stopped in front of her desk and removed his sunglasses. "Sorry, Ms. Dasher. I had some business to take care of and got caught in a little bit of traffic coming back." He glanced at his watch, and then back at her. "But I'm not late. I have five minutes to spare."

Margaret was shaking her head as she rose from her chair. "You must have *Mrs.* Ford on the brain. Is that where you were? I'll bet you did have business to take care of. Did you have *lunch* with her?" She made quotation marks with her fingers when she emphasized the word. "That's about the only person who could make you forget that you had an important one-fifteen conference call with Pastor and the KBA Education Ministry Board."

Neil slapped himself on the forehead. He hated it when Margaret insinuated that he and Shaylynn had already consummated their relationship, and he disliked it even more when she referred to Shaylynn as *Mrs.* Ford. But he was too disappointed with himself for not remembering the important business call to scold her for either offense. "CJ is gonna kill me. How in the world did I forget?" The question was more to himself than her, but Margaret was ready with a reply.

"Dr. Taylor, when you're with that young thing, you forget your own name. It's a wonder you remembered to come back to work at all. I done told you to watch yourself. You can't spend too much time with a person you're in love with and attracted to. The devil will sneak in the mix and have you doing all kinds of ungodliness. Do you understand what I'm trying to say?" She looked at him over her reading glasses like some crazy mix of schoolteacher and over-bearing mother. Then with an accusing tone, she added, "Of course you do."

Neil released a sigh. He knew he didn't owe Margaret an explanation, but it was the only way he would be able to shut her up. "First of all, Ms. Dasher, I was not with Shay; I was taking care of business just like I said. Okay? Secondly, as I've told you a million and one times already, *Ms.* Ford and I have not broken any rules. We've not gone there, and have no plans to go there, so you can stop worrying." In the back of his mind, Neil wondered if the thought of going *there* with him had ever even entered Shaylynn's mind. He'd be lying if he said it had never entered his, but he couldn't help but wonder if her desires to *go there* with anyone had died right along with her beloved Emmett. Neil swallowed the bitter bile that rose in his throat.

"Never underestimate the power of the enemy," Margaret warned. "The Bible tells us that that filthy, lowdown, stankin' devil is out to kill, steal, and destroy. All you have to do is let your guard down just a little bit, and he'll slither his way in and trip you up. Not a single one of us is so saved that we don't get tempted once in a while."

Without replying, Neil walked the fifty feet that would deliver him to his own office space, removed his jacket, and hung it on the coat rack behind his desk. He placed his hat, scarf, sunglasses, and gloves on the nearby credenza before pulling out his chair and sitting. He didn't need Margaret to fill him in on the woes of temptation. He and temptation weren't only on a first-name basis; they sometimes ate dinner and watched movies together. He looked that little imp in the eyes every time he touched Shaylynn or she touched him. Neil knew all too well that he wasn't beyond being tempted, and he knew he wasn't beyond yielding to temptation either. He'd denied his flesh for more years than he cared to calculate, but that hadn't always been his testimony. Even so, Shaylynn was different. She was worth waiting for. He just wondered how long he'd have to wait.

"Are you hearing me, Dr. Taylor?"

Neil looked at Margaret, who was now standing in his doorway, but he avoided her examination. It was time to change the subject. "What did Pastor Loather say when

I wasn't here for the conference call?" He was one of the few church members who knew the pastor intimately enough to refer to him as CJ, but he rarely did so around others.

"He didn't seem upset, if that's what you're worried about." Margaret rested her ample hips against the frame of Neil's open door. "I'm surprised he didn't just call you on your cell."

Neil slapped his forehead again, and then swiveled his chair around so that he could reach for the coat he'd just hung. Just before entering the jewelry store, he had set the volume of his ringer on silent and dropped the phone in his pocket. After leaving the store, he never thought to change the setting. As Neil slipped the BlackBerry from its case, the first thing he noticed was the message on the screen that notified him that he'd missed three calls. "Aw, man!" he whispered.

"What's going on with you, Dr. Taylor?" As loveable as she was, Margaret's prying was rarely subtle. She stepped farther into the office space. "For the past few weeks I've noticed that you've had a lot on your mind. You sure that you and that li'l girl are okay? No matter how mature she might be, she's still her age and you're yours. Although the age gap might not seem like a problem going into a new relationship, it could develop into one the more you get to know a person."

While Margaret's nosiness was obvious, her feelings about Shaylynn weren't. Whenever Shaylynn dropped by the office to see Neil, she and Margaret always exchanged pleasantries and got along well. But sometimes Neil wondered how genuine it was on the part of his executive assistant. When she spoke of Shaylynn in Shaylynn's absence, Margaret's tone sometimes carried an edge. Neil could detect that edge right now, and it caused him to clench and unclench his jaws. He and Margaret had worked together now for nearly seven years, and because they attended the same church, he'd known her even longer than that. By all accounts, Neil considered Margaret Dasher his friend more than his employee despite the fact that they never referenced each other by their first names. Margaret was fifteen years his senior, and for a while Neil had carried a secret schoolboy-like torch in his heart for the attractive, divorced mother of two. But all of that notwithstanding, if Margaret ever crossed the line and said anything disrespectful about the woman he loved, Neil would introduce her to a side of him that she'd never met.

"You mind closing the door on your way out?" He made the abrupt request while quickly typing in the password that would allow him access to his own cell phone. Neil was growing weary of the small talk and the needless insinuations. It was time to get back to business.

"Does that mean everything *isn't* okay?" Margaret could be relentless.

Neil wished he could say something that would convince Margaret that there was absolutely no need for concern, but first he had to convince himself. There was no real evidence of trouble in paradise, but his instinct detected something on the horizon. His hesitations about buying the ring . . . the increase of Emmett's name creeping into his and Shaylynn's conversations . . . the knot that gradually tightened in the pit of his stomach . . .

"Well, does it?" Margaret's voice snatched him from his thoughts.

An exaggerated inhale and exhale non-verbally accused his secretary of being a hopeless case. Neil pressed the code to listen to his messages, and then placed the phone to his ear. He shooed her away with his hand and forced his voice to be confident and unwavering when he replied with,

"What it means, Ms. Dasher, is close the door on your way out."

# TWO

Life for Shaylynn Ford was one big hustle. It always had been. Nothing worth having had ever come easy for her, but when she decided to take her life's biggest faith leap and become her own employer, she had no idea the magnitude of the challenge that lay ahead. Shaylynn desperately needed to prove to herself that she wasn't the failure she'd been defined as for the majority of her life. Emmett's life insurance policy had left her with a nice nest egg, but if she lived off of that, it would validate what her former in-laws had always said about her — that she would be nothing if it weren't for their son.

Despite proving her genuine love for Emmett, his parents, both successful corporate attorneys, were determined to hold fast to the accusation that the Ford family fortune was what had most attracted her to him. As true as it was, they never believed her story that she didn't even know about their class and ranking prior to falling for Emmett. To solidify their "liar" status once and for all, Shaylynn had to make this business venture work. She had to show attorneys William and Melinda Ford that she had a net worth aside from the small fortune that Emmett had willed to her.

When she first metaphorically opened the doors of Shay Décor, Shaylynn spent the better part of her days praying for God to send business to her home-based interior decorating company, so that defeat wouldn't force her back into corporate America. That was over a year ago, and just as it is promised in scripture, God had done exceeding abundantly above all that she'd asked. These days, she sometimes found herself praying that He would allow her a breather between assignments. Shaylynn loved what she did, and she knew that a prosperous Shay Décor signified a blessed Shay Décor, but still . . . she needed a break, or at least a good assistant. She would love for Saturday to be a day of relaxation for her, but it just wasn't possible with her workload. There never seemed to be enough time in the weekdays to get it all done.

"Mama, can we go to the park or something?"

And now, here was someone else who wanted to shorten her Saturday. Shaylynn stopped flipping through her design binder and looked up in time to see her son stomping his way down the stairs. Considering Chase's slim build and early growth spurt, most would probably think the boy would be interested in basketball, but that wasn't his sport of choice. Chase had a genuine leather regulation-sized football tucked under his right arm, and a helmet dangled in his left hand. Was he crazy? Saturday morning had greeted them with twenty-eight-degree temperatures. As the afternoon settled in, it had warmed to thirty-six, but that was still too cold for Shaylynn. Plus she had far too much to do to donate time to the park. She sighed. Moments like this one caused her to miss Emmett even more than normal. If he were still alive, regardless of the outside elements, she was sure that he would have no qualms with taking Chase to the park for some outside playtime.

"No, son, we can't do that today." Shaylynn watched him stop midway down the stairwell. His shoulders slumped and his face fell. The sight of it sank her heart. She never took pleasure in disappointing her only child, but . . . "Mama has a lot of work to do, Chase. Besides, it's just too cold outside. The park is really for spring and summer, maybe early fall. But in the winter it's too frigid for playing outdoors. Nobody plays outdoors in this kind of cold unless they're playing in the snow."

"Ah-huh." Chase bobbed his head up and down as he challenged her declaration. "We still go outside and play at school. When you run around, it gets your blood pumping and warms you up. It helps you to think better too. That's what Dr. Taylor says when he runs around with us on the playground."

Shaylynn placed her design binder on the coffee table and gave Chase her full attention. "Dr. Taylor goes outside and plays with the kids during recess?"

With one elbow propped on the banister of the staircase, Chase looked at her with a know-it-all expression. "Yes, ma'am. Not every day, but sometimes."

Shaylynn cocked her head and eyed her child. His story wasn't believable; it didn't make sense. "Dr. Taylor wears a suit to work. Are you trying to tell me that he goes outside and plays in his dress clothes?"

Chase's laugh made Shaylynn feel like she was on the verge of crossing into idiot territory. "Of course not, Mama. He couldn't run around with us in a suit. He changes clothes when he plays with us, and then he goes back inside, takes a shower in the bathroom that's in the back of his office, and puts his good clothes back on. He says that getting our blood pumping helps us to get our work done better and faster."

"He would say something like that." Shaylynn mumbled the words to herself.

"Hey." Chase said the single word as though a light switch in his head had just been flipped into the on position. "Maybe if you go outside and play with me, you can get your work done faster too."

Shaylynn couldn't help but smile at both Chase's rationale and at the mental picture she had of Neil on the playground running after children or having them pursue him. The newsflash shouldn't have taken her by surprise. Neil's energy level had reaped the benefits of his new, healthier lifestyle. He'd been carrying on a love affair with the treadmill for more than a year now. His body was cashing in too. Shaylynn liked that best of all, but that was a secret she kept to herself.

Neil was becoming quite the sportsman. He'd participated in the six-mile Peachtree Road Race last July, and though he didn't even come close to winning it, for a middle-aged rookie, he had a very impressive fifty-eight-minute finish. And Neil had always taken special interest in the children at his school, so it only made sense that he'd take his interaction with them to such a level. At first, Shaylynn thought it was just a "Chase thing." In the early days of their courtship, Shaylynn figured that Neil was trying to impress her by being so actively involved with Chase. But the more she got to know him, the clearer it became to her that he wasn't being biased. He genuinely loved children. Still, she had no idea that he took it as far as roughhousing with the students on the playground. Neil had never told her that. Shaylynn's chest warmed at the realization of it all. The longer she knew Neil, the more reasons she found to love him. He would make a good dad one day. Maybe even to Chase. . . .

"So can we go to the park?"

"I really can't." Shaylynn blinked rapidly as her trance broke. That last thought had entered her head without warning, but it wasn't the first time. As she continued speaking, she reclaimed her binder for visual effect. "I have to put together some ideas to show a client by Monday morning, and I'm doubtful that I'll have time to do much tomorrow with church and all. Plus, I'm not going to be running around like Dr. Taylor does, so I'll be freezing if I went out there. If you want to go out into the back-yard and play, you can. You'll just need to stay in the area where I can watch you from the bay windows." She pointed toward the kitchen, which was set in the rear of their split-level townhouse.

"By myself?" Now Chase was whining, and Shaylynn didn't like that. Little boys shouldn't whine. Emmett used to say that repeatedly, and he was cringing right now if he could somehow hear his son. "It's no fun if I have to play by myself."

"Well, we'll have to consider it for another day then," Shaylynn said. "Why don't you go play video games, or what about watching that karate movie that stars Will Smith's son, who you love so much?"

Chase's top lip curled upward. "I've seen that a hundred times already. Plus he ain't all that. I mean, he's a good actor and stuff, but Willow is the one who's hot. I just give him points 'cause he's her brother."

Shaylynn's eyes widened. Wasn't it about five years too early for her son to be notic-ing girls? And had he just used the adjective *"hot"* to describe one? Shaylynn didn't know whether to laugh at Chase or scold him, so she decided to do neither. "Go read a book, then. You can't convince me that you've read all the books on the list that your teacher gave you at the beginning of the school year. Remember what I told you before. It's better to be ahead than to fall behind."

Apparently none of Shaylynn's options appealed to Chase. "Can I call Dr. Taylor? Maybe if he's not doing nothing, he'll come and play with me. He likes playing with me."

Shaylynn often wondered just how much Chase understood about her relationship with Neil. She'd never told him how she felt about the director of his school, never figured that he'd understand anyway. But now, with him using words like *"hot"* to describe the opposite sex . . . maybe he would. Neil visited her home often, and the three of them spent time together nearly every weekend, but Chase probably thought he visited all the kids' homes just as regularly. Both Shaylynn and Neil were conscious of the boy's presence whenever the three of them were in the same place. They never kissed, hugged, or even held hands if there was a chance that Chase might see them. It wasn't a mutual agreement. Neil totally opposed her insistence to conceal the relationship from her son, but Shaylynn was adamant. As strongly as she felt about Neil, she wasn't yet fully convinced of how their relationship would pan out.

The handsome, talented educator, who also served on the deacon board of Kingdom Builders Christian Center, was one of the kindest, most loving men Shaylynn had ever known. But he was also older and, undoubtedly, far more experienced than she. Plus, she wasn't blind. Shaylynn knew that she wasn't the only woman who liked what she saw when she looked at Dr. Neil Taylor. He was admired by several of his female business and church associates, many of whom were closer to his age. What if one of those smart, educated women he worked with wormed her way into his heart? Add to that the fact that Neil already had one failed marriage to his credit, and Shaylynn had even more reasons to be cautious. And she didn't even have to put a "what if" in the equation where *that one* was concerned. If Shaylynn had ever wondered if Audrey Taylor was still interested in Neil, that question was answered when Ms. Thing and her Mary Kay Career Car made their grand appearance at the Taylor family reunion back in July.

Shaylynn had heard the stories, and she knew Audrey was probably going to show up, but that didn't stop her from feeling uneasy. Audrey was pretty fabulous for a woman her age. Shaylynn hadn't expected her to be so attractive. She found herself struggling to hold together her mask of security and self-confidence. When Audrey had to leave suddenly, it was an answer to a prayer that Shaylynn had begun praying the moment the woman stepped out of her car. Neil promised that he had absolutely no interest in his ex-wife, and from what Shaylynn could see he wasn't being untruthful about that, but what if Audrey's persistence eventually paid off? During their marriage, they'd separated and reunited two or three times. What if, somewhere down the line, Neil decided to give it one last try? Shaylynn was still very protective of her son. Chase had already lost one dad. Granted, Emmett was a father her son had never known, but he was his father still. And the last thing Shaylynn wanted was for Chase to get too accustomed or attached to Neil, and then be left with a broken heart if it didn't work out.

"Today is Saturday, Chase. Dr. Taylor spends five days a week with children. It's not fair to ask him to come here and spend his weekend with children too." The explanation she offered didn't nearly address Shaylynn's real concerns.

Chase shrugged his shoulders. "What's the big deal? He's over here all the time anyway."

The kid had definitely inherited his father's gift for gab and flair for quick comebacks. But the traits that Shaylynn had found appealing in her late husband she sometimes found annoying in her son. It was at that moment that she decided she had allowed the debate to go on long enough. "How 'bout you go back upstairs and take off those cleats? You want to move around and get your blood pumping? Fine. While you're upstairs, clean up your room. That ought to do the trick."

"But, Ma —"

Shaylynn held up her hand to stop any further deliberation. "And stop whining," she ordered. Chase said nothing more, but remained standing in place looking down at his mother with those big brown eyes that usually got him his way. He'd inherited those from his father too. Shaylynn fought the urge to give in. The image of her shivering in the near-freezing temperatures helped her find the strength to stand her ground. Her tone thickened when she added her single order and pointed a stiff finger toward the top of the staircase. "Go."

While he obeyed her command, Shaylynn basked in the relief of her victory as she began flipping through her book once again.

She had never been one of those mothers who spanked her child as a first-string disciplinary action. In Chase's lifetime, he'd only endured corporal punishment four or five times, and even then she'd used nothing harder or heavier than her open hand. She had endured so many unmerited beatings as a little girl that she found it hard to pass along the tradition, even when one would be justified. Overall, Chase was a well-mannered and obedient child. Today he was just antsy. He got that way periodically. Shaylynn remembered being that way as a kid too. She surmised that it was one of those things that came along with being an only child. There were no built-in playmates to pal around with, and sometimes that became a problem . . . for both the parent and the child.

Thumping sounds coming from upstairs indicated that Chase was making his normal valiant, but poor, attempt to tidy his room. Shaylynn would go behind him and tweak it later. She didn't expect him to be an expert. At his age, she just needed him to give it his best effort. She didn't want him growing up to be ill-equipped to take care of himself. One of Emmett's flaws was his inability to do anything deemed "woman's work." His mother had done everything for him in their well-to-do home. Even after he was an adult and had moved from under his parents' roof, housekeeping was a woman's job. A hired maid came by Emmett's home twice a week to tidy it for him, and Melinda Ford would insist that her son bring his dirty laundry to her to wash on a weekly basis. Even his meals came compliments of his mom. Emmett could name all of the US presidents in order of their servitude, fill in the names of the fifty states on a blank map, convert centimeters to feet, and decimeters to yards, but he couldn't properly iron a shirt even if his life depended upon it. Shaylynn leaned back on the cushions of her loveseat and chuckled. Thoughts of Emmett almost always made her smile.

She set her design book to the side as her telephone rang. Her smile widened when she looked at the caller ID. "Hello?"

"Hey, suga."

She liked it when Neil called her Shay, but she *loved* it when he called her suga — mostly because she didn't personally know anyone else who referred to their love interest as such. Where she came from, sugar was something that was added in cake mix. She knew a lot of honeys, dears, babies, and sweethearts, and since moving to the South, she'd even met her share of muffins, pump-

kin pies, and cupcakes, but as far as Shaylynn was concerned, sugar or *suga* was hers
alone. There was just something especially
endearing about the manner in which Neil
said it.

As for her, she didn't need to find a
nickname for him. "Hi, Solomon." She'd
developed a habit of labeling him by his
middle name even before their relationship
turned serious. Shaylynn began doing it
because to her, he just looked more like a
Solomon than a Neil, but the fact that he
seemed to relish it made it stick.

"I love that smile," he cooed.

"What smile?" Shaylynn looked up like
she expected to see him inside her house,
peeking down at her from the same spot on
the staircase where her son once stood.

"The one I hear in your voice. I hope it's
for me."

Shaylynn took in a breath, and then
released it. The sound of Neil's voice always
moved her, but over the phone his mellow,
raspy tone sounded especially appealing.
She imagined him wearing one of those
Nike running outfits that made him look so
enticing. Neil sounded calm and relaxed, so
he was probably sitting in his recliner, or
maybe resting in his bed. No . . . not the
bed. She shook the thought from her brain

like the devil himself had put it there. Envisioning Neil in bed wasn't something that she needed to be doing.

"Well, is it?" A twinge of concern had crept into his voice.

"Is it what?" Shaylynn used her fingers to rake her long braids over her shoulder. What was he talking about? She couldn't believe she'd drifted.

"The smile," Neil said, bringing her up to speed. "Is it for me?"

Shaylynn searched her general area. She almost always kept a bottle of water nearby as she worked, but of all days, not today. Her tongue felt pasty when she used it to try to moisten her parched lips. "Of course it is." She felt justified with her response. Hers had started out as a smile that developed from memories of Emmett, but Neil certainly didn't need to know that. And anyway . . . the smile expanded when she saw Neil's name on the caller ID. So technically, it was for him. Right?

"Good." He sounded satisfied with her confirmation. "I know when we spoke last night you mentioned that you needed to catch up on some work today, but I was wondering if you were at a place where you could break for a couple of hours." Shaylynn was already shaking her head in a negative reply, but unable to see it, Neil continued. "I'm over at Ms. Ella Mae's house, and she's about to start cooking dinner. She asked me to invite you and Chase. What do you say?" After a pause, he added in that sexy voice of his, "I'd love to see you."

Shaylynn felt the onset of goose bumps. Seeing Neil would make her day too, and his mother, the woman he lovingly called Ms. Ella Mae, was one of the best cooks she'd ever met, but Shaylynn's reality was that she couldn't afford to spend time away from work. "I'm sorry, but I don't think I can do that," she replied with regret. "I have too much on my plate, and I'm so far behind. From the looks of it, I'll probably be spending at least a part of tomorrow working on this project as well."

"Wow. That busy, huh?"

Shaylynn could hear the disappointment in Neil's voice. Inside of fifteen minutes, she'd managed to burst the bubbles of both the men dearest to her heart. "Yeah. I'm sorry, Solomon; believe me, I am. But I just can't chance not having these samples together by Monday."

"No need to apologize," Neil said. "I understand." After a brief silence, he added, "So with all this work you have to do, what are you and Chase gonna eat for dinner?"

Shaylynn hadn't even given dinner a thought. It was four o'clock now and she hadn't even begun to prepare anything. "Don't worry about us; we'll eat." She tried to sound confident, but it was apparent that Neil wasn't fully convinced.

"Well, listen. Let me at least come and get Chase. Ms. Ella Mae hasn't seen him in a couple of weeks, so I know it would make her day. Plus if you're that bogged down with work, I'm sure getting him out of the house will help you be able to better concentrate and give the project your full attention. Maybe the two of us can toss the football around for a while until Ms. Ella Mae finishes dinner. Then he can eat over here so you don't have to break from your work unless you absolutely want to. You eat like a bird, so you'll probably just throw a sandwich or something together. Chase is a man. He needs more."

Shaylynn laughed. "A man? Really?" Then she thought about her son's earlier remark about Willow Smith. "Well, maybe you're right. That would be great. I'm sure he'd like to play outside, and then eat a full meal." She didn't want to tell Neil that Chase had actually asked for him earlier. Neil would be offended that she hadn't called him. "Are you sure you don't mind?"

She hoped he didn't somehow feel obligated.

"Not at all. Why would I mind?"

"I don't know." Shaylynn shrugged. "I mean, it's Saturday, and there are a whole lot of more important things that you might need to get done on your off days."

"More important?" Despite her effort not to offend Neil, he sounded offended anyway. Shaylynn heard the wind of his sigh as it blew into the telephone, and then he said, "Just get him ready, Shay. I'll be there in about half an hour. And if you think you're gonna have to pull a late-nighter with this project, it's okay if you want to pack an overnight bag for Chase. He can crash at my house tonight. It'll be fun. We'll all be at the same church in the morning anyway."

Allowing Chase to spend the night with Neil was something she'd never done. It was a nice gesture on his part, but Shaylynn didn't know if they were ready for that yet. Something like that could have dire consequences if things between her and Neil didn't work out. "Thank you. He'll be ready by the time you get here." Shaylynn decided to leave it at that. The overnight bag would never get packed, but she didn't want to insult Neil any more than she already had.

He'd discover her decision when he arrived to pick up her son.

# THREE

Pastor Charles Loather Jr. sat behind the desk of his office with his eyes closed. If he sat like that long enough, he knew he'd fall asleep. It had been an extraordinary Sunday morning worship service that had left him feeling spiritually charged, but physically drained. Although they were still a few minutes away from the benediction, CJ had excused himself from the pulpit just after praying over those who had come to give their hearts to the Lord and/or pledge their membership to Kingdom Builders Christian Center, a church of which he'd served as pastor for the past five years — ever since the death of its founder and CJ's beloved father, Dr. Charles Loather Sr. Between his delivering today's message and the energy he spent while laying hands on the twelve people who had gathered for prayer and church discipleship, CJ had worked up quite a sweat. He had made the early departure so that he could change into dry clothes and have a few moments to wind down before the counseling session that had been scheduled for this afternoon.

"Here's your cranberry juice, sweetie."

CJ's eyelids lifted at the sound of the voice that came from behind him. From the side of his eye, he watched one hand place the pastor's official monogrammed flute on the desk in front of him, and then felt that hand join the other in a firm but gentle caress of his shoulders. CJ closed his eyes again. Theresa always knew just where the tension would gather. His only response was a pleasurable groan.

"I'm so good at this, aren't I?" It was rhetorical. She knew the answer.

"You're the best. I don't know what I'd do without you."

Theresa lowered her face and brushed her lips against his ear. Then at a level barely above a whisper, she said, "And don't you forget it, Pastor Loather."

Chills engulfed CJ. She was just messing with him now, and this was not the time or the place for her to tease him. He took special pleasure in hearing Theresa call him by his ecclesiastical title, and she knew it. All things considered, the sound of it probably shouldn't awaken his sensual side, but it did. They would be celebrating their sixth anniversary in less than five months. CJ was forty, and Theresa was thirty-two at the time that they exchanged wedding vows. It was a first marriage for both. By most standards, they'd gotten married late in life, but CJ was more than glad that he'd listened to his late parents and waited for the right one. They told him that if he waited for God to allow him to find his soul mate, he'd have no regrets, and they were right. Resa, as he called her, had been everything he'd ever prayed for in a life mate: smart, sophisticated, saved, and sexy.

He reached over his shoulder and grabbed her right hand. "Come here, woman." CJ navigated her to the side of him, slid his rolling executive chair away from his desk, and then gently pulled her down until her perfectly round behind rested in his lap. His hand briefly caressed her knee, and then traveled to her stomach, where it lingered. Lately, it was his favorite place to touch her. Not only had Theresa been everything he'd ever needed, now she was giving him everything he'd ever wanted: a family.

Pregnancy had little or nothing to do with her full bottom. CJ had described Theresa as a woman with baby-making hips long before they made the baby. They were three months away from being introduced to their firstborn. Now forty-six and thirty-eight, they were getting a late start at parenthood too, but as far as CJ was concerned, the timing was perfect. They had agreed not to find out the gender of the baby until Theresa gave birth, but CJ had a feeling that he already knew who was growing in his wife's womb. "How's Daddy's namesake?" He pressed his lips against the side of Theresa's protruding belly and delivered a lingering kiss that didn't end until she stroked his head and spoke.

"Are you gonna be disappointed if we have a daughter?"

CJ looked up at her. He couldn't believe what he'd heard. "Of course not. Why would you ask me that?" He kissed her stomach again. "I just want to be the father of a healthy, happy baby; you know that."

Theresa nodded in agreement, but when she spoke, she didn't exactly sound persuaded. "But you're always calling him . . . or *her* . . . your namesake. What if we don't have a Charles Loather III? What if he's a she and can't carry on the name you're so proud of?"

She was right. He was indeed proud of his name. Not so much because it was his name, but because it was his father's name, and there was no one CJ admired more than his dad. Dr. Charles Loather Sr. had passed away less than a year after officiating the ceremony that legally bonded CJ and Theresa. It made CJ a bit sad that his child would never know his . . . or *her* paternal grandparents. "The name doesn't have to be Charles in order to be my namesake." A grin crossed CJ's lips despite the sadness that threatened to creep in at the thought of his deceased parents. "There are a lot of girl names that could do the trick. Charlie, Charlene, Charma, Charlotte —"

"You've been thinking about this thing, haven't you?" Theresa's new tone indicated that he had lessened her previous concern.

"Wait." CJ held up a finger. "I'm not done yet. Charlese, Charlissa, Charo, Char—"

"Okay . . . stop," Theresa interrupted. "Charo is out; I can tell you that right now. The world already has one of those, and she's quite enough. And Charlie . . . well, when it's given to a female it always comes with an old-fashioned middle name like Mae, and that's just not gonna happen, preacher man. No daughter of mine is gonna be named Charlie Mae."

CJ laughed. "You'd better not let Ms. Ella Mae hear you say her middle name is old-fashioned. Besides, it sounds a whole lot better than some of the four- and five-syllable names we find attached to our children these days. Would you rather your daughter's name be Charlie Mae or Charlie MaeQuaneesha?"

Theresa broke into a loud laugh. With his hand still on her stomach, CJ could feel the baby make a sudden movement. He couldn't help but wonder if her vigorous outburst had disturbed their child's sleep. When Theresa finally calmed enough to answer his question, she said, "Neither. I wouldn't choose anything tongue-tying, but I don't want old-fashioned either." She freed herself from his lap and walked around his desk so that she stood in front of it, facing him. CJ knew it was only a matter of time before she started pacing the floor like she always did when she got worked up about any topic, and he prepared himself to enjoy the sight of it. "CJ, I don't want our child to have a name that ages him or her one way or the other. I want to give our baby a strong, timeless name like both of us have. You find newborns named Charles and Theresa, and you find senior citizens with the same names. They aren't trendy or generational names. They cross age lines, and they also cross ethnic lines, which is also important to me."

CJ strongly agreed with that last part, and his firm nod said so. They had been having conversations like this one ever since they found out Theresa was expecting, and CJ never tired of them. When they discussed anything, whether it was as carnal as baby names or as spiritual as scriptures, he enjoyed the manner in which he and his wife were able to communicate. They were both analytical thinkers, which meant deliberations like this one could go on for days, but somehow they were almost always able to hash out any topic without their discussions getting heated, even when they disagreed.

"Neither of our names gives away our race." As soon as she completed that sentence, Theresa began pacing, and CJ's eyes followed. "As much as we'd like to believe that racism is dead in the twenty-first century, we know that it's not," she continued. "People just find less obvious ways to practice it. Any executive who wants to indiscreetly avoid calling in a qualified black woman for a job interview will toss aside all the resumes with names like Shaniqua and LaQuisha. Even the ones with less flamboyant names like Ebony, Imani, and Essence will get skipped, because although they're pretty names, everyone knows that they are overwhelmingly more likely to be tagged onto a female of African American descent. And not only that but . . ." Her voice trailed for a moment, and then she said, "CJ, are you listening to me?"

He raised his eyes to meet hers. "Yeah, baby, I'm listening."

"No, you aren't. You were doing it again, weren't you?"

"Doing what? I really was listening to you, Resa." CJ laughed, knowing full well what she was accusing him of.

"My lips are up here, CJ." She pointed at her mouth. "If you were listening to me, you'd be looking up here. You're not listening, you're watching my behind shake when I walk."

CJ leaned back in his chair and laughed harder. "I don't have to do either/or, baby. I'm not deaf; I don't need to look at your lips in order to know what you're saying. I heard every word you said *while* I was watching your butt jiggle." He laughed some more.

"I don't *jiggle,* for your information." Theresa folded her arms and tried to give him a stern look, but CJ could tell that she was flattered. "I'll have the last laugh. You've only got three more months to enjoy your insanity."

"Yeah, like I wasn't looking before you got yourself knocked up."

The smile she'd been trying to withhold spilled onto her face despite her efforts. Placing her palms on the top of his desk, she leaned in and said, "First of all, *Pastor Loather,* I wasn't the one who knocked me up. Secondly, yes, you were looking before I put on these additional twenty pounds, but now you're gawking."

Slowly bringing himself to a standing position, CJ matched her stance, which put his face only inches from his wife's. His eyes scaled the details of her face, and he could see her tense as his eyes locked into hers. CJ knew she had read both his eyes and his body language. He knew that he really didn't need to verbalize anything, but he did it anyway. "You keep calling me that, *First Lady,* and I just might forget where I am."

Theresa lifted her hands and gently tugged at his clergy collar until it slipped from its place. "You've got a meeting," she whispered, placing the soft, pliable piece on the desk between them without ever taking her eyes off his.

CJ licked his lips. Theresa had always had a healthy appetite for him, but this pregnancy thing had made her ravenous. CJ could easily get used to this. Maybe they'd have two or three more kids before it was over. Proving that he was up to the challenge, he reached forward, removed her eyeglasses, and placed them on the desk beside his collar. "I could forget the meeting too."

"Oh, really . . . *Pastor Loather?*"

This wasn't funny anymore. CJ's heartbeat was set on hypersonic, and the temperature in his office was on a steady incline. "Don't test me, woman."

With a smoldering look that matched his, Theresa replied, "Too late. The test has already been administered. The question is . . . will you pass or fail?"

"Baby, I don't fail anything." CJ had barely finished the sentence before he attacked her lips with his. Her responding groan was so pronounced that he wondered, for a moment, if he was hurting her. His concerns were short-lived and immediately dissolved when he felt Theresa's fingernails rake through his short, coarse hair as she pressed her lips even harder into his.

"Oh, c'mon! This is the house of God. Have you no shame?" They parted immediately at the sound of the booming voice that came from the area of CJ's office door. CJ tried to catch his breath and regain his composure at the sight of the arrival of his appointment. "I'm gonna report this to the pastor," Neil added. And then with an animated thoughtful look, he concluded with, "Oh, that's right. You *are* the pastor."

"You always did have bad timing," Theresa told him as she stood up straight and brushed away a loose strand of hair from her face. She gave CJ a brief, apologetic look, and then turned to face their intruder. "Don't you know how to knock?"

"Well, pardon me." Neil walked inside and closed the door behind him. "I've never had to knock prior to entering the pastor's office before. Not when I have an appointment. But now that I know he might be in here getting it on, I'll try to be more mindful."

CJ was embarrassed by his own actions. Sure, Theresa was his wife, but still. What if it had been someone other than his best friend who walked in on them? It would have been hard to explain this to one of the other lay members. "Nobody was *getting it on,* Neil," CJ said through a sigh.

"Not yet, maybe. But if I had arrived about two minutes later, I would have wanted to gouge out my own eyes."

"We weren't going to do anything. I wouldn't do that on church property." CJ hoped he was telling the truth, but the fire that still raged in his body's field said differently. "I don't think kissing is out of order. It's not like Resa is my personal secretary or something. She's my wife, and I think God is okay with me kissing my wife on church property."

"Kissing her lips is one thing. Eating her face is another."

"We were just discussing baby names," Theresa claimed.

Neil laughed like she was a stand-up comedienne and had just delivered her best punch line. "Oh, yeah? Well I'd sure like to hear you pronounce the name you were just discussing when I walked in."

CJ looked at his wife and steadied his voice while picking up her glasses from his desk and handing them to her. "Baby, do you mind giving Neil and me some privacy?"

"Not at all." Theresa took the spectacles and put them back on her face. She then grabbed his clergy collar from the desk and gently returned it to its place around CJ's neck. "Do you want me to wait for you?" she asked as she tucked and tugged until it was neatly secure.

"I'll bring him home," Neil said before CJ could speak. "This might take a while, and

I'm sure you don't want to be waiting around that long." He turned his attention to his best friend. "I can bring you home, CJ, can't I?"

CJ gave him a long, hard stare. That innocent look plastered on Neil's face wasn't fooling him at all. He was doing this mess on purpose. It had been an exhausting day. CJ just wanted to get this meeting over so he could go home and grab some rest, grab some dinner, and before he retired for the evening, he hoped to grab some Resa, too. Neil was jacking up his plans big time.

"Is that all right with you, sweetie?" Theresa asked after seconds lapsed without CJ responding.

CJ clenched his jaws. He wanted to smack Neil for making this appointment, and then turn around and smack himself for accepting it. If he answered his wife truthfully, he would have to admit that it *wasn't* all right with him. Theresa had ignited a desire inside of CJ that made him want to throw Neil out of his office with the same fervor in which God had cast Satan out of heaven. CJ wanted nothing more right now than to take his wife home and finish what they'd so ill-timely started. "Sure." He forced a smile and made his best attempt to ignore the needs of his flesh. Touching her stomach, he added, "You go home and get off your feet. I'll catch a ride with Neil."

"Okay." Theresa kissed his cheek again, and then stepped away and allowed CJ to walk around the desk and help her put on her coat. She picked up her purse, and headed for the private exit that would lead directly to the parking lot. Just before closing the door behind her, Theresa looked over her shoulder and said, "Don't be too long."

CJ knew that tone. She wanted him as much as he wanted her. He released a heavy sigh, and then turned to the object of his disappointment and stared at him in silence. There Neil stood near the door, wearing a stupid grin that assured CJ that his friend was not oblivious to the fact that he'd not only walked in at an inopportune time, but he also knew that although CJ was honoring his word to serve in the capacity of counselor, he was now aching for a different kind of therapy of his own.

"Whew. I thought she'd never leave." Neil's continuous struggle to keep from having a good laugh at CJ's expense remained obvious, even while he took the liberty of sitting comfortably in the chair across from his pastor's desk. "Women," he added, shaking his head theatrically. "They

70

just don't know when they're imposing and overstaying their welcome, do they?" Then, rubbing his hands together like they were about to get down to business, he asked, "You ready to start our session now?"

Using slow motions, CJ returned to his chair and sat too. He nibbled at his bottom lip and looked Neil straight in the eyes. After a lengthy silence, he said, "You know what? Somewhere in the Bible, in the book of Acts, the seventeenth chapter, and somewhere around the twenty-ninth and thirtieth verses, we find that there was a time, in the Old Testament days, when God would *wink* at the ignorance of His children; meaning that His wrath and judgment wouldn't be swift when they were found doing things that were against His will." CJ pointed a menacing finger in Neil's direction. "I wish God would *wink* at me for just a few moments; because if I thought for one cotton-pickin' minute that I would get away with it and that He would just chalk it up to my ignorance, I'd lock my office door right now and beat the living crap out of you." Neil could no longer contain himself, but CJ didn't see the humor. "No. No. I'm for real, boy," CJ said over his friend's loud belly laugh. "I mean it. If I thought I could get away with it, I'd climb across this desk and whoop you like you stole something."

# FOUR

By the time they reached the ninetieth minute of what was supposed to be a sixty-minute meeting, nothing was funny anymore. Not to Neil, anyway. In truth, the humor had dried up well before now. The meeting started with Neil talking to CJ, his best friend, but about twenty minutes in, the man sitting on the other side of the desk had gone through an obvious metamorphosis, changing into Pastor Charles Loather Jr.: his spiritual leader. Neil had sought counsel from CJ before, so none of it should have blindsided him, but somehow he was ill-prepared for the tongue-lashing. CJ's words stung. Some of the realities of what were discussed in the meeting had been a bit hard to swallow. But then again, those proverbial bitter pills generally were.

CJ showed no mercy. Was he using this meeting as an excuse to punish Neil for breaking up his little rendezvous with Theresa? They were coming close to knocking on the door of two hours, and CJ continued to bring up new things, challenging Neil to consider and then reconsider them. "Yes, you're an eligible bachelor," he was now saying, "but you're no longer that young heartthrob you used to be when we were walking together on the campus of Morehouse College, hoping to look across the way and catch a glimpse of some cute Spelman chick. I ain't sayin' you're in your twilight years or anything, but if you think for one minute that you've still got your whole life ahead of you, you're definitely in the Twilight Zone."

Neil took offense to the insinuation. "Are you calling me old?" He sat forward in his chair. "You tryin'a say I've lost my appeal?" The last part was what concerned him the most. Neil didn't mind getting older. Nobody ever believed him when he told them his age anyway. Young genes ran in his family. Even his mother had stumped some of the best age-guessers out there. But Neil still didn't need to feel like he was being called an old man, especially not when the woman he loved was more than a decade his junior.

CJ shook his head. "First of all, I'm a grown man. And most grown men . . ." He caught himself, grunted, and then started again. "Most *straight* grown men don't go around citing other grown men as *appealing*." He paused to chuckle, then added, "Besides, you and I are only a few months apart in age. So to say you've lost it would be the same as saying I've lost it, and my wife's got a baby in the oven, so I *know* I still got it."

Whereas CJ popped his collar with pride after he said the words, Neil tugged at the Windsor knot around his neck until it loosened. He'd worn the blue silk necktie throughout Sunday morning worship with no problem, but now it suddenly felt nooselike. Neil had long ago accepted his childlessness as God's will for his life, but every once in a while — like now — he felt a twinge of misery that he had never experienced fatherhood. Well, there were the children at Kingdom Builders Academy, but as much as Neil cared about the wellbeing and development of those little ones, it wasn't the same. To them, his title was Doctor. He wanted the title of Daddy. And not having it wasn't due to lack of trying; that was for certain.

In the years that his marriage was good, it was *very* good, and Neil remembered praying often that God would give him the child that he and his wife so desperately wanted. He would have been content with a healthy child of either gender, but in his heart of hearts, a son was what he desired. In the end, he may have not succeeded as a husband, but Neil had no doubt that he would have been a great dad. Despite his fervent prayers, in the ten years that he and his ex were married, they'd never even had as much as a "pregnancy scare." Not even one. And like everything else that went wrong in their marriage, Audrey swore their empty nest was Neil's fault, but he refused to even consider the possibility. After all, Pop had given Ms. Ella Mae ten children, and all of Neil's siblings had children of their own, so it just didn't seem possible that sterility would be his lot in life. Neither he nor Audrey had been brave enough to go to the doctor to see who was really to blame. Not knowing was better than finding out the truth. That, apparently, was one of the few things they could still agree on at the end of their marriage.

In the long run, Neil had found a reason to be thankful in spite of the prayer that was never answered. He realized now that God had denied him for his own good. In one of the talks Neil and Shaylynn had early in their courtship, she'd admitted that she found relief in the fact that he had no children. Shaylynn told Neil that as wonderful as he was, she would not have entered into a relationship with him if he'd had kids; not if the mom was still alive. Where she'd grown up, and in the environment where she'd spent her youth, Shaylynn had seen more than her share of baby mama and baby daddy mischief. She liked her drama-free life and aimed to keep it that way. So if Shaylynn was the reward Neil would get in exchange for whatever it was that had hindered him from having babies with Audrey, the trade-off was well worth it as far as he was concerned. Besides, when . . . *if* . . . when . . . he married Shaylynn, Neil reasoned that he would have the son he'd always wanted in Chase. *But will Shaylynn allow Emmett's son to call another man Daddy?*

Neil cleared his throat as his mind reconnected with his body. He looked across the desk and saw CJ staring at him in silence. Neil hoped that his pastor hadn't said anything that his wandering mind had caused him to miss. He loosened his tie some more. "So if you're not trying to say I'm old, what are you saying?"

"I'm simply pointing out the fact that from the moment you met Shaylynn, you've been captivated by her." CJ rose from his chair, and calculated steps brought him to the front of his desk. He stood, resting against the brown oak furniture for a moment before hoisting himself up, and then sitting on top of it. From there, he looked down at Neil, who sat in a chair to his left, and continued. "Admit it, bruh. Even in the early weeks, when you were denying your true feelings, she had you hook, line, and sinker. It didn't take long for that initial bud of interest you had in her to blossom into full-blown love."

All Neil could do was nod. It was all true. He was sometimes hesitant to admit that he'd fallen so far so fast, because even to his own ears the truth sounded a little too mushy. Neil was a man's man. It had never been a part of his persona to be sentimental and sappy. Before Shaylynn, he had never been the first to "fall." Every woman with whom he'd had a serious relationship in the past had fallen for him first. Even Audrey. Everything about his relationship with Shaylynn was different from anything in his past. He didn't know if he'd go so far as to call it love at first sight, but it wasn't far from it.

Neil's dad used to call it "the thunderbolt," and Pop claimed that very few men were fortunate enough to experience it. Pop insisted that the thunderbolt was a good thing. A man shouldn't fight it, and he certainly shouldn't be embarrassed by it. It was that *thing* that hit a man at first sight and made him know almost immediately that she was the one. According to Pop, the thunderbolt only hit men. Since Proverbs 18:22 stated, *whoso findeth a wife, findeth a good thing,* Pop said it wasn't possible for the thunderbolt to hit a woman. A woman wasn't supposed to be out looking. And he didn't care how much society changed or what people said about the evolution of the female gender, Neil's dad was adamant in his belief. Based on the Word of God, the thunderbolt was reserved for men, and Pop said it had hit him within minutes of meeting his Ella.

Countless times he'd told his growing sons, "If any one of y'all ever be lucky enough to be hit by the thunderbolt, I hope to God that you ain't dumb enough to let her get away." Their father would look them in the face and point an unbending finger. "Marry that gal, you hear me, boy? Don't let her get away. Marry her," he'd reiterate. "You ain't got to be courtin' forever. A thunderbolt relationship is a lifetime relationship. You can take that right there to the bank and cash it any day of the week." And Pop must have known what he was talking about, because he was twenty-three when that thunderbolt hit him, and he said he would have married Neil's mother instantly, but her daddy wouldn't let him. Ella was only thirteen at the time, and her father said she had to be fifteen before she could marry. Pop hung in there, because despite the marked age difference, he knew she was the one. Once she turned fifteen, it was a wrap. They were married twenty-four short hours after the day he proposed, and they remained happy and in love 'til the day Pop died.

"Am I right; yes or no?"

The fog of memories lifted from Neil's head just in time for him to hear CJ's query. He had no earthly idea what question he was expected to answer. Were they still on the subject of how quickly Neil had fallen for Shaylynn, or was his pastor now talking about something else?

"Well?" CJ leaned forward so far that he almost toppled off his desk. And when Neil's pause lingered, worry lines etched their way across CJ's forehead. "Has something changed that you haven't told me about? You do still want to marry Shay, don't you?"

"Yes . . . yes . . . of course I do . . . why wouldn't I? . . . Of course I want to marry her . . . yes." Neil's words were so quick they strung together like a run-on sentence. The last thing he needed was to plant seeds of doubt in the head of the man who he would ask to be the presiding minister over the wedding. Neil knew CJ like the back of his hand. Friendship and brotherhood aside, if he thought for one moment that Neil wasn't completely sure that he wanted to make a lifelong commitment to Shaylynn, CJ wouldn't give a second thought to presiding over the ceremony. "That's not it at all," Neil added. He felt like he was talking to the Jewish jeweler all over again; only this time he wasn't confiding in a stranger. "I'm sure of what I want, I'm . . . I'm just not a hundred percent on what she wants."

When CJ scooted off of his desk in one swift motion and stood silent on the floor beside his chair, Neil felt hot under the scope of his pastor's eyes. Although he wasn't looking at CJ, Neil knew CJ was looking at him. The room was so quiet that Neil could hear the seconds as they ticked away on the wall clock. He could hear the soft humming of the water cooler in the corner. He could hear himself breathing.

"Please tell me that this isn't still about

Emmett Ford," CJ finally said.

With his eyes locked on the wooden cross that was mounted on the wall behind CJ's desk, Neil forced himself not to grimace at the sound of his rival's name. He said nothing as he nibbled lightly at his bottom lip. His silence must have given consent.

"It is, isn't it?" CJ sounded disgusted.

"You just told me not to tell you."

"Don't get coy with me, Neil."

With frustration lacing his voice, Neil looked up at CJ and blurted, "What do you want me to say?" He stood and rubbed his hands over his graying temples. "Look, I know it sounds crazy, but —"

"It doesn't just sound crazy, it *is* crazy." CJ sounded equally as frustrated, and Neil knew why. They'd had this conversation so many times that it was stale, bordering on molded. "Neil, Mayor Ford died eight years ago."

"Physically, that's true, but in Shay's mind, I think —"

"Okay, stop right there," CJ ordered. He stepped a little closer to Neil. "Did you say you think? What do you mean, you think? I can't believe we're still having this conversation. At this point in your relationship with Shaylynn, you shouldn't be *thinking* anything. When we talked two weeks ago, you said —"

"I know what I said." Neil plopped back into his seat. "You don't have to remind me."

"Apparently I do," CJ challenged, and then proceeded to do so. "You told me that you were gonna talk to her and get a clear understanding of where her head is. Even then you were telling me stuff that you *thought*. And now, here we are, two weeks later, and you're still *thinking*. What are you afraid of?"

Neil eyed him. "I ain't afraid of nothing."

"The devil is a lie," CJ replied, returning his glare. "You're afraid of *something,* that's for sure. That part isn't even a question. What I need you to reveal is the identity of that something." Neil didn't have the opportunity to voice another denial before CJ continued. "You keep telling me how much you love this woman, and Resa tells me that Shaylynn feels the same way about you. But every time we talk, you're still strapped into the bucket seat of this same frightful theme park ride that is apparently called The Emmett Ford. You've brainwashed your own self into thinking you're in some crazy tug of war with this man."

"Emmett isn't some figment of my imagination, CJ," Neil spat. Just like that, he was back on his feet. He wanted to pound his fist on CJ's desk, but suppressed the urge. Nobody understood, and Neil was sick and tired of trying to explain it. "You act as though I'm making this junk up, and I'm a candidate for first dibs in the loony bin." Realizing he was on the verge of screaming, Neil took a breath and lowered his voice. He looked his friend square in the eyes. "You've been here for every day of my relationship with Shay. I ain't telling you nothing that you don't already know, so don't make me out to be some kind of hallucinating cuckoo bird. You know about the ring. You know about the dried violets on her mantle. You know how she brings his name up in every other conversation. You know all that."

CJ leaned against his desk and crossed his arms. "Yes, I do know all of that, Neil. But I don't read into the same things that you do. You see all of those things as yellow caution lights and red stop signs; I see it as normal human behavior. Granted, her wearing the ring for seven years was excess, but people have different ways of dealing with certain issues. Just because I wouldn't do it doesn't make it wrong. How many times have I told you that?" CJ didn't wait for an answer. "Shaylynn may have needed to do that to get through that phase of her grieving process. The important thing shouldn't be what she *did,* but what she's doing now. She met you, she fell in love, and she removed the ring. Meeting you made her do something that she hadn't been able to do in seven years. That should mean something to you."

Neil blew out a puff of air. "It does mean something, but that's just one piece of the puzzle. What about those dead flowers? What about how she talks about him all the time?"

"She was married to him, bruh. What do you expect?"

Neil wasn't buying that. "I was married before too. Do you hear me throwing Audrey's name up in everything? I wonder how she'd feel if I all of a sudden started saying stuff like, 'Audrey would have enjoyed this movie,' or 'That's the perfume Audrey used to wear.' "

"In the first place, it's not the same thing, because Emmett died, whereas you divorced Audrey. Your termination of your marriage from Audrey was a choice that was ultimately made by both of you. In utter contrast, an assassin's bullet forced the dissolution of Shay's marriage. Emmett is no longer around and can't serve as a threat to your and Shaylynn's relationship. Audrey, on the other hand, is still alive and well, and as I understand it, she still makes guest appearances at Taylor family functions. There's a big difference in the situations, and if anybody has a right to be apprehensive, it should be Shaylynn."

Neil rolled his eyes in silent protest, but he knew he didn't have a leg to stand on. How could he argue the point? The evidence had the scales tilting in CJ's favor. Less than six months ago, Audrey drove her signature pink Cadillac in the yard of Neil's childhood home in Mississippi. Her uninvited appearance was no real surprise to anyone. Audrey had shown up at eleven of the fifteen reunions Neil's family had had since the divorce. The most recent showing made it an even dozen. Knowing the likelihood was great, Neil thought it was best that he gave Shaylynn fair warning. He didn't know how she would receive the news that she would probably meet his ex-wife at the very same family gathering where he was taking her to meet his siblings and other family members, but Neil knew that it wouldn't be right to withhold the information. Shaylynn didn't even seem thwarted when he made the big reveal, and as they stood in the yard along with the other Taylor clan that day,

Neil's sweetheart showed no signs of insecurity when Audrey stepped out of her car, looking like the Mary Kay professional that she was.

Ella Mae couldn't be convinced that Audrey didn't make it her business to look especially good when she knew Neil would be around. She had packed on a few pounds since their divorce, but she carried them rather well. Even still, she was no match for the much younger, much shapelier, much prettier new lady in Neil's life. Audrey must have heard the standing eight count very shortly after she set eyes on Shaylynn, because less than an hour after she arrived, she made a remark about having a meeting to attend, and then she was gone. Neil couldn't prove that she was lying, but if he were a gambling man, he'd put his money on it. It was too much of an irony that in all the years before, she'd been one of the very last to leave the reunions.

"You know I'm right," CJ was saying. When Neil parted his lips to interrupt, CJ held up his hand to stop him. "And in the second place, I have to put myself in Shay's shoes. I love Theresa." He pointed toward the door that his wife had exited through earlier. "I love that woman with all my heart. And, God forbid, if my phone rang right now and somebody on the other end said, 'Pastor Loather, your wife just got killed in an automobile accident,' I would be devastated. I'd be *more* than devastated." A pained look that crossed his face made Neil wonder if he was imagining that it was all true. CJ seemed to snap out of it as he added, "I wouldn't get over that in a day, a week, a month, or even a year. Me and Resa have made a life together. We have hopes and plans and dreams for our family that a sudden death would snatch away.

"Seven or eight years from now . . . ten or twelve years from now . . . fifteen or twenty years from now, I'd still be talking about her. There would be sights, sounds, smells, music, television shows, even biblical passages that would remind me of her. And if ever God gave me the strength and courage to move on with my life, whatever woman would even have a remote possibility of sharing in it would have to be able to deal with that. You know why? Because Resa ain't going nowhere. Not when it comes to this right here." CJ pressed his index finger into his chest several times using quick hand motions. "And if you're gonna be with Shaylynn, you're gonna have to get over it, bruh, 'cause Emmett Ford, as dead as he may be, will always, on some level, live in that sister's heart."

# FIVE

"Come on in, baby." Ella's grin was wide as she stepped aside to allow the surprised dinner guest to enter Neil's bachelor pad. She practically had to pull Shaylynn inside before quickly closing the door, barricading them from being battered by any more of the outside frigid temperatures.

The shock of seeing her had slowed Shaylynn's movements, but she managed to return Ella's hospitable smile. That must have been why Neil's SUV was parked in the driveway instead of the garage. His mom's car must have been there. When Neil called and asked if she would allow him to take Chase to his house after school, and then she join them for dinner later, Shaylynn was under the impression that it would be just the three of them.

"Hi, Ms. Ella Mae." Shaylynn loved Neil's mother; she just didn't expect to see her. It had taken her some time to get used to calling her Ms. Ella Mae. When Shaylynn first met Eloise Mae Flowers Taylor as a decorating client, she became accustomed to calling her Ms. Flowers while Chase called her Ms. Eloise. It wasn't until she began dating Neil that she tagged the name on his mother that the rest of the family used when addressing her.

Ella always offered the warmest greetings. "Give me a hug, baby. How you been?"

"Busy, but fine. It's so good to see you." While she accepted the hug that Ella offered, Shaylynn's eyes scanned the space for any signs of her son.

"Good to see you too. It's nice and warm in here, so let me take that." Ella reached for Shaylynn's full-length navy blue coat. When Shaylynn removed it and handed it to her, Ella stepped back in admiration. "You looking mighty, mighty pretty this evening, but then again, you always look pretty."

"Thank you." A timid smile stretched Shaylynn's lips, and she arbitrarily ran her fingers through her signature braids that cascaded over her shoulders.

"I don't know if I've ever seen you in all white before," Ella remarked as she hung Shaylynn's coat on the rack near the door. "Is that new?"

Shaylynn reached up and touched the cowl neckline of the sweater dress that she wore, then gently fingered the silver chain of the necklace that was largely hidden by the thick fabric. Technically the dress wasn't white; the color was closer to cream. Shaylynn pondered for a moment, wondering what Neil's mother would think if she told her that she'd just bought it today . . . just for Neil. Consciously, and sometimes subconsciously, Shaylynn found herself often wearing beige, ivory, taupe, and other neutral colors along that line when she was around Neil. Ever since she found out that they were among his favorites. Even the décor of his house reflected his choice colors. "I bought it not too long ago," she finally answered, "but this is my first time wearing it." Shaylynn released a soft sigh, relieved that she could tell the whole truth without telling the *whole* truth.

"Oooh," Ella sang out. "And look at them shoes!"

Robotically, Shaylynn looked down at her three-inch-heeled Anne Klein boots. The stretch material hugged her legs all the way up to the calves, and their shade of cream matched the dress's to perfection. She'd complemented the entire ensemble with dangling pearl earrings and an oversized silver, flower-like ring with pearl accents that she wore on the middle finger of her left hand. Shaylynn had been pretty proud of herself when she gave her image a final once-over before leaving her home to head to Neil's, but now, as she looked at Ella's casual top and slacks, Shaylynn felt over-dressed and suddenly self-conscious.

"You have a seat right over there, and make yourself comfy." Ella pointed at Neil's tan leather couch.

Shaylynn smoothed the back of her dress as she sat down, but making herself comfortable wasn't as easy, and her self-consciousness wasn't the only reason. She was still getting accustomed to allowing her son to be in places that she wasn't. Where was Chase? "Is Solomon here?" Shaylynn figured she'd ask that question instead of the one that was really on her mind. She didn't need Neil's mother to think she didn't trust them with her son.

"Oh yeah, he's here." Ella laughed and reached for her cane that was leaning against the loveseat. "That young'un of mine and that li'l linebacker of yours were outside playing football a little earlier. They're upstairs getting cleaned up and changed. They ought to be down any minute. I hollered up there and told Sol that you were here when I saw you through the window as you pulled up in the driveway."

Shaylynn leaned against the back of the seat and tried to relax. If Neil and Chase came down in jeans and T-shirts, she would just die. Why did she get all dressed up? It was Tuesday, for goodness sake! Why didn't she just assume that it would be a casual affair?

The delicious smells floating from the kitchen area were starting to intoxicate her and free her mind from the bondage of worry. She smelled collard greens, some type of fish, and something sweet. On cue, Shaylynn's stomach released a soft rumble. She had no idea that Neil could cook like that; though it should not have shocked her with Ella Mae Taylor for his mother. "Did he cook seafood?" It was Shaylynn's favorite, and she hoped the answer was yes.

Ella laughed out loud. "Chile, *he* didn't cook a thing. I baked stuffed salmon and prepared some long-grain wild rice, and collards. For dessert, y'all got some homemade peach cobbler." She began walking toward the kitchen. Her cane helped her to move a little faster.

"You did the cooking?" Shaylynn was surprised, but she had eaten Ella's award-worthy food too many times to be the least bit disappointed.

The woman flashed a grin and said, "What you think I'm over here for?" before disappearing in the kitchen.

Did that mean she wasn't staying for dinner? Shaylynn inhaled deeply and became too hypnotized by the aromas to care one way or the other. Oddly enough, in all the months that she and Neil had been dating, he had never invited her to his home for dinner; they always ate out. As a matter of fact, their time alone at his condo had been very limited. Usually if they were there longer than an hour, it was because the three of them — she, Neil, and Chase — were all there together playing board games or watching movies. That was another one of her rules to which Neil had grudgingly agreed, but for once, Shaylynn wanted to do it God's way. She'd grown up with such little self-worth and so deprived of love and affection that every boyfriend she'd had since the age of seventeen had been able to talk her out of her clothes without much effort. Even Emmett had done it, but unlike the three before him, he really did love her, and he'd proven it during their brief life together.

This time, though, Shaylynn would do it right. Not that she thought Neil would try anything; he had been nothing but respectful and honorable. If the harsh truth be told, he probably wasn't the one she didn't trust. Shaylynn's emotions had the tendency to run amok when she was with Neil, and that was especially true when they were alone. The thought of it all sometimes still boggled her mind. Shaylynn had never thought she could love again, let alone *desire* at a level like this. After Emmett's death, the thick body of ice that she had built around her heart was soundproof, yet somehow, when Neil talked, she could hear him. And though the glacier was guaranteed unbreakable, Neil managed to shatter it to smithereens.

Theirs was a relationship that never should have developed, but it had, and when she was with him, she found herself letting her guard down more and more and allowing Neil greater entrance into her heart. But Shaylynn was determined that despite her past record, her heart was all that she'd allow him to enter. This time, she knew she could abstain in spite of her fleshly desires. Not because she had found some great secret to celibacy between the time she dated Emmett and now, but because between then and now, she had found Christ. She had to believe that the Holy Spirit would be her keeper and would bring her flesh under subjection, but there was no mistaking that the Holy Spirit had His work cut out for Him.

Neil was handsome, and his sexiness wasn't limited to his physical makeup. Even the way he walked, talked, ate, and breathed were sexy. He had a level of coolness that probably only came with age and experience. Shaylynn had never even considered dating an older man prior to him. A man in his mid-forties could never have gotten her attention a couple of years ago, but now she wondered, if things didn't work out between her and Neil, if a man without graying temples would even get the courtesy of a second look from her. There was something about the way Neil talked to her . . . and looked at her . . . and treated her. No man her age had ever compared. Emmett loved her, no doubt about it, but chivalry wasn't a subject in which he excelled. Neil, on the other hand, majored in it. If that PhD he held didn't license him to teach a class on it, it should. Opening doors for her, helping her put on and remove her coat in the colder months, draping his suit jacket across her shoulders if she caught a draft inside a restaurant or movie theatre in the warmer months, pulling out her chair for her whenever they dined together, even standing up whenever she had to leave the table to visit the ladies' room.

At first, Shaylynn thought it was a regional thing since she'd never seen it before moving to the South and meeting Neil. But now, after living in Atlanta for nearly three years, she realized that it wasn't *where* he was raised, but rather *when* he was raised. Shaylynn had yet to see even one guy in her generation do all of those things. *How* he was raised probably had a lot to do with it too. At Neil's family reunion, she noted that all of his brothers did the same with the women in their lives. It made Shaylynn sad that she'd never gotten to meet the man Neil fondly called Pop. She felt like she owed him a thank you, a hug, *and* a box of chocolates. He had trained his sons well.

"Hey, Ma!"

Speaking of sons, Shaylynn's wrenched her from her thoughts as he ran down the steps and into her awaiting arms. She barely had time to stand up before he reached her. "Hi, Chase." She kissed his forehead and detected the scent of Irish Spring soap. "How was school? Did you have homework? Did you get a chance to do it?"

He loosed his arms from her waist and said, "Yes, ma'am. I'm all done, and Dr. Taylor checked over it."

"Good. That's good." Shaylynn smiled and sat, pulling him onto the space beside her. She noticed his casual outfit: jeans and a pullover hoodie with the Kingdom Builders Academy emblem on the front. Her self-consciousness returned, and she wished she could go home, change clothes, and be back before Neil came down to join them. "What else did you do today?" She figured the small talk might help take her mind off her inappropriate attire . . . at least for a while.

"Me and Dr. Taylor played football while Ms. Ella Mae was cooking."

"You did?" Shaylynn widened her eyes like she didn't already know. She plucked a particle of lint from the front of his hoodie. "Who won?"

"He let me win." Chase grinned wide. "He always lets me win."

"I did not *let* you win. You won fair and square."

Shaylynn looked up at the sound of Neil's voice, and for a moment, she felt suffocated by her own breath. Her earlier concerns disappeared in midair at the sight of him. Using calculated steps, he descended the stairwell dressed in a chocolate brown suit accented by a dress shirt and shoes that matched the tan of his living room furniture. He wore no tie. Instead, the first two buttons of his shirt were undone, giving him a casual yet dressy appearance. This man was just too debonair for words. He came to a stop on the other side of the coffee table, appearing to be careful not to stand too close in the presence of Chase. Shaylynn's mind told her to follow her son's lead and stand up to greet Neil, but her legs wouldn't cooperate.

"Na-ah." Chase shook his head and grinned up at Neil, seeming clueless to how thick the air in the room had grown. "You let me win, and you know it."

"What I know is that you're a whole lot better than you think you are," Neil replied. "You're gonna be a heck of a quarterback one of these days." Then he turned his eyes to the place where Shaylynn continued to sit. "Good evening, Shay. You look . . . lovely, as usual. How are you?"

She swallowed. Hard. It had been over a year now. How was he still able to do this to her? There was just something about those eyes . . . and that voice. She swallowed again. Harder. "Thank you, Solomon. I'm fine."

"Yes. Yes, you are." His eyes seemed to reach into her soul.

Shaylynn blinked. She couldn't believe he'd said that. Her eyes darted to Chase, and then back at Neil. With her eyes, she tried to tell him to cut it out. In return, his eyes seemed to be daring her to try to make him. Shaylynn hoped Chase couldn't read morse code.

"I hope you're hungry," Neil said.

Shaylynn released a nervous laugh. "Why? Could you hear my stomach growl from upstairs?"

Neil laughed too. "No. But I'll take that as a yes."

"Right on time," Ella said, emerging from the kitchen. "Food is all ready, and the table is all set."

"Thanks, Ms. Ella Mae." Neil kissed his mother's cheek and pressed a few folded bills in her hand. "Let him eat whatever he wants, okay?"

"He done already told me that he wants chicken fingers from Zaxby's," she replied. Then she looked at Chase. "Ready?"

"Yes, ma'am." He bounced with excitement.

Shaylynn's legs quickly found their strength and stability, and she rose to her feet, looking from one of them to the other. Ready? Ready for what? Where were they going? She was totally lost. Had she missed something? "Wait a minute. You're leaving?" She reached for Chase's arm.

"It's okay, Shay." Neil's voice was soothing. "Please let him go with Ms. Ella Mae. I'm sorry I didn't ask earlier, but my plans . . . I mean, the dinner . . . it's just for the two of us. I'll drive over to her house and get him and bring him back here to you once we're done. It'll only be a couple of hours. I promise."

This would be groundbreaking in their relationship. If Ella and Chase left, it would leave only the two of them. Neil had to know that she wouldn't have agreed to this had he mentioned it when he first asked her to come over for dinner. Of course he knew. That was probably why he didn't mention it. Shaylynn didn't like being put on the spot like this, but she liked the man who had put her on the spot far too much to deny him. Something in Neil's voice and eyes was pleading, and Shaylynn couldn't stop the nodding of her head that granted the permission that he requested. She could visibly see his body relax as he breathed a sigh of relief.

"Thank you," Neil said.

Shaylynn quietly hugged Chase and again kissed his forehead, all the while praying that God would help her to keep her vow and her virtue tonight. "You behave yourself, you hear me?" She knew Chase wouldn't misbehave. That charge was more to herself than her son.

"Yes, ma'am." The glee could be heard in his voice when he turned to Ella and said, "Give me just a minute. I'ma be right back. I gotta go get my coat and my backpack." Chase's fast legs already had him at the top of the stairwell before he finished the last sentence.

"He'll be fine, baby," Ella said, giving Shaylynn's arm a reassuring touch. "Chase don't never give me no trouble. Don't you worry your pretty head none."

Shaylynn nodded again and watched in silence as Chase bounded back downstairs wearing the Falcons jacket that Neil had purchased for him. Her silence reigned as she watched Neil help his mother into her coat before walking them both outside. She heard the garage door open, heard Ella crank up her car, and heard the fading sound of the car's motor as she drove away. Shaylynn hadn't moved. Her feet remained planted in the exact same place when Neil returned, closing the door behind his reentrance. When he turned the deadbolt, the sound of it locking into place seemed to bounce off the walls of his home.

Neil turned to face her, and then cupped his hands to his mouth and blew several lungfuls of warm breath into them. Apparently satisfied, he took several steps that brought him within inches of Shaylynn. "It's okay, suga," he whispered. "I just feel very selfish tonight, and I need to have you all to myself so we can . . . talk. You aren't mad, are you?"

Like a deaf woman, Shaylynn watched the movement of his lips as he spoke. Then like a blind woman, she reached up with both hands and used her fingers to trace his face. His skin was always smooth and clean-cut, just the way she liked it. He closed his eyes momentarily, released a pleasurable moan, and then reopened them. How could she be mad at eyes like those? Like a mute woman, she finally answered his question with a slow shake of her head.

"Thank you." He followed that with, "I love you," and then brushed his lips softly against each of her cheeks before finding her lips and parting them for a deep kiss that seemed to last an eternity.

*Lord, help me.* Shaylynn hoped that God heard the prayers of blind deaf-mutes.

# Six

He went to Jared.

Twice.

Once on Monday to purchase the ring, and again on Wednesday to return it.

Neil hadn't seen or spoken to Shaylynn since they parted ways on Tuesday night. He was lying on the sofa with his back to her as she left. He'd had to settle for a good night kiss that she planted on his right cheek, but he didn't care. By then, all he wanted was for the evening to end.

On most days, Neil had no problem keeping his personal and business lives separate. If something went awry at work, he knew how to leave it behind when he clocked out for the day. By the same token, if anything got off track in Neil's personal life, he knew how to leave that at home. But his growing dissatisfaction with this Shaylynn thing was getting harder to mask these days. And as keen a gift she had for sniffing out trouble, it was no real surprise when Margaret strolled into Neil's office during the lunch hour on Thursday with her famous frames resting on the end of her nose.

"Okay, Dr. Taylor. I've tried to mind my own business for the last two days, but I can't hold my tongue any longer."

"I really wish you would, Ms. Dasher." Neil knew where this was headed, and he really wasn't in the mood. He removed the reading glasses he sometimes wore when he did paperwork, and then he stood and filed away the folder he'd just completed.

"Well you can wish all you might; it's not gonna happen. Not today."

"Yeah. As if it happens any other day." Neil mumbled the words under his breath, but Margaret must have been wearing her hearing aid today.

"Look. Don't be taking the anger you got for *Mrs.* Ford out on me."

Neil's movements froze. For her information, he wasn't angry, he was annoyed. And furthermore, Shaylynn wasn't *Mrs.* Ford, she was Ms. Ford. Neil didn't verbalize any of that, but when he slammed shut the file drawer, and then turned and glared at Margaret, she heard his thoughts loud and clear. Her hearing aid must have been set on supersonic.

"Sorry," she said, holding up both her hands in surrender.

"Oh, really? Then why don't I believe you?" Neil didn't even try to hide his reservation.

"Look, Dr. Taylor —"

"No . . . you look."

"No . . . you look."

"No. *You* look!" Neil knew that nothing about the volume or tone of his voice reflected professionalism, but at the moment, he didn't care. Besides, he and his longtime assistant often crossed the lines of professionalism at work, so this was nothing new. "I don't like the way you seem to take joy in blaming everything on Shaylynn, and I'm sick and tired of correcting you when you *mistakenly* refer to her as Mrs. Ford." He threw up the index and middle fingers on both his hands to signal quotation marks around his stressed word. "I'm gonna need you to have a little more respect for her than that." If Neil thought his authoritative tone would immediately humble Margaret and send her to her corner of the boxing ring battered and bruised, he had another thought coming.

"Respect her?" Margaret twisted her mouth like she'd swallowed a spoonful of castor oil. "You would have done better to ask me to have enough respect for *you,* Dr. Taylor. At least that would have been an order I could have filled."

Neil's back stiffened. "What?" He had never heard Margaret flat-out admit that she didn't care for Shaylynn, but that seemed to be what he was hearing buried between the lines of her retort. "Are you telling me you don't respect Shay? Where is this coming from? You used to like her. What has she done to you to change that?"

"It's not what she's done to me, it's what she's done to you." Margaret paused long enough to close the door that separated her workspace from Neil's, barricading them and their voices inside the privacy of Neil's office. Most days, nobody would walk in during the lunch hour, but Neil guessed she wanted the added insurance. "Yeah, I used to like her," Margaret continued, "but that was because she was making you happy. When the two of you first got together, I thought she was a gift from God to you. You were happier than I'd ever seen. I always said you were too good a man to be without a wife, and well, when Ms. Ford came along, I thought she was the cat's meow."

*The cat's meow?* Neil looked at Margaret and shook his head. Every now and then, her word choices gave away the age that her skin's good elasticity didn't show. He wanted to verbally tell her that, but he didn't want to interrupt. Neil was curious to see where Margaret was going with this rant of hers.

"If my attitude about her has changed, it's because my perspective about her has changed," she continued. "I consider you my friend, and I just happen to be one of those people who don't like it when somebody messes with my friends."

Neil scowled. "And what? Shay is messing with me? Is that what you think?"

"You're not happy anymore, Dr. Taylor, and I've had enough experiences of my own to know when a bad relationship is the culprit."

"Bad relationship?" The hard hit of Margaret's words made Neil stagger backward. "Is that what you think? You think I'm in a bad relationship?"

"Honey, any relationship that makes a man as unstable as this one makes you is a bad relationship. You're changing. And not for the better. It's getting to where I don't know which one of your personalities I'm gonna be dealing with when I come to work every day. Monday and Tuesday, you were happy. Wednesday and today, you're temperamental. Only God knows what Friday is gonna bring. If you were a woman, I'd think you were going through the change." She looked over the rim of her glasses at Neil. "I don't claim to be the smartest woman in the world, but it don't take a rocket scientist to see that you're not as sure about Ms. Ford as you used to be. You're a decent man, Dr. Taylor, and decent men aren't quick to walk away from a relationship; especially when they're the ones who initiated it. When men like you have to fight to win over a woman, you feel like you should fight to keep her. But believe me when I tell you that some things just ain't worth fighting for."

Neil released a heavy sigh. *Not again.* First Rabbi Bernstein, then CJ, and now Margaret. Everybody was starting to question what he and Shaylynn had, and since they were all drawing their conclusions from his actions and reactions, Neil couldn't help but feel responsible. It was never his intent to turn anybody against Shaylynn. Even in the face of what they were going through right now, she was an exceptional woman. "You're so off base, Ms. Dasher. So off base." It was all he could say before sitting in the chair behind his desk and rubbing his tired eyes. Neil felt spent. He hadn't gotten much sleep since Tuesday night, and this conversation was draining him of what little energy he had.

"Is that so? Well, fine then, Mr. Reggie Jackson." Margaret's tone dripped with sarcasm. "If I'm so off base, then use that strong right arm of yours to throw me out."

In spite of his irritation, Neil couldn't help but chuckle. "Ms. Dasher, do you know how long Reggie Jackson has been retired from baseball?"

"I'm not a dummy, Dr. Taylor. I know he retired in the late nineties. I don't follow sports like you do, therefore, his name just happened to be the first that came to mind."

"Try the late eighties," Neil responded. "And since he was a lefty when it came to batting and throwing, I don't think he would have used a strong right arm to do much of anything that was baseball related."

Margaret sucked her teeth. "Like I said, I don't follow sports like you do."

"Then maybe you should stick to comparisons that you know more about, like cooking . . . or meddling." Neil jiggled his mouse to get rid of the Kingdom Builders Academy default screensaver and found himself staring at a picture that he, Shaylynn, and Chase had taken together following a recent Sunday morning worship

111

service. They were the vision of a family, and a smile tugged at the corners of his lips.

"Good friends always meddle," Margaret reminded him.

Neil heard her, but at that very moment, something about the image on his screen had arrested his attention. It arrested his smile also. Arrested it, stripped it, locked it up, and threw away the key. Neil had never noticed this detail of the photo before, but now it was all he could see. How long had this been going on right under his nose? He wished he could will the screensaver back, but it would be another five minutes before it would activate.

"Are you all right, Dr. Taylor?" His extended silence had apparently begun to concern his assistant.

Neil forcefully averted his eyes from the picture that now seemed larger than life. "Can we talk about this later, Ms. Dasher?"

"Dr. Taylor —"

"Okay, let me rephrase that." Neil needed Margaret to leave. And he needed her to know that he needed her to leave. Looking her straight in the eyes, he said, "We can talk about this later, Ms. Dasher." There wasn't a question mark anywhere in his restatement.

She rolled her eyes, blew out a sigh, and

shook her head, but as long as she got the message and acted accordingly, Neil couldn't care less about her body language. Without saying another word, Margaret turned around and headed for the door.

As soon as she closed it behind her exit, Neil reached for his cell phone. He stared at it for a few minutes, wishing that he had someone to call other than CJ. Neil already knew what CJ would say. He would never understand why Neil would purchase a ring one day, and then return it less than forty-eight hours later. In times like this, Neil missed his brother more than ever. Dwayne was only four years Neil's senior, but he was wise beyond his years. Dwayne knew everything about Neil — the good, the bad, and the ugly — and he'd prayed him out of a few pitfalls that none of his other family members were even aware of. Neil had no doubt that if his brother was still alive, he would be able to offer some sound advice. Neil had other older brothers, but he'd never confided in them with personal issues like this before, and he wouldn't feel quite comfortable doing it now either.

After another moment's thought, Neil picked up his cell phone, went to his address book, and clicked on the name he was looking for. "I must really be desperate."

# SEVEN

This was more than a long shot. Deacon Homer Burgess was old by any definition. He had celebrated his ninety-second birthday just a month ago, and the church held a special service in his honor, as not only the oldest member of KBCC, but also the member who had been connected with the ministry the longest. At Deacon Burgess's request, Neil sang "Center of My Joy," a classic by Richard Smallwood that took the gospel world by storm back in 1986. The aging deacon was one of the wisest men that Neil knew . . . at least, on his sane days. But that was the problem. Alzheimer's had been the archenemy of Deacon Burgess's mind for the last five years. At the onset, he had more good days than bad, but as time passed, the good days were coming fewer and farther between. Deacon Burgess hadn't fully been in his right mind a single Sunday since his birthday celebration. Neil's heart went out to the man. He'd grown rather fond of him over the past couple of years. When the call connected, the telephone only rang once.

"Burgess residence; Teena Marie speaking."

Neil snickered. He always got a kick out of hearing Deacon Burgess's personal caregiver answer the phone. Nurse Teena Marie Mitchell's first and middle names matched the stage name of the late, great blue-eyed soul singer who brought a new flavor, and color, to the Motown Record label when she hit the scene in '79. But with her full lips, copper skin, and big hair, this Teena Marie looked far more like Tina Turner than she did the Ivory Queen of Soul. Still, she enjoyed flaunting the name.

"Good evening, Ms. Teena. This is Dr. Taylor. How're you this afternoon?" Teena was only a few years older than he, but Neil always felt the need to put a "Ms." in front of her name.

"Oh hey, Dr. Taylor." What little tone of professionalism that Teena's voice initially had dissolved like ice on hot coals. "Any day above ground is a good day, so I'm doing just fine. How 'bout you? You good?"

The normal reply would have been a simple yes, but today, the normal reply would also have been a lie. "Well, I'm alive too, so I guess I can't complain," he chose to say. "How about my buddy? What's the good deacon up to today?"

"Running me half crazy, that's what he's up to," Teena replied. "Funny you should call, 'cause I just told him a little while ago that I was gonna call you and have you come over here and string him up if he didn't quit cuttin' the fool."

That was a good sign. If Homer Burgess was acting up, that meant God had granted him another day with at least a portion of his good mental capacity.

"Is that Deacon Taylor you talkin' to?"

Neil heard the familiar voice from somewhere in the background of the phone call, and it made him smile. If the aging deacon was sane enough to pick up on who his caregiver was talking to, that was a *really* good sign.

"Yeah, this him," Teena said, "but he didn't ask to speak to you, so you just stay at that table and finish eating your lunch."

"Hand me that phone," Deacon Burgess ordered. She must not have done it fast enough, because his next words were, "All right now, don't make me have to get up from here."

On his end, Neil was thoroughly enjoying

the live entertainment. He couldn't see either one of them, but he'd seen those two go at it before, and the looks that he knew were on both their faces had him laughing out loud.

"Are you kidding me?" Teena's already high voice got even higher. "By the time you get up and shuffle your way over here, it'll be tomorrow."

"And once I get over there, it'll be next week by the time you wake up out that coma I'ma put you in when I beat you wit' my stick."

As entertaining as it was, Neil knew that it was time to step in and play referee. "Let me speak with him, Ms. Teena."

"Okay, but while you got him on this line, tell him to stop treating me like I'm some kind of maid. I'ma be asking for a raise if he don't stop running me crazy."

"I'll talk to him." Neil laughed, but he meant every word, because unbeknownst to Deacon Homer Burgess, Neil was the one who paid Teena's fees.

"Deacon Taylor," Homer said immediately upon getting on the phone, "you know how you and your brother used to sing, and God would chase demons outta folks?" He didn't even give Neil time to respond. "Well, I need you to come over here and stand in front of this woman and just go to singing your heart out."

Neil laughed. "You'd better behave yourself, Deacon Burgess. You know Ms. Teena is a godsend for you. You need that woman, so stop fighting with her."

Homer had outlived two wives and all of his siblings. Between both marriages, he'd had eight children, and he'd outlived some of them too. The ones who were still alive didn't reside in metropolitan Atlanta, and collectively, they'd decided that it was time for their father to live out the remains of his twilight years in a nursing home. Deacon Burgess didn't want that, and Neil didn't want it either. Once he found out that their fellow church member, Teena Mitchell, was an unemployed LPN looking for work, Neil pitched the idea to her to provide private care for Homer, and she accepted. And the two of them had been in a love-hate relationship ever since.

"She got her traps set for me, that's what it is," Deacon Burgess said, drawing another laugh from Neil. "I know a woman wit' a trap when I see her. That's how the women-folk act when they on the hunt for a husband."

"Ain't nobody tryin'a trap you," Teena called out from somewhere in the house.

"I'm only fifty years old. You old enough to be my daddy. As a matter of fact, you could be my granddaddy."

Deacon Burgess kept talking to Neil like he hadn't heard his nurse's rebuttal. "She tryin'a marry me, son, and I done been there and done that . . . and then I had the nerve to go back there and do that again. I'm tired now. This old back ain't what it used to be."

Neil was wiping moisture from his eyes now. The laugh felt better than good. He needed it. "How are you, Deacon? You sound good today."

"I'm in the land of the livin', thank the good Lord. I been doing good for the past four days. Ever since you sung my song at my birthday party."

That wasn't four days ago; it was four weeks. But Neil didn't correct him. "Glad to hear it, Deac. I just . . ." Suddenly he wondered if now was the right time, or if Homer was the right person for the conversation that was weighing heavily on his heart. "I just wanted to call and check up on you. I didn't get to speak to you after church last Sunday. I had a personal meeting with Pastor Loather following service."

"Oh. I didn't even see you at church last Sunday. I thought maybe you and that sweetheart of yours had done rode off into the sunset or something."

Neil sighed. Deacon Burgess had certainly been out of it Sunday if he couldn't recall seeing him. Neil was sitting right beside him in the deacons' corner, and he'd spoken to Deacon Burgess upon his arrival. The two of them almost always sat side by side. Not because the church had individual assigned seating or anything, but because none of the other deacons ever wanted that space. Deacon Burgess had to be tone deaf, because when he sang, it sounded like he was gargling rocks . . . and he sang loud every Sunday. The other deacons avoided sitting next to him because of it, but Neil had learned how to stomach it.

"No, sir. I was there," Neil replied. "Both of us — me and Shay — were at church Sunday."

"Shay, yeah, that's her name." The smile on Homer's face could be heard in his voice. "Boy, you sure do have yourself a looker, you hear me? And she young. Got pretty legs, too. Young, pretty, and sanctified: now them's some good qualities to have. That's a good woman you got, son. If I was younger, I'd fight you for her."

Neil wanted to blurt, "You wouldn't be fighting me, you'd be fighting Emmett Ford, and I can tell you from experience that that's a fight you can't win," but instead, he held his tongue and remained silent. Some things were better left unsaid.

"Emmett Ford? Who is that?"

Neil's heart threatened to pound a hole in his chest. He couldn't believe he'd said it out loud, but evidently he had since Deacon Burgess had responded. "Sir?" Neil didn't know what else to say.

"I said, who is Emmett Ford, and why in the world would I be fighting him for your lady?" When Neil remained silent, still unable to conjure up a lie that would explain it away, Homer Burgess proceeded with caution. "That girl ain't . . . she ain't married or nothing, is she, Deacon? I seen her son, but I just thought maybe she had a baby out of wedlock. You ain't messing with no other man's wife, are you?"

It was the perfect segue, and Neil decided to go with the flow. "Not technically."

"You talkin' to a man with a third grade education, so you got to use smaller words. What you mean by technically?"

Neil relaxed his back against his chair, but he felt anything but relaxed. "She's widowed. Her husband died over eight years ago, but she still has an attachment to him. She still loves him." That sick feeling was returning to Neil's stomach again. He always got that way when Emmett's name came up in the conversation.

"So what?" was Homer's response. "What that got to do wit' anything? She yours now, ain't she? Boy, if your biggest problem is a dead man, you better go 'head on and marry that woman."

"I want to, but —"

"But what?"

"I don't think you heard what I said, Deacon Burgess. She's still in love with her late husband."

"Ain't nothing wrong wit' my ears. I heard you the first time. If you want her, that ought not to stop you. You think I ain't still in love with Odette?" Neil was familiar with the name. Odette was Homer's second wife — the one he called the love of his life — and they were married for over forty years before she passed away. "I'm gonna always love Odette," the old man continued, "but just 'cause I love her don't mean I'm off the market. Didn't I just tell you that this one I got over here at my house right now wants to take more than my temperature?"

Neil stifled a laugh and shook his head. "Even if that's true, it's not the same. If Ms. Teena wants you, that's like me want-ing Shay. That part's not the problem. The problem is her wanting me back. She loves Emmett so much that I don't think she'd ever want another man. Not in that way."

"Don't kid yourself, son. Everybody wit' the good sense God gave 'em wants to love. And they want to love somebody who can love 'em back. Sometimes they just need that other person to be the one to make the move. That girl might just be waiting for you to do what you think you can't do."

Neil gnawed at the skin on the inside of his left cheek and mulled over what the deacon had said. It all sounded good, but Neil doubted it more than a little bit. As an afterthought ran through his mind, he chuckled and said, "If that's true, Deac, that means that you're just waiting on Ms. Teena to make the first move."

"I'm old, I need this stick to get around, and I done had the same name for ninety-two years, but there are some days that, hard as I try, I can't even remember it," Deacon Burgess said. "But so long as I got breath in this old body, there's always hope."

Neil broke into a laugh, and Deacon Burgess laughed with him. Neil supposed that if Teena Marie Mitchell was anywhere within listening range and could guess what they were talking about, she was probably laughing too. *Real* hard.

Neil caught his breath. "So what you're saying is —"

"What I'm saying is, stop being scared of the dead, and go buy a ring."

"I'm not afraid of Emmett."

"Look like it to me," Homer said. "You just said a minute ago that you wanted to marry that girl. If you wasn't scared, you would've bought a ring by now."

"I did," Neil blurted. The resulting noise on the other end of the line made Neil wonder if Homer had passed out at the news, or if he had just dropped the phone.

"You did?" he finally replied. "Well, glory to God! Why you ain't said that 'fo' now? When's the wedding?"

"Don't shine your shoes just yet," Neil said. "I took it back."

Silence.

More silence.

"Deacon Burgess?" The silence was deafening. Neil sighed. "I know you're still there. Don't do this to me, Deac. I need you to talk to me."

"If I talk . . . you gonna listen?"

"Yes."

"Good, 'cause I ain't never know you was a dummy 'til now."

Neil pulled the phone from his ear and looked at it in disbelief. Had Deacon Burgess just called him dumb? Was his Alzheimer's kicking in or something? Neil put the phone back to his ear. "Excuse me?"

"You heard me." He was pulling no punches. "That's about the dumbest thing I ever heard in my life, and that's a long, long time. You mean to tell me that you bought a ring and took it back 'cause she still loves her dead husband?"

"Okay, can you at least listen to the whole story before you draw conclusions?" When the deacon said nothing, Neil accepted that as permission to continue, and his words flowed like water from a faucet. "I was so ready to propose, Deacon Burgess. At first, I was gonna wait for Christmas; it's only a couple of weeks away and seemed like the perfect holiday to get engaged. But then I thought, why wait? So Monday, during my lunch break, I went to the jewelry store and purchased the ring. By the time I got off work, I had planned it all out. Had it all set for Tuesday. I didn't tell anybody because I didn't want any added pressure. I just asked my mother to babysit Chase — that's Shay's son — for a couple of hours while we shared a private dinner at my house. Two hours," he reiterated. "That's all I needed."

When Neil stopped to catch his breath, Deacon Burgess said, "Go on." It was the first sign of life in a while from the other end of the line.

"Everything was perfect," Neil said. "Shay was beautiful . . . downright killing that outfit she was wearing. And a brotha wasn't looking too bad either, if I do say so myself."

"What were you wearing?" Deacon Burgess asked.

"A Ralph Lauren number I purchased back in February. I wore it for the men's ministry conference banquet. You kept telling me how sharp I was in it, remember?" Neil knew he wouldn't.

"That brown one that almost feels like silk?"

Shocked at the deacon's recall, Neil said, "That's the one."

"Yes. Very good choice." Deacon Burgess sounded impressed.

"I'm telling you, I was on it. Everything was perfect."

"What y'all had for dinner?"

"Stuffed salmon."

"Humph. That's city folk food. I'd rather have food from the country, like plain ol' fried catfish, but was the salmon good?"

"My mama cooked it. And she's from the backwoods of Mississippi, so what do you think?"

"Have mercy," Homer replied. "Okay . . .

clothes was good; food was good. What about the lighting? Did you light a few candles?"

Neil was taken aback that a man of Homer's years would ask such a question. "As a matter of fact, yes. Nothing but the candles on the dining room table and the Christmas tree lights in the adjoining living room."

"Good . . . good," he said in approval. "Music?"

Grinning, Neil was suddenly seeing Homer Burgess as an old-school playa. Even at ninety-two, he had enough good looks to prove that he had been quite the handsome one back in the day. "Remember the brother who played the saxophone at the Valentine's Dance that the church had last year?" Neil knew for sure that Deacon Burgess wouldn't be able to think back that far, so he just continued without awaiting a reply. "His name is Antonio Allen, and I bought his *Forever & Always* CD at that dance. I knew Shay loved it, so I played it during dinner."

"Sounds like you thought it all out real good."

"Deac, I'm telling you, there was nothing I could have done to make it better." Neil ran his hand over his low haircut. Reliving how much thought and effort he'd put into the evening was making it all seem even more hopeless. In essence, he had given it his best, and his best wasn't good enough. "The mood, the dinner, the ambiance . . . it was all flawless. I had the ring tucked in the inside pocket of my suit jacket, and I was sixty seconds away from kneeling when I saw it."

"Saw what?"

Neil tried to shake the snapshot from his head, but couldn't. "When I talked to Pastor Loather last Sunday, this is what we talked about. And the thing he said to me that made the most sense was when he brought it to my attention that seven years after Emmett Ford died, Shay was still wearing his ring. It wasn't until after she met and fell in love with me that she removed it. The more I thought about that, the bigger deal it became."

"My, oh my," Homer said. "They say actions speak louder than words, and that sounds like action that was using a bullhorn, if you ask me."

"Yeah. I thought so too."

"What you mean, you *thought* so? You say she was wearing that man's ring all them years after she buried him, and she stopped when she met you. What else you want from her?"

"I want her to stop wearing his ring. He was her husband. She loved him. I understand all that, and because of it, I'm willing to compromise on some things, but not this. As long as she's wearing his ring, she can't wear mine."

After a brief silence, Homer said, "But I thought she already stopped wearing his ring."

"I thought so too, until Tuesday night." Neil clenched and unclenched his jaws. "She hasn't stopped wearing it; she just changed where she wears it. Emmett Ford's ring now dangles from a chain that Shay wears around her neck."

"Say what?"

The knot that formed in Neil's stomach was so tight that he felt like he would vomit. Just like on Tuesday night. "Don't make me repeat it."

"You seen it?" Homer's voice had dropped to a near whisper.

"Even the low lighting couldn't hide the haunting sparkle of that thing." Neil grunted. "The worst part about it was the timing. We had just finished eating dessert, and she said, 'I've never kissed you after peach cobbler before. I wonder what that tastes like.' That threw me, because she'd never said anything quite that *sexy* to me before. It was quite the turn-on, I might add."

"My temperature just rose a hundred degrees from hearing it," Homer injected.

Neil would have laughed, but he had no laugh left. "When she stood to lean across the table to kiss me, that's when I saw it." He grabbed a stress ball from the credenza behind his desk and began squeezing it as he continued. "The necklace slipped from behind the collar of her sweater. I saw the object dangling at the bottom of her chain when it first fell out, but I was too busy looking at her mouth that was closing in on me to recognize what the object on the end of the chain was. But when the kiss ended, and she pulled back to return to her seat, the light from one of the candles caught the diamond, and when that rock sparkled, it darn near burned my corneas."

"And what happened then?" Deacon Burgess sounded guarded, like he was bracing himself for Neil's answer. "You ain't snap or nothing, did you?"

Neil shook his head. "You know me well enough to know that's not my style, Deac. I didn't even mention it, but it totally killed my mood. *Totally.*"

"Once words come out your mouth, you can't never take 'em back. So even though you was mad, I'm glad you didn't say nothing you would've regretted. Ain't nothin' worse than living wit' regrets, son. I'm glad you kept enough sense not to go off on her."

"I didn't go off on her, but I didn't propose to her, either." Neil wondered if he would live to regret that too. "I ended the evening earlier than planned. Within ten minutes of seeing that ring, I literally got sick to my stomach. I was supposed to drive out to Ms. Ella Mae's and get Chase once our date ended, but I was too sick to do that. And Shay was trying to make it better, but she was only making it worse."

"Worse how?"

"She was being all caring and attentive. She offered her lap for me to lay my head in, and she kept trying to rub the pain from my stomach with her hand. She even prayed for me."

"Well, I'm old, and a long time done went by since I dated Odette. I know a lot done changed 'tween then and now, but back in my day, that would've been a good thing."

"But I didn't need her to be there for me, Deac. What I needed her to do for me was leave. Don't you get it? Her presence was what was making me ill. I don't care how much laying on of hands and praying she did; I wasn't gonna feel any better until she left my house and took Emmett with her."

It was a while before Homer replied, and for the first time ever, Neil felt like somebody might actually understand where he was coming from.

Deacon Burgess released a labored sigh before he finally spoke. "So what you plan to do now?"

"I don't know." Neil was being honest. He had no idea what his next move would be.

"Have you talked to her since your dinner?"

"No, sir."

"She got to know something's up with you, Deacon Taylor. Don't you call her on a regular basis?"

"Yeah. Every single day." Most days, Neil called her more than once.

Another sigh from Homer blew into the phone. "I'm surprised she ain't called you."

"Actually, she has," Neil admitted after a moment of hesitation. "She called last night, but I didn't answer, and she didn't leave a message. Plus, she picks up Chase after school every day. Yesterday I left early so that I could make it to the jewelry store to return the ring before they closed, so I wasn't here when she picked him up. Today, when it's about time for her to arrive, I'll find something outside of my office to do to make myself scarce and unavailable."

"What you sayin', son? You breakin' up with that pretty girl?"

"I . . . I don't know." Just the thought of ending his relationship with Shaylynn made his heart hurt. Neil actually felt like crying.

"Returning that ring makes it sound so over and done wit'," Deacon Burgess pointed out. "You ought to really rethink this thing. Like I said, some things you can't take back once you say 'em. Don't do something you gonna live to regret."

"I don't know. Maybe we just . . . Maybe we just need a break from each other." Neil couldn't believe the words that were coming out of his own mouth. A break from Shaylynn? Just the two days that had passed without him seeing or speaking to her was killing him.

"What you need to do is talk to each other," Homer said, now sounding like the voice of CJ. "*Talk* to her, son. Stop being a coward."

Neil rubbed his forehead. Deacon Burgess was name-calling again, and although Neil knew for certain that he was no coward, he chose not to interrupt.

"Tell that girl just how this whole dead husband thing is rubbin' you," Homer continued. "If it's one thing I learned in twenty years of marriage to Esther and forty-one years of marriage to Odette, it's that talkin' to each other is important in any relationship. *Talk to her.*"

"You know what the scariest part about this is, Deac?" Neil stared at Shaylynn's name and face as they flashed on the screen of his BlackBerry, indicating that she was calling him yet again. "Whether I have that heart-to-heart talk with Shay or take the cowardly way out . . . either way, I have a feeling that I'm gonna lose her, because if I give her the ultimatum of wearing his ring or mine, she'll choose his in a heartbeat."

# EIGHT

"Hi, Solomon, this is Shay, calling to check up on you. I'm kind of worried that I haven't heard from you in the last couple of days. The last time I saw you, you weren't feeling well, and I just want to be sure you're doing okay. I'm guessing you're at least feeling better since Chase told me that you've been at work. When you get this message, please call me back. I love you. Bye."

Shaylynn disconnected the call and dropped her cell phone in the pocket of her apron. Then she slipped her right hand back into the latex glove she'd removed just moments earlier and climbed back up the stepladder to resume working on her current assignment. This was the first time she had ever decorated a nursery, and although it was coming together nicely, Shaylynn would probably enjoy the process more if she weren't so consumed with thoughts of Neil. *Where is he, and why hasn't he called?*

Once she was back at the top of the ladder, Shaylynn dipped the natural sponge into the golden yellow paint that she had stirred and poured into a sturdy paper plate, blotted the excess onto the newspaper that lay beside the paint, and then began carefully dabbing at the second of four walls that she had covered with two coats of red paint yesterday. Red, white, and gold. This was going to be the oddest-colored nursery she had ever seen, but both Shaylynn and the baby's mother had been unsuccessful in their attempts to talk the father out of it. Boy or girl, he'd said, this baby was going to be an Atlanta Hawks fan.

"I can't believe I'm actually starting to like the way these colors look in here."

The voice behind Shaylynn startled her, and she had to catch herself so that she didn't take the short tumble from the ladder.

"Ooh, girl, please don't fall." Theresa held out her hands as though she could have caught Shaylynn from the spot where she stood in the doorway. "Sorry. I didn't mean to scare you."

Shaylynn felt flustered, embarrassed. "You didn't. I mean, you did, but I'm okay. I guess my mind was just somewhere else. I didn't hear you come in." The floors were wooden, and Theresa was wearing mules. Shaylynn should have heard her approach. She used the sleeve of her smock to wipe away the perspiration that, at some point, had begun beading across her forehead in spite of the cool temperatures; then she looked around the room and tried to get the subject back on track. "It actually does look a lot better on the walls than it did in my head when Pastor Loather first described what he wanted."

"Yeah, it does." Theresa walked farther into the room. "You're doing a great job, Shay. I'm glad we took Neil's advice and hired you. After seeing the magic you worked on Ms. Ella Mae's house, I guess I shouldn't be so surprised. I think you've definitely found your calling."

"Thank you." It was a high compliment, and smiling shouldn't have been a chore, but the corners of Shaylynn's mouth just wouldn't cooperate, so she turned back to her task and again began dabbing the walls with her sponge.

"Are you okay?"

Shaylynn didn't break her eyes from the wall. "Yes, I'm fine." Lying to her first lady probably wasn't helping the situation any.

"Are you sure?" Theresa pressed. When Shaylynn didn't answer, she added, "I'm not trying to pry or anything, I'm just concerned. You just seem a little distracted. I noticed it yesterday when you were here, but today it's even more obvious."

Shaylynn took in a deep breath, and then released it before turning to look down at Theresa. The mother-to-be was glowing beautifully in her turquoise and black maternity sweater and black leggings. Her stomach appeared larger now than it did when Shaylynn arrived at the house two hours ago. Maybe it was just the angle at which she was currently viewing her. Although Theresa was her pastor's wife, and six years separated their ages, Shaylynn felt comfortable around her; more than she had with any other female in her life. Theresa never acted as though her status in the church made her untouchable. She acted more like a big sister than the first lady of one of the largest churches on the eastside of Atlanta. Even so, Shaylynn had never really confided in Theresa regarding anything as personal as her love life.

"Is everything okay between you and Neil?" She'd practically read Shaylynn's mind.

"Yes." As soon as the word escaped Shaylynn's mouth, she made the decision that one lie to her first lady had been enough.

She quickly followed that with a slow, "I think so," and then again with an even less confident, "I guess."

Theresa picked up the Atlanta Hawks blanket that was on the arm of the nearby rocking chair, wrapped it around herself, and then took a seat. All of the baby room furniture was white like the chair, but for now, it was the only piece of furniture in the room. Everything else was stacked in the corner of their den and would be moved in once Shaylynn finished painting. "You want to talk about it?"

Shaylynn remained on the stepladder, but she carefully laid the sponge on top of the newspaper. She did *want* to talk about it, but *should* she? Sharing her insecurities had never come naturally for Shaylynn. Life had handed her a multitude of reasons not to be so trusting of others, but desperation made her throw caution to the wind. "I think something's going on with him."

Theresa tilted her head to the side. "Something?"

Shaylynn directed her eyes to the window she'd opened to help with ventilation. "Or maybe it's *someone*." Her body shuttered when she said it. Maybe it was due to the cold air coming from the open window. Or maybe the chilling thoughts that were swarming in her head had caused it.

"What are you saying?" Concern laced Theresa's voice. "You're not suggesting that Neil is —"

"I don't know." Shaylynn couldn't bear to hear the word released in the atmosphere. She didn't want to believe that Neil was capable of sneaking around behind her back. He'd wooed her tirelessly, and she'd finally given in to her heart's desire and allowed him in. Surely he wouldn't work that hard for her affections, and then turn around and do this. *Would he?* There had to be another explanation. "I have no idea what's going on with him. All I know is that we had a date Tuesday night, and everything was perfect. Candles, dinner, music . . . at his house. Just the two of us. But I haven't heard a word from him since." Shaylynn willed her tears to keep at bay. "He hasn't called me. He's not answering my calls. He hasn't been in his office when I go to pick up Chase. I think . . . I think he's purposefully avoiding me."

Theresa looked perplexed. "What did you talk about on Tuesday? Did you argue?"

"No. That's the part that makes this entire thing even more senseless. We didn't argue at all. Not even once. Like I said, the night was perfect. I mean, Solomon is spontaneous and he has great taste, so he and I always have wonderful dates, but Tuesday might have been our best. He went all out." Shaylynn closed her eyes to recapture the images as she gave Theresa the CliffsNotes. "Ms. Ella Mae cooked, and then she took Chase to her house so that Solomon and I could have a private dinner for two. We talked and laughed and ate by candlelight. It was all so amazing." She opened her eyes and again looked at Theresa. "There was something different about Solomon. For a minute, I thought he was . . ." She released a sigh and shook her head. "I don't know."

"You thought he was what?"

Shaylynn should have known she wouldn't be allowed to just gloss over her near slip of the tongue. "Nothing," she replied, hopeful that Theresa would accept that answer, but knowing full well that she wouldn't.

"No." Theresa shook her head as expected and leaned forward in her chair. "You have to tell me what's on your mind, Shay. Together, I'm sure we can figure this out, but I need you to trust me with all of the details. You thought he was what? Are you saying you thought he was gonna try to go all the way with you? Is that it? You think he put together the whole candlelight dinner to get you in bed?" Theresa was still shaking her head. "I can understand why it might have appeared that way, but I've known Neil for a long time, and he's really not like —"

"That's not what I meant, that's not it at all." The thought hadn't even entered Shaylynn's mind. Well, it sort of had early in the night, but that's not at all what she thought by the time the evening came to an abrupt close.

"What, then?" Theresa asked.

Shaylynn slowly descended the ladder and once again removed the glove from her right hand. Could she really be transparent with her pastor's wife? She looked at Theresa and saw nothing but concern in her eyes. "You promise not to tell Solomon?"

"I promise." With her right hand raised, Theresa looked like an over-aged Girl Scout.

Glancing down at the glove that dangled in her grasp, Shaylynn whispered, "I thought he was going to propose." Slowly, her eyes met Theresa's. "The setting was perfect for it, and Solomon was being so mysterious and attentive and romantic. If he had proposed, I think the only thing missing from my dream would have been a song."

A smile had stretched across Theresa's face at the onset of Shaylynn's admission, and it lingered as she spoke. "A song?"

"Yeah. In my dream, right before he proposes to me, he sings."

"So you dream of Neil proposing to you?"

The invisible flame that heated Shaylynn's face seemed to be set on high. Even the wintry air coming through the open window wasn't enough to douse it. She looked down at her clasped hands again. "Once."

"And in the dream, did you say yes?"

"I don't know." She shrugged her shoulders. "I woke up before I answered."

"So if he had asked you to marry him the other night, would you have accepted?"

Slowly, but surely, Shaylynn's head nodded. She was unsure about a lot of things in life, and taking chances had never been her strong suit. But despite all of her misgivings, she knew that if it came down to it, she'd take a risk on Neil. "But it doesn't matter now, because he didn't ask," she told Theresa. "Instead, he all of a sudden got sick. And once that happened, the night came to a screeching halt."

Theresa stood. "What do you mean, he all of a sudden got sick?"

Shaylynn shrugged her shoulders again. "He got sick." She wasn't sure how else to explain it, but she gave it her best try. "He just said his stomach and head were hurting, and from that moment on, it was like he didn't even want to talk anymore. He all but asked me to leave. I thought that maybe the food disagreed with him or something. Or maybe he had an allergic reaction. But now that I haven't heard from him at all, I'm thinking that maybe it was something else. Maybe something happened between then and now."

Theresa tightened the blanket around herself as she walked the length of the bedroom floor, looking like a black Jessica Fletcher, trying to put together the pieces of a mystery in an episode of *Murder, She Wrote.* She stopped walking and turned to look at Shaylynn. "What was said right before he got sick?"

After a moment's thought, Shaylynn felt her face heat another twenty degrees. If her skin wasn't a shade of dark chocolate, she was sure that her face would have turned a bright strawberry.

"You don't remember?" Theresa asked.

Oh, she remembered all right, but there was no way that Shaylynn could say it. Not to her first lady. How would she say, "I had just told him that I'd never tasted his lips after eating peach cobbler" without feeling like a hussy? A moment later, Shaylynn gasped and her hands flew to her lips. That was it! Theresa had questioned whether Shaylynn thought Neil was going to try to get her to go all the way, but the fact of the matter was Neil thought *she* was trying to get *him* into bed. That was the only explanation that made sense. *Oh my God.*

"What?" Theresa walked toward her. "What, Shay? What happened?"

"It's me." Shaylynn couldn't bring herself to admit the details, but one thing she knew for certain: "I messed up."

# NINE

Four days. That's how long Neil had allowed the madness to continue. Four days of not seeing or speaking to Shaylynn, and four days of only having short exchanges during school hours with his favorite little guy, Chase. If the notion of "three strikes and you're out" applied to his situation, Neil had already been sent back to the dugout, defeated.

*What on earth was I thinking?*

By now, the word had spread, and he'd been duly reprimanded from all sides. CJ, Theresa, Ella Mae; even his younger sister, Val, had called from New Jersey to weigh in on the issue after their mother telephoned her and blabbed. Neil had grown weary of hearing his friends and family members tell him how disappointed in him they were, but he understood, because none could come close to matching his disappointment in himself. They each had different suggestions about what he should do next, but the one thing they all agreed on was that he needed to make it right. Neil was beginning to feel like God Himself was talking through his closest confidants, and time was running out for him to take heed. That was especially true when Homer Burgess miraculously retreated from the edge of insanity long enough to offer sound, almost fatherly-like advice. As deteriorated as his mind had become in recent months, that was about as big a miracle as God speaking to Moses through that burning bush.

It was just six o'clock in the morning on Saturday, and Neil had already surpassed mile three on the treadmill he was using for this weekend's exercise routine. A steady stream of up-tempo music from his MP3 player helped to keep him energized and the pace of his steps on beat.

Today, he'd chosen to work out at the LA Fitness Center on Peachtree Road in the Buckhead district of metropolitan Atlanta. This wasn't the location that he normally visited for his weekly cardio blasts. Neil chose it today for one major reason: he needed some solitude. Not that he was there alone. The gym opened its doors somewhere around five o'clock each morning, so there were people all around him, working toward achieving better health and fitness, but he didn't know any of them, and they didn't know him. The Northlake/Tucker facility that he normally frequented was much more convenient to home, but had he gone to that one today, not only would it have been jam-packed with its normal swarm of Saturday patrons, but Neil also would have been sure to run into Adam Schmitz, his unofficial, yet self-proclaimed, trainer.

Adam was the carrot-top fitness fanatic who had encouraged Neil to take up the sport of running in the first place. He was a great kid, a genius when it came to technology, but sometimes Neil wondered if the computer programmer forgot that in their relationship, the mentee was nearly twice the age of the mentor. Adam had been running religiously for thirteen years, and since he was only twenty-five, that was more than half his life. Neil, on the other hand, had been at this for less than two years. He was in commendable health, but at the end of the day, he was still forty-six, and sometimes Adam's endless energy, and his constant peps of "Come on, Neil . . . don't give up . . . you can do it!" could get downright annoying.

Funny thing was the personality trait of Adam's that annoyed Neil the most was also the one that he appreciated most. He owed Adam much of the credit for his improved health and more toned physique. Neil felt stronger and looked better now than he did ten, maybe even fifteen years ago, and that had become of particular importance to him since entering into this May-December romance with Shaylynn. There were as many years between them as there were between Ashton Kutcher and Demi Moore . . . only in Neil's equation, the script was flipped. He didn't know if Demi ever felt the need to work harder than other women just because she had a younger man, but Neil sure felt the need to do so for the sake of his younger woman.

He came from good genes on both sides of his family, so despite the premature graying of the hairs on his temples, people had always told Neil that he looked about ten years younger than his age. Each of his siblings received the same compliment on a regular basis. Their bodies, however, aged just like everyone else's, and Neil knew that if he was going to be in a relationship with a woman fifteen years his junior, he needed a physique that could compete with those of men closer to her age. Because of Adam's pushing, Neil's confidence about his body image had tripled over the past year. But all those positives notwithstanding, he still didn't feel like entering any fitness challenges today. Neil wasn't in the mood to try to keep up with the man who would be running on the belt beside him. He didn't feel like playing the psychological game of pushing beyond the pain and the fatigue so that he would beat his personal best. Today, Neil was running to clear his head. He needed to come up with a strategy to save his relationship. He needed to think. And he needed to think *fast.*

All of the lectures and scolding that had come by way of his family and friends had really been unnecessary. By the time Neil ended his call with Deacon Burgess on Thursday, he had been convinced that he needed to make things right with Shaylynn; he just didn't know exactly how to go about doing it. In his procrastination, two additional days had passed, and he couldn't help but wonder if whatever he did at this point would be too little too late. Neil's initial plan had been to answer the phone the next time Shaylynn called, and the two of them could talk about it and begin to mend. But the opportunity never came. The success of his plan was depending on that "next time" phone call, but it never happened. Shaylynn's name and photo image hadn't lit up on his cell screen since Thursday afternoon, and Neil could only imagine what was going through her head. She was probably wondering what was going through *his* head. Sometimes Neil wondered about that one himself.

Shaylynn made him crazy. Plain and simple. Love had lived in Neil's heart before, but it had never occupied every nook and cranny like this. Women had rented his heart in the past, even leased it, but Shaylynn was the first to own it outright. Yes, this one had changed the drapes, painted the walls, and put her name on the mailbox, and Neil knew that it would be insane of him to let her go over something as silly as her lingering attachment to her deceased husband. But as childish as it might seem to others, Neil couldn't totally shake the urge to do something to cut the heartstring that remained adhered to Emmett all these years later. As much as everyone tried to convince him that it shouldn't be such a sore spot for him, Neil still found it disheartening to know that the woman he defined as his soul mate already had a soul mate . . . and it wasn't him. The fact that Emmett was deceased didn't make it any easier to accept.

At four miles, Neil's favorite Nike shirt

was clinging to his hairless chest, and in his ear, Jennifer Lopez was singing a song that said love didn't cost a thing. Neil disagreed. If that were true, he wouldn't be in the predicament that he was in right now. Love may not cost money, but it definitely came with a price, and if a person wasn't willing to pay it, they ended up alone. There was a time in Neil's life when he thought lifelong bachelorhood was the order of the day, but not anymore. Shaylynn had changed all that, and being alone was no longer appealing. He had to get their relationship back on course.

Sweat seemed to be oozing from every pore of his upper body, but he could still breathe without struggling. He remembered a time, not too long ago, when he couldn't do that. At five feet seven, Neil stood at a modest height for a man. Glancing to his right, he noted that the stride of his jog was in perfect sync with that of the man on the treadmill beside him. Had that been Adam, it would have been a different story. Adam was six feet tall and had longer legs. When he ran, it was as though he had lungs in his chest, and then an extra pair in his feet. He seemed to never get winded.

Neil glimpsed at the man beside him once again. He was an Asian gentleman who appeared to be in his mid to late thirties, and he wore a wedding band. As desperate as Neil was at this point, he seriously contemplated pulling the earphones from his ear and asking the guy's opinion on what he would do if he were in his situation. This fellow was married, so it was safe to assume that at one time he and his wife had to be in the dating stage. Relationship problems weren't exclusive to black folks, so he should know a little something, right? Neil decided against disrupting the stranger's workout. It wouldn't do any good. CJ was married too, and Homer Burgess had been married twice, but neither of them owned a crystal ball with any magic answers. Neil knew that the man running beside him wouldn't have the answers either.

Homer indicated that Neil was acting like a coward. Neil still thought that was far too strong a word. True, he had some apprehensions, but he wasn't scared. It was *apprehension* that had tied that knot in his stomach and made him too sick to end Tuesday night's date on a good note. It was *apprehension* that had him making a rash decision to jump in his car on Wednesday afternoon and return the engagement ring he'd purchased. It was *apprehension* that stopped him from answering Shaylynn's last call on Thursday. And it was *apprehension* that had him tossing and turning on Friday night, up at such an early hour on Saturday morning, and now jogging for the past hour. *Apprehension . . .* not fear.

Neil snapped from his rampant thoughts when his treadmill began to slow down on its own accord. He had preset it for five miles and couldn't believe he was already there. Fatigue had caught up with him somewhere along the way, but he hadn't noticed it until now. As the fog of thoughts cleared from his head, Neil gripped the handlebar in front of him while he caught his breath. The guy who had earlier been jogging beside him had, at some point, left the scene, and had been replaced by a leggy black chick who didn't look a day over twenty-one. She was scantily clad in a red sports bra and matching spandex shorts, and her shoulder-length ponytail swung from side to side as she ran at an impressive speed. In his mind, Neil wondered how long she could keep up that relay runner's pace, but he wouldn't be sticking around to find out. His treadmill's belt slowed to a stop, and he paused long enough to turn off his MP3 player, and then used a hand towel to wipe his face. When he stepped off the apparatus and made eye contact, the girl flashed a grin and winked her right eye. *Is she flirting?* Neil was too flattered not to return the smile. She was pretty. Too tall, too thin, and too young for his taste, but pretty just the same.

Once he was in the locker room and inside the shower stall, Neil's mind was consumed once again. "You can't let this go another day," he whispered into the waterfall that beat directly on his face. "Come on, Neil . . . make it right . . . you can do it!" He shook his head at his own pep talk. "I can't believe it," he muttered as he turned his face to the wall and allowed the water to rinse the lather off of his back. "I'm turning into Adam Schmitz."

By the time he stepped out of the shower, he had devised a tentative plan. Neil dried his head and his body, and then took his time getting dressed. He knew what he had to do, but he was in no big hurry to do it. Neil had waited so long to do something that anything that he tried to do at this point could backfire. Taking ownership of his error in judgment was way overdue, and he wasn't at all sure that Shaylynn would be so quick to accept his apology; *if* she accepted it at all.

"It's easier to reach the heavens . . . than for us to work this out . . . I haven't prayed

155

in so long . . . but if it brings you back somehow . . . then I guess I need a miracle, right now . . ."

Neil stopped at his locker door and listened to the lyrics that were streaming from the gym's speakers. It was the voice of Abraham McDonald, the man whose amazing voice virtually blew the competition out of the water when Oprah held that karaoke challenge on her show a couple of years ago. The song was so befitting because Neil felt like he needed a major miracle if he was going to win back Shaylynn. Not that they had broken up. At least he hoped not.

Dressed in the grey sweatshirt and blue jeans that he had rolled inside his gym bag before leaving home this morning, Neil sat on the bench in front of his locker door and bent to tie his shoes. His head remained lowered even after his task was complete. He had failed to pray this morning, and the song had just reminded him of it. Now was as good a time as any, because Neil had a feeling it was going to take more than his youthful looks and toned body to get him back in Shaylynn's good graces after four days of silence. After a whispered, "Amen," he grabbed his coat, pulled the strap of his gym bag over his shoulder, and headed for the exit door.

The windchill that met him on the outside of the gym energized Neil to rush to his SUV despite his fatigue. He'd forgotten his hat, and on top of all the other misery he was dealing with, the last thing he needed was a head cold. He climbed inside the vehicle, but the temperatures there didn't seem to be much better. Neil quickly started the engine, pulled a peppermint candy from his ashtray and popped it in his mouth, and waited impatiently for the air coming from his vents to turn warm.

"One heaven . . . one forever . . . there's just one eternity. One heaven . . . one everlasting . . . and one chance for me to go. I don't wanna miss my chance . . ."

Neil shook his head. Was God trying to talk to him through music today? The harmonizing voices of gospel legends The Williams Brothers streamed from Praise 102.5 radio station and filled the space inside Neil's Toyota Highlander. He pressed his back against the seat and exhaled. The inside temperature was so cold that he could see his breath. Neil knew that the group was singing about actual heaven and how they didn't want to do anything that would cause them to miss the opportunity to spend eternity there with Jesus, but somehow the song made Neil think of Shaylynn. He hoped to God that one chance to spend a lifetime with her wasn't all he had. If so, he'd blown it big time.

As Neil gathered himself and began the drive back toward Stone Mountain, the traffic was noticeably heavier than it had been when he made the early morning trip to Buckhead. Twenty minutes into the journey, he heard his cell phone ringing from somewhere in his gym bag just as he approached a major intersection. The red light allowed him the chance to reach into the side pocket of the bag to retrieve his Bluetooth. He didn't have time to fish for the phone itself. "Hello." Neil had barely attached it to his ear before pressing the button to answer the call. He hoped it was Shaylynn. Even if she was calling to chew him out, he'd be happy. At least she'd be talking to him, and he'd have the chance to try to explain himself.

"Hey, Doc. I'm just pulling up at the gym and don't see your truck in its usual spot. You're coming this morning, right?"

Neil would know that slight German accent anywhere. He didn't understand why his trainer insisted upon calling him Doc, as though he was some top surgeon or something. He was a PhD, not an MD. People didn't widely refer to one who held a doctorate in philosophy as *Doc,* but Neil had no real qualms with it. "What's up, Adam? I've actually already hit the gym for today, man. I needed to get my five miles in early because I have another appointment."

"You've been here already and gone? Wow, dude; you're on the ball. I like that. You didn't let your appointment be an excuse to skip. What was your time today? Did you challenge yourself to beat your time from last Saturday?"

This is what Neil got for giving Adam his cell number. If the boy couldn't push him at the gym, he'd do it away from the gym. To be honest, Neil had no idea what his time had been; his mind had been too occupied to pay it any attention. "It was about the same," he reported, hoping it was true. "I'll take it up a notch the next time out. I didn't need to tire myself out too much . . . you know, with my appointment and all."

The spontaneous explanation seemed enough to satisfy Adam. "Oh yeah. Good thinking. Wouldn't want you to do that. All right then. I'm about to go for mine now, so I'll see you next week, dude. Okay?"

"Yeah. See ya," Neil replied. Between *Doc* and *dude,* he'd take Doc any day.

Shaylynn only lived about twelve miles from Neil. His first thought was to jump off on the Glenwood Road exit, which would get him to her area quicker. But considering the kind of trouble he was in, Neil bypassed it and merged on the Covington Highway exit instead. That was closer to his home, and if he had a prayer of making amends with Shaylynn today, he'd need to go all out. His sweatshirt, jeans, and gym shoes weren't going to do. He needed to come correct, and Neil knew the kind of gear she appreciated seeing him in: the kind of clothes he wore when she seemed not to be able to keep her hands off of him.

When he pulled into the driveway of his three-bedroom home, Neil didn't bother to open the garage door. This would be a quick stop. He'd already had a shower, and it shouldn't take more than half an hour to get changed. Neil let himself in, tossed his keys and his jacket on the sofa, and disappeared inside of his master bedroom, peeling off his shirt en route. Twenty-three minutes later, he emerged freshly shaven and dressed in a pair of pressed Calvin Klein khaki slacks and a black, short-sleeved Perry Ellis shirt that showed off his muscle tone. A pair of polished black Florsheim Brinsons had taken the place of his Air Jordans, and he smelled of L'Eau d'Issey by Issey Miyake.

Neil took one last look at himself in the

circular mirror mounted on his living room wall, rubbed his hands over the short hair he had just brushed, and then reached for the keys and jacket that he'd thrown on the sofa earlier. When he heard his doorbell ring, he froze. *Not now.* This visitor's timing couldn't be worse. Neil had places to go and people to meet, but with his truck being parked out front in plain sight, it was hard to pretend that he wasn't there. His only option was to get rid of them fast. He wasn't expecting any deliveries, he wasn't buying anything, and he wasn't converting to any new religions; so this would be a very short conversation.

"Shay?" Neil's eyes stretched when he swung open the door. He certainly wasn't expecting to see her. "What's the matter, suga?" Her eyes were red and puffy. She'd obviously been crying, and she looked to be on the verge of tears again. Neil wanted to reach out and grab her, but unsure of whether his embrace would be welcome, he restrained himself. "What's the matter?" he asked again.

Shaylynn gasped before blurting, "Oh, Solomon . . . I'm so sorry!"

They were the only words she managed before falling into Neil's chest. His arms quickly responded, wrapping around her, and then pulling her inside his home and out of the cold. Why was she sorry? Neil's mind raced to catch up on a conversation that they'd never even had. He wanted to ask Shaylynn why she was apologizing, but now just didn't seem like the right time for a questionnaire. Her tears were falling heavily. She was crying like she'd mistakenly run over Neil's beloved cocker spaniel, but he knew that couldn't be it, because he didn't have a cocker spaniel.

Together they stood in the space directly in front of the front door, her sobbing and him comforting. When her weeping increased, Neil tightened his hold, wondering what on earth had brought on this flood. He had seen Shaylynn cry before, but never like this. He couldn't think of anything that would cause a meltdown like this except maybe . . .

Neil's heart pounded, and he had to pry her away from the grip she had around his waist. "Shay . . . Shay, where's Chase?" He lifted her chin and forced her to look him in the face. "What is it? Did something happen to Chase?"

Her eyes were a watery, red mess when she shook her head in reply. It took her a moment to say the words that matched the gesture, but she finally did. "No. He's fine.

He's . . . he's with your mom," she said between gasps.

Ella Mae had Chase? Now Neil was doubly confused. Why did his mother have Chase this early on a Saturday morning? This had to be serious if Shaylynn had driven her son all the way to Powder Springs. "He's with my mom? Why?" Neil gently led Shaylynn to the sofa and sat down next to her. They hadn't sat there together since Tuesday night. It felt good to have her in his arms again, but her wrecked emotions worried Neil. He used his thumbs to wipe tears from both Shaylynn's eyes. "What's the matter, suga?" He reverted to his original question that had never gotten answered.

She gasped a few more times, like a little girl trying to catch her breath after a hard cry. She sat up straight, but turned her eyes away from him when she said, "I asked Ms. Ella Mae to keep him so I could talk to you."

This sounded major. Neil wanted to offer to take her coat, but if this was what he thought it was, she probably wouldn't be sticking around long. Neil felt his insides tense. Was she about to officially end their relationship? Is that why she was so broken? Was she apologizing in advance of the "It's not you, it's me" speech that she was preparing to deliver? Neil didn't want to think the worst, but in light of the picture sitting before him, he didn't know what else it could be. He wanted to tell her to go on with what she wanted to talk to him about, but if it was what he suspected, Neil didn't want to hear it. He pulled his hands from her face and slowly laid them in his lap. His heartbeat was slowing to a snail's pace as though it were preparing to stop beating all together.

"I would have come by earlier, but I couldn't even figure out what to say." She wrung her hands as she spoke. "I just want you to know that it wasn't what you thought. I promise, that wasn't what I was trying to do."

With narrowed eyes, Neil searched Shaylynn's face and saw new tears trail down each of her cheeks. The hole of confusion was getting deeper and wider. What was she talking about? As loud as the question echoed in his head, he wasn't quite ready to verbalize it, so he sat quietly and allowed her to continue.

"I didn't realize what happened Tuesday night until I had left here," she said. "Actually, it was Thursday before it all came clear to me." Shaylynn sniffed, and then blew out a lungful of air as though saying what she was trying to say was one of the hardest things she'd ever done. Even as she continued, she still refused to make eye contact. "I knew something was wrong when you started avoiding me and wouldn't answer or return my calls."

"I'm sorry," Neil jumped in. "That was stupid and childish of me, but —"

"No." Shaylynn shook her head. "I mean, it may not have been the way to handle it, but I understand."

She did? Neil's eyebrows furrowed. "You do?"

Shaylynn nodded. "If I were in your place, and you had done what I did . . . or what you *thought* I did . . . I wouldn't have known how to handle it either. I probably would have cut you off cold turkey too." She eased her hands on top of his and squeezed. "I promise I wasn't trying to . . ." She shook her head and started again. "I wasn't trying to seduce you, Neil. I wasn't trying to get you in bed. I promise; I wasn't."

*Get me in bed? What on earth?*

"When I said . . . well, you know . . . and when I kissed you like that, I wasn't trying to cross any lines. I think I just got caught up in the moment." Her voice quivered. "The candles . . . the music . . . everything was so romantic, and you had made the night so perfect. I think I just got lost in you for a minute, and . . ." She finally looked up at him, and her eyes were pleading. "I'm sorry."

Neil's heart swelled. The album on the record player in his ears was skipping, and all he was hearing over and over again was *I think I just got lost in you . . . I think I got lost in you . . . I think I got lost in you.* Outside of "I love you," that had to be the most touching thing a woman had ever said to him. "I . . . uh . . . I . . ." He was literally at a loss for words.

"Please," she added. "Please don't be mad at me anymore. I didn't mean it like it sounded. I wouldn't try to jeopardize either of our integrity like that. You believe me, don't you, Solomon? I didn't mean it like it sounded."

Neil saw the anguish in her eyes, and it tore at his heart. He reached up and touched Shaylynn's cheek, then ran his fingers through her long, braided hair. What she'd said to him that night, and the impassioned kiss that followed, had absolutely nothing to do with the last four days, and he was on the verge of telling her so when reality hit him like a ton of bricks. Shaylynn's misinterpretation was the key to the door of the doghouse in which he thought he was indefinitely confined. A strange relief washed over Neil. He no longer had to concern himself with how to admit he'd been a jealous, moronic nincompoop.

Looking into Shaylynn's soggy eyes, Neil wanted so desperately to tell her the truth. But he couldn't. He just couldn't. This was the opportunity of a lifetime, and he had to grab it while he could. It was his turn to break eye contact. If he were going to ride the wave of this charade, he couldn't do it while looking into her eyes. "It's okay, suga," he whispered, pulling her into his chest and holding her there. "I'm not mad. Let's just forget it. I believe you."

A part of him was happy, and a part of him was sad, but all of Neil was disappointed in himself. Deacon Burgess was right. He *was* a coward . . . and a dummy.

# TEN

With Christmas falling on a Sunday, most churches in the area decided to close their doors so that families could stay home and celebrate the holiday together. But that wasn't the case with Kingdom Builders Christian Center. Pastor Charles Loather Jr. said Christmas was the day that most believers celebrated the birth of Christ, and it just didn't make sense to him that on the day set aside to recognize Jesus' birth, people locked up the church and celebrated everything except that as they sat home eating, talking, laughing, exchanging gifts, watching television, and then eating some more.

"When I was growing up," CJ said, trying to wind down the spirited Christmas message that he had just preached, "nobody could throw a party like my daddy. Charles Loather Sr. would put together the absolute best birthday parties. My mama would make the cake, but that was as much as she did, because even she knew that when it came to celebrating birthdays, my daddy was the man for the job. And going to a park or a restaurant on my birthday every now and then was cool, but there just wasn't no party like the ones held at my daddy's house."

Neil broke into a grin because he knew where CJ was going with this analogy.

"What I'm trying to say," he continued, "is celebrating Christmas at your house once in a while might be all right." Many of the audience members jumped to their feet, and if CJ said much more on the subject, they looked ready to start the shout-a-thon they'd had earlier all over again. "But since it's Sunday anyhow," their pastor challenged, "what better place to hold Jesus' birthday party than in His Daddy's house? The invitation sent from heaven said that RSVPs weren't necessary and walk-ins were welcome; so come on in, 'cause can't nobody throw a party like *His* Father."

"Go 'head, Pastor," Neil heard himself say.

"We love to say, 'Jesus is the reason for the season,' " CJ pointed out, "but is He truly at the forefront of our minds on this day?"

*Ouch!* Neil felt like that one was tailor-made for him. The plans he had for later today had been priority in his mind all day long.

"I'm gonna just let that one marinade, 'cause I'm done," CJ said, using a blue hand towel to wipe perspiration from his face. "We're just about ready to go home, but we have to pray first." He pointed toward the center section of the church. "Didn't our youth department do a beautiful job re-enacting the birth of our Lord?"

A collective, loud "Amen" echoed in the sanctuary. It was followed by rousing applause. Some of the members of the congregation remained on their feet, giving the youngsters a standing ovation.

From the deacon's corner, Neil's eyes focused on Chase, who sat on the front row along with some of the others who had actively participated in the dramatization. Chase had played the part of one of the wise men who sought the Christ child. He only had one line, but he recited it well. He was still clad in his white sheet and headdress, and in his lap he held the box that was supposed to contain the gold that was brought to the manger scene. Chase caught Neil looking at him and smiled. Returning the grin, Neil threw up his hand and motioned like he was giving the boy a high five from across the room. Chase raised his hand and did the same. How ironic that they were both left-handed. Neil had often wondered if Emmett was a lefty too, but he'd never bothered to ask. It didn't matter.

In Neil's heart, Chase was *his* son, and in the glove compartment of his truck, he had a box tucked away that contained a little gold of its own that would make it official. Over the two weeks that had passed since mending things with Shaylynn, their relationship had strengthened. If it were possible, Neil had fallen even deeper in love; so much so, that his dreams of her were bordering on becoming unrighteous. There was just too much adoration and attraction for her bottled up on the inside of him, and Neil desired to share it with her . . . in every way. Margaret would have a field day if she knew that. She'd repeatedly warned him of what could happen, but Neil wasn't about to continue like this. He had no intention of starting the New Year without Shaylynn as a fiancée, and their engagement couldn't last more than six months. If it drew out any longer, he'd explode. Of course, all his plans were contingent upon her accepting his proposal, and Neil knew that there was a possibility that she wouldn't, but he had to trust his heart on this one. It was time to go for it.

School was out for the holiday, so Neil had spent much of Friday morning at Deacon Burgess's home, delivering Teena's weekly pay and then sitting with her over cups of hot coffee and fresh-baked cinnamon rolls, discussing Homer's well-being. Physically, he was doing about as well as could be expected of a man of his advanced years. Mentally, though, the outlook wasn't so bright. It concerned Neil how quickly Homer's mind was deteriorating. It didn't seem that long ago that Alzheimer's was just beginning to creep in. Neil wasn't an expert on the subject, but he'd always thought the progression was much slower. Over the past ten months or so, the change in Homer had been drastic.

Not only was he chronically forgetful, but now they had to concern themselves with him wandering off if no one was around. There were days when he still thought he could get in his car and drive himself, and days when he thought he could turn on the stove and cook his own meals. Those were no-no's, and in the past two weeks, Teena had virtually moved in the man's house so that he could be under constant surveillance. She said she didn't mind the change.

For her, it wasn't exactly an inconvenience. Deacon Burgess's house was larger and nicer than hers. Moving in with him rescued her from the long commutes to and from his home each day and from hearing the noises of the planes as they took off and landed at Hartsfield-Jackson Airport, which was located so near her apartment complex that she rarely had a peaceful night's sleep.

For the duration of Neil's visit, Homer sat on the living room sofa, watching the Game Show Network while eating his favorite egg salad finger sandwiches that Teena had made for him. He still had a healthy appetite, and that was good. Neil sat on the sofa with him for a while and tried to have a normal conversation, but most of the things Homer would say in reply didn't make much sense. However, just as Neil was ending his visit and was preparing to walk out the door, Homer said seven words that stopped him in his tracks.

"You bought back that girl's ring yet?"

When Neil turned from the door to face the living room, Homer was looking him square in the eyes, but only for a moment before the old man shoved a sandwich in his mouth and shifted his eyes back at the television screen. Neil had lost him before he ever had a chance to respond. It was easy to see from the far-away expression on Homer's face that he was again back in his own world . . . population one. But his momentary sanity was enough to send Neil straight to the jewelry store. This time, he didn't go to Jared; he went back to Menorah Jewelers and was elated to find that the ring that had initially captured his attention was still there waiting. Like it didn't want to be purchased by anyone but him. Like it had been made for Shaylynn's finger only. Just as in times past, Rabbi Ezra Bernstein greeted Neil warmly by name and with a knowing smile, but this time when Neil walked out the door, he didn't walk out empty-handed.

"In John 1:1, the Bible tells us, *'In the beginning was the Word, and the Word was with God, and the Word was God.'* So Jesus Christ is the Word," CJ stressed, getting Neil's full attention once more. "That being the case, when He came to us wrapped in swaddling clothing and lying in that manger, that was the Word made flesh. Amen?"

"Amen," several voices replied.

Despite the fact that CJ had closed his Bible said that he was finished sermonizing for the day, a familiar female voice in the crowd called out, "You preaching good, Pastor."

Neil couldn't see Margaret, but he knew it was her. Apparently, CJ did too.

"What can I say, Sister Dasher? It's what I do." CJ's quick wit drew a wave of laughter from the audience, and without skipping a beat, he continued. "People could actually see Jesus. Do you know how awesome that had to be? With their own eyes, they could see the Son of God. The Christ Child. The Great I Am. The everlasting Promise. The Word. They didn't just hear about Him. They *saw* Him. They watched Him grow. Anybody could converse face-to-face with Him. Anybody could see Him perform miracles. Anybody could hear Him preach and teach. Anybody could touch Him as He passed by. Anybody could follow Him from city to city. Anybody *could* . . . yet so many chose not to." CJ shook his head, and again used his towel to wipe residue sweat from his forehead. "Imagine that. Seeing Jesus Christ in the flesh, but still not believing."

"Lawd, ha' mercy. Imagine that."

Neil looked at Deacon Burgess, who sat right beside him. He had passionately muttered the words like he fully grasped what CJ had said, but Neil saw no connection in his face. He looked as distant now as he'd looked all service long. Neil reached over and patted Homer on the knee. The old deacon looked at him and gave a mechanical smile.

"People who saw Jesus didn't believe in Him," CJ continued, "yet He continues to require that we, who have never seen Him, will trust and believe in Him. We have to walk by faith, and not by sight. It may not be easy, but when we do it, God rewards us in ways unimaginable. In John 20:29, speaking to Thomas, the disciple who said he'd never believe Christ had risen from the dead until he could see the nail piercings in His hands, Jesus said, *'Because thou hast seen me, thou hast believed: blessed are they who have not seen, and yet have believed.'* " CJ held the cordless microphone in his right hand, and stretched his left hand toward his audience. "Do you believe?"

"Amen," they said in chorus.

"Do you believe?" CJ challenged again.

"Amen." The reply was louder this time.

"This child who was born of a virgin during this time that we celebrate as Christmas. This very God, yet very man, who healed the sick, raised the dead, opened blind eyes, unclogged deaf ears. This Son of God, who hung on the cross and died for the sins of the entire world. Do you trust Him? Do you follow Him? Do you believe the One you have not seen?"

More chants of "Amen" filled the edifice, and Neil felt chills as the Spirit filled his heart.

"If you don't know Christ as your Lord and Savior, there's no better day than today." CJ slammed his hand against the cover of his Bible that still lay closed on the book board and said, "God Almighty! There's no better gift that you can give Jesus on His birthday than your heart." When CJ said those words, he turned and looked at Neil. Neil knew that look. It didn't happen often, but when it did, he knew what was coming next. "Come up, please, Deacon Taylor. I need you to minister in song as we open the altar for lost souls on this Christmas Sunday."

There was a time, not too long ago, when Neil would fight CJ on this. Everybody who knew Neil well, and even some who didn't, was aware that Neil didn't like singing as much now as he did when his brother Dwayne was alive. Neil had an amazing voice, but as far as he was concerned, he wasn't a solo artist. He was one half of a duo, and without Dwayne, it just wasn't the same. Still, singing was in his blood, and it was a gift and calling that God had given him that had blessed many; even since

Dwayne's passing. And the congregation relished those rare moments when Deacon Taylor's gift was called upon. Neil had stopped giving grief to his pastor every time he dared to put him on the spot, because it had become clear, even to him, that the only time CJ did it was at the leading of the Holy Spirit.

He slipped from his seat and began his trek to the podium, knowing exactly what he was going to sing. He had been humming the tune for much of the past two weeks. It had come on the radio following the "One Chance" song by The Williams Brothers that he'd heard during his ride home from the gym that Saturday. As it turned out, the station was playing a marathon of songs by the group that day in honor of their fiftieth anniversary, and this one was a perfect fit for today's sermon.

Amid applause and cheers, Neil walked onto the platform and accepted the mic from his pastor. Without introductory words of any kind, he looked toward heaven and began singing the words, "It's amazing to me . . . all the things that you do for me . . . and I've never seen your face . . ." Neil continued the anthem, telling Jesus how much it would satisfy his curiosity on the day that he was finally able to see Him face-to-face. He sang of how awesome it was that Jesus would go so far as to die for his sins and give him the gift of everlasting life, even though he didn't even know Him as the Son of God. The words of the song were powerful. When Neil brought his eyes down to the crowd, he saw the floor filling with people, mostly from the youth department, who were standing or kneeling at the altar, giving their lives to Christ as he sang.

Neil's heart did a special two-step when he saw that Chase was among them. Still in his wise man get-up, the boy had his eyes closed and his hands lifted, and CJ was standing in front of him, dabbing blessed oil on the child's forehead in preparation to pray. Still singing the words of "Never Seen Your Face," Neil searched the audience. He knew when he found Shaylynn, she'd be weeping, and sure enough, there she was. Theresa had gone to stand beside her and was allowing Shaylynn to cry on her shoulder as they embraced. Neil could only imagine her delight at seeing her son make such a monumental decision at such an early age and on such a pivotal day. The only thing that could make this day more beautiful was a marriage proposal, and Neil had never been more ready.

■ ■ ■ ■

Ella's house smelled of everything delicious when Neil, Shaylynn, and Chase entered. They'd driven two separate vehicles to church; therefore, they drove separately to Ella's house too, but they arrived at the same time. Chase chose to ride with Neil in his SUV, and Shaylynn followed them in her Chrysler New Yorker.

"Welcome, welcome." Ella's voice was chipper as she held open the door.

"Ho ho ho . . . Merry Christmas!" Neil's Santa impression left much to be desired.

"Merry Christmas to y'all too. What's all this?"

"We come bearing gifts." He set his armload on the floor by his mother's tree, and then proceeded to relieve Shaylynn of hers.

"Me too." Chase handed Ella the single box he was holding. "This is for you."

Accepting the neatly wrapped present, Ella said, "Well, I sure do thank you. Is it from you?"

Chase nodded. "Me and Mama."

"Well, I can't wait to see what it is."

"That's too bad, because you're gonna have to." Neil eased the box from his mother's hand and placed it under the tree with the others. "We'll open gifts later. I'm about to starve, and this whole house smells edible. If I don't get a plate soon, I'm gonna just start gnawing on the walls."

Shaylynn giggled and slapped his arm playfully. "You want me to fix his plate, Ms. Ella Mae? I took a lot of care in redecorating your house. The last thing I need to see on your walls is a grown man's teeth marks."

Laughing, Ella said, "No, chile; I don't want you fixing nothing. I want you, Sol, and Chase to wash up and sit at the table." While Shaylynn was the only one who referred to Neil by his full middle name, the short-cut "Sol" was occasionally used by several of his immediate family members. Ella nudged Shaylynn in the direction of the hallway. "While y'all doing that, I'll fill the serving dishes and set them on the table."

While Shaylynn obediently headed for the restroom to wash her hands, Neil kissed his mother's cheek. "Ms. Ella Mae, you did more than enough by cooking it all. Why don't you take a load off? You and Shay can sit down, and let the men serve you. How's that? Me and Chase will fill the serving dishes and set them on the table." He looked down at Chase. "Won't we?"

Chase's eyes grew with excitement. "Cool!"

"Fine by me." Limping slightly without the help of her cane, Ella headed for the table that was already decorated with her best china.

Neil bent down slightly and raised his hand. He remembered a time when he used to have to stoop much lower. Chase was growing. "Let's do it."

"Yes, sir!" Chase said, slapping his palm against Neil's.

The men used the kitchen sink to wash their hands, and they were hard at work when Shaylynn joined Ella.

"We're fixing the table, Mama," Chase announced as he set the bowl of macaroni and cheese on the table beside the bowl of collard greens and the plate of cornbread that Neil had placed there just moments earlier.

Shaylynn kissed his cheek. "Well, aren't you two just full of surprises?"

Neil smiled to himself. *You don't know the half of it, suga.* He almost wished all his siblings had traveled to Atlanta to share the holiday with their mom. Not only would Ella have liked that, but it would have opened the door for the people closest to him to be witnesses to his moment of happiness. Neil's smile widened at the thought of his brothers poking fun at him well into the evening for doing the one thing he'd said he would never do again.

From the kitchen counter where he stood,

carving the turkey into slices, he turned and looked across the room into the adjoining dining area and winked at Shaylynn. Then he looked at his mother, who sat beside her. "Speaking of surprises, I think Chase has something to tell you." When Chase threw him a confused look, Neil said, "Tell Ms. Ella Mae what you did today."

"Oh." Chase turned to face Ella. "I got Jesus today."

"You got Jesus?" It was clear from the expression on her face that she didn't understand.

Chase bobbed his head, grinning from ear to ear. "Yes, ma'am. I went up to the front of the church, Pastor Loather prayed for me, and I got Jesus."

As it all became clear to her, Ella gasped, and her hands fluttered to her chest. "Oh, baby," she said as tears filled her eyes. Ella didn't cry that often, but Neil knew that one would get her. It had gotten him too. "Come give Ms. Ella Mae a hug." Chase ran around the table and obliged. "You just made the best decision of your life. You know that?"

"Yes, ma'am." He was wrapped so tight in Ella's arms that his voice was muffled.

Ella pulled him away from her and looked him in the eyes. "You done made Ms. Ella

Mae so happy." She picked up a napkin and dabbed at her eyes. Neil noticed Shaylynn wiping hers too. "If you hadn't bought me nothing for Christmas, this would be my Christmas gift right here."

"Dr. Taylor said when I got Jesus, they started having a party up in heaven," Chase said.

Ella clapped her hands and laughed. "That's right, sweetie, they sure did. That's what Jesus said. He said that the angels in heaven rejoice over one soul coming to Christ." She held up her index finger when she said the word "one," and Chase's eyes followed her gesture. "That means they threw a party today, just for you. The angels were up there rejoicing," Ella concluded.

Shaylynn sat forward in her chair. "That means your daddy was rejoicing too, Chase."

Neil gasped and stifled an "Ouch" as he snatched his hand back from the blade of the knife that had just nicked the index finger on his right hand. The excruciating pain from the cut made him bite down hard on the inside of his bottom lip. Not the cut of the knife, but the one caused by Shaylynn's words.

"Your daddy is happier than all the other angels combined." She was bordering on giddy now, and her chipper tone was like grinding broken pieces of glass into Neil's flesh. "You know, Christmas was Daddy's favorite holiday," Shaylynn continued. "I wish he were alive and there in the church to see you get . . . Jesus today."

*I wish he were alive.* Those words rendered the deepest stab of all. She was still talking, but Neil tuned her out. He had to in order to contain his fury. He snatched off a sheet of paper towel and wrapped his finger with it before picking up the tray of turkey and delivering it to the table. When he placed it down, he dropped it harder than necessary. The resulting thud got everyone's attention.

"Be careful, Sol," Ella said, probably thinking the tray had slipped from his grasp. Then she took note of his hand. "What's the matter? What happened?"

"I'm fine," Neil lied. His finger may have been fine, but he certainly wasn't. "I cut myself a little bit while I was carving the turkey."

Shaylynn stood. "You want me to —"

"No." Neil tried not to sound snappish, but he didn't know if he succeeded. "No, thank you," he added. "I'm gonna go to the bathroom and put something on this. I'll be back. Don't wait. You all just go ahead and bless the food and eat." He was already halfway down the hall when he completed the sentence.

"There's some peroxide in the medicine cabinet," Ella called after him, "and some Band-Aids in the first aid kit on the floor of the linen closet."

Neil closed himself in the bathroom, taking special care not to slam the door . . . even though he really, *really* wanted to. What did she mean she wished he were alive? If Emmett was alive, then Neil and Shaylynn wouldn't be together. To Neil's ears, what she had said was as good as saying she didn't want to be with him; she was just with him because she couldn't have the man she really wanted. He ripped the makeshift dressing from his finger and discarded it in the trash can. There were only a few specs of blood on it. The wound was almost superficial.

In frustration, Neil shoved his hands in his pockets. That's when he felt the ring. He had taken it from the box of his glove compartment and hidden it there . . . waiting for just the right moment. Every day since he made the purchase, he'd taken the ring out of its casing and admired it with a smile; sometimes even rehearsing his lines in preparation for today. Looking at it now brought him no joy, and he knew that every time he looked at it from here on out, it would remind him all over again of the ill-timing of Shaylynn's little salute to the great Emmett Ford.

Melancholy began to replace his anger. Why did she have to do this today? Not only was she refusing to let Emmett die, but it was like she was on some kind of mission to keep him alive in Chase's mind too. How could Neil propose to her? Not only was she not willing to allow him to be her husband, she also wasn't willing to allow him to be Chase's father.

Defeated once again, Neil dropped the ring back into his pocket and washed his hands with soap and water. Peroxide wasn't necessary. Instead, once he dried his hands, he proceeded to hunt through the first aid kit for a Band-Aid that was the right size for his minor wound. Neil was so dejected that he'd lost his appetite. He didn't know how he was going to manage to put on a brave face and pretend to enjoy the rest of Christmas Day, but one thing he knew for sure: the only piece of jewelry that would get presented today was the birthstone cuff watch that Shaylynn and Chase had purchased for Ella Mae.

# ELEVEN

"I still can't believe you didn't propose." The disappointment was written all over Theresa's face, not to mention how obviously detectable it was in her voice. She had been in the kitchen preparing dinner when Neil first arrived at the Loather home. Now she was stretched out across the sofa, getting pampered, like preparing a meal for two had been a chore and a half.

Neil wanted to laugh. He sat on the loveseat directly across the room and watched as Theresa lay with her bare feet in CJ's lap while he massaged them. Ella Mae had given birth to ten children and never had an ounce of painkillers while doing so. As a matter of fact, most of the Taylor children weren't birthed in a hospital or by doctors. Ella had midwives, and she had pushed out most of her babies while lying on the same bed she'd gotten impregnated in, in their country home. And as much as

Pop loved her, Neil never saw him rub his mother's feet. No doubt, childbearing was an assignment for which he definitely wouldn't volunteer . . . even if he could. But he still often wondered what modern women would do if they lived in yesteryear.

Neil bit down on the remains of the dissolving peppermint he had been nursing for the past few minutes, and between crunches, he replied, "Well, I can't believe you can't believe I didn't propose. I think I did just what any man would have done if he were in my shoes."

"You're gonna mess around and let her get away if you don't learn how to deal with your male ego."

"What male ego?" Neil swallowed the last of the candy. "This has nothing to do with ego."

Theresa sucked her teeth. "Are you kidding me? Of course it does. It has everything to do with male ego, and yours is so inflated that everything's gotta be your way or no way at all."

Neil couldn't believe the words coming out of her mouth. "This isn't about having everything my way, this is about having *one* thing my way."

"Yeah, one *humongous* thing," Theresa said. "Your one thing is like a hundred regular-sized things."

"You make it sound like I'm being unreasonable." Neil looked to his best friend for support. "Am I being unreasonable, CJ?"

"That all depends upon what your expectations are, bruh. I've told you that already. You know how I feel on this matter. It's not gonna go away. You're either going to have to learn to deal with it, or not. But if you choose not to, then I'm afraid you've taken this relationship with Shay about as far as it's gonna go."

"Man, don't say that," Neil said in reply.

"I'm just stating the facts as I see them."

"In other words, yes, you're being unreasonable," Theresa inserted.

Neil sighed and crossed his right foot over his left knee. He felt like he was in some crazy sort of courtroom and not a single member of the jury believed his testimony. The only person who seemed to be able to understand his pain at all was Deacon Burgess, and as senile as he'd been lately, Neil knew better than to verbally cite that. Calling Homer Burgess's name as his sole witness wasn't going to make his case any stronger. "Come on, Theresa. Are you telling me that you'd be cool with sharing my boy's heart with some other female, dead or alive?"

Theresa propped herself up on her elbows. "You see this?" She pointed her eyes toward her stomach. With only a few weeks to go, it stuck out like the fully expanded top of one of those old-school Jiffy Pop stovetop pans that people have to continuously shake while the popcorn pops. "If this turns out to be a girl, I may never get any love from *your boy* again, because he'll be giving it all to her."

CJ squeezed his wife's foot. "Oh come on, baby. You know that's not true."

"Of course it's not," Neil said. "There's a big difference between the love a man has for his kid and the love he has for his woman. You won't lose any of CJ's love, 'cause those two loves actually come from two entirely different aortas of the heart."

"What?" Theresa looked at him sideways. "The heart only has one aorta, boy. You're just making junk up."

"I'm a PhD," Neil said, "I'm licensed to make junk up."

Theresa chuckled and lay back on the throw pillows that were positioned behind her head. After a moment of silence, she restated her stance. "You should have asked her, Neil."

"Did you hear a single word of the story that I just told y'all about my Christmas

Day fiasco?" Neil shook his head. "It literally blows me away that you're still saying I should have proposed."

"She would have accepted."

"No, she wouldn't have." Neil's voice raised an octave. "I don't think Shay's ever gonna say 'I do' again . . . to me or anyone else, for that matter. That's the one positive in this whole mess. At least it ain't personal. She's not gonna marry me, but I won't have to stand by and watch her marry somebody else, either." Neil tried to laugh it off, but the sting of his statement wouldn't let him. He was beginning to believe it more and more.

"Haven't you ever heard that saying about how you're only a failure when you don't try?" CJ grunted. "I can't believe you're giving up without even trying."

"I'm not saying I'm giving up. I'm just saying . . ." Neil rubbed his forehead, and then muttered, "I don't even know what I'm saying anymore."

"She would have said yes," Theresa reiterated in a sing-song tone.

Neil looked at her and frowned. "Will you stop saying that? What makes you so sure? You're some kind of prophetess now?"

"Maybe I am."

"Yeah, right," Neil said through a sigh.

"I refuse not to remain very optimistic about this. I like the thought of you and Shaylynn being a wedded couple," Theresa said. "She did such an amazing job on the baby room."

That was true. The room looked fantastic. Neil had come by on New Year's Eve, before Watch Night service, to help CJ set up all the furniture. "So what? You want her around so you can have a built-in designer who'll give you the family rate every time you want a room redecorated?"

Theresa twisted her lips. "Of course not. Well, yeah . . . I guess that would be a perk, but that's not the reason I like the idea of her being Mrs. Neil Taylor. I like Shaylynn for several reasons. For one, she's very mature. Maybe life forced her to become wise beyond her years, but whatever the reason, she's mature. When she's around, I don't feel like I'm talking to someone four years younger than me."

"How 'bout six," Neil corrected.

"How 'bout shut up," Theresa warned, and then proceeded without missing a beat. "And Shaylynn is different than a lot of the sisters at KBCC. When she talks to me, it's just Shaylynn talking to Theresa. I mean, she respects me and everything, but she never gives me that stupid 'Oh my God; I'm talking to the first lady' act that a lot of the members do. Around me, she's herself and she's comfortable. I like that. Plus anyone who knows me knows that I like to talk and discuss things in detail. Shaylynn is a great conversationalist. I know she didn't graduate from a four-year university like I and a lot of the other women at the church did, but she's smart and knowledgeable. When we're talking, I forget that she's someone who, when I was graduating *from* high school, was just getting *in* high school."

"Middle school."

"Shut. Up." That time Theresa said it through clinched teeth, and it was accompanied by a look that told Neil that was his last warning. "The point is I like her, okay? She's like the ever-so-slightly younger sister I never had. I just happen to think she's right for you."

CJ nodded in agreement. "I do too. Of all the girls I've known you to date since we met on the campus of Morehouse College — including Audrey, who I actually thought was pretty cool — I like Shay the best. Spiritually, mentally, physically . . . I think she's your perfect fit. She supports you. She encourages your ministry. She loves your mother. You're crazy about her son. She gets along with your whole family and, let's face it, that's a heck of a lot of people to get along with."

Although the things CJ and Theresa were saying were true, they only increased Neil's frustration. Where was he going to find another woman like Shaylynn? He loved her too much not to make this work, but he had to snatch her from under the spell Emmett had cast. Someway. Somehow. "You guys are talking like you have to sell me on her or something. I'm already sold. I know that we're another Ossie and Ruby Dee."

"He was amazing, but he's dead," Theresa injected.

"Another Bill and Camille Cosby."

"Another good one, but he had an outside love child."

Neil looked at CJ. "Can't you do anything to control your wife's mouth?"

CJ laughed. "I've only found one way to shut her up, and you'd have to leave before I could do that."

Neil huffed and looked at his surroundings. "I can't believe I actually sit on y'all's furniture when I come over here. I'll bet all kinds of ungodliness takes place on this loveseat. I gotta remember to bathe when I get home. And to throw all my clothes in the washer."

CJ laughed some more. "You're stupid, bruh."

Neil got back on subject. "But for real. Can one of you call Shay and start your speeches all back over again? Maybe between the two of you, one of you will be able to make her see it too."

"I think she already does," Theresa said. "I still say she would have been glad to have you propose to her."

Neil rolled his eyes and decided not to even respond to her repetitious psychosis. Instead, he turned his attention back to CJ. "When you hear people say stuff like, 'A marriage takes three,' they're talking about the groom, the bride, and God, not the groom, the bride, and her ex."

"But he's not her ex," CJ explained further. "If Emmett was an ex-boyfriend, ex-fiancé, ex-husband, ex-anything, I'd agree with you wholeheartedly about this. But he's not. He's her *former* husband. A man she was with until death parted them."

"And even after that." Neil dropped his head against the back of the loveseat.

"Have you spoken to her since Christmas?" CJ asked.

Neil stared up at the fan attached to his friends' ceiling. It would be at least two more months before they'd need to turn it on. "Sure, I have. It's not like we broke up. She doesn't even know how upset I was at the Christmas gathering, so we've talked every day as usual. I'm the one who drove them to the airport on Friday, so they could catch a flight to Milwaukee for Chase to spend the first few days of the New Year with his grandparents." Neil hadn't been particularly happy when he first found out that Shaylynn and Chase wouldn't be with him when the old year made its exit, but taking Chase to Milwaukee to see the other side of his family was sort of tradition for them. Just as he'd done every year for as far back as he could remember, Neil brought in the New Year in church. Watch Night was a great worship experience, but it would have been even better had Shaylynn and Chase been there with him instead of on the other end of the country.

"How's the visit going?"

Neil knew why CJ was asking. Shaylynn wasn't exactly fond of Emmett's parents, and they weren't in her fan club either. "I spoke to Shay last night. She hasn't seen the ex . . . *former* in-laws since she dropped off Chase at their house on Friday afternoon. He's staying with them, and she's staying with a couple who used to be her neighbors back in the day. She went to her old church home for Watch Night service, and she said it was good to see the lady who used to be her pastor."

"They're coming back tomorrow, right?" Theresa asked.

"Yeah. They have to be back by then. That'll be the last day of the holiday break. School starts back on Wednesday."

"Just so you know," CJ said, "when I asked you if you'd spoken to Shaylynn since Christmas, I wasn't talking about your normal daily conversations. I was asking if you'd talked to her about the thing that upset you, but you've already answered my question." CJ shook his head. "I guess if she doesn't even realize that you were put off by her mention of Emmett, it's a safe assumption that you're still avoiding the inevitable."

Neil sighed. *Here we go again.* His pastor/best friend hadn't been all that subtle when letting Neil know that he was disappointed in his hesitation to be totally honest with Shaylynn on how he felt about her posthumous relationship with Emmett. "I haven't talked to her about it yet, but I plan to."

CJ released his wife's foot long enough to fan a carefree hand at Neil. "Yeah, right. How many times have I heard that one? You wouldn't happen to be related to the boy who cried wolf, would you?"

Theresa laughed like it was the best joke ever, but Neil didn't see the humor. "I *am* going to talk to her," he stressed. "I just . . . didn't want to do it so soon after the other misunderstanding that had just happened a couple of weeks earlier, nor did I think our Christmas gathering with Ms. Ella Mae was the right time. I didn't want to ruin the holiday. What would I have looked like bringing up something like that on the day that celebrates Jesus' birth?"

CJ made a grunting noise. "So you're gonna talk to her tomorrow, then? No holiday falls on tomorrow."

"I . . . I hadn't thought about it. Maybe. I don't know."

"Christmas is gone, New Years is gone." CJ shrugged. "Let's see . . . Martin Luther King Day is coming up. You gonna use that for your next excuse? Maybe you won't want to mess up the day that celebrates Dr. King's birth either."

Theresa thought that was funny too. Apparently, to her, it was even funnier than the wisecrack about the boy who cried wolf.

Neil stood. "Okay, I'm about to go. It's obvious that I've worn out my welcome."

"Boy, sit down." Theresa wiped moisture from her eyes.

"No," Neil protested. "Apparently you and your sidekick husband here think this is some kind of joke. I'm dealing with a very stressful situation, and the two of you are getting your jollies off of it."

CJ looked up at him. "Do you see me laughing? Am I laughing?"

"I don't *see* you laughing, but I hear it. The two of you are working together. You're the ventriloquist, and the sounds are coming out of your dummy's mouth."

In a flash, Theresa was back on her elbows. Getting to her feet wasn't nearly as easy, but she didn't have to struggle for long. Before Neil could even figure out what he'd said to generate such a reaction, CJ was standing in her stead.

"What did you just call her?" CJ was three inches from Neil's face, and he looked about two seconds away from speaking in unknown tongues . . . and not the holy kind.

"What?" Neil batted his eyes while the ticker tape in his mind tried to reverse and detect the error. "What?" he repeated.

"You just called Resa a dummy, and not only is that inaccurate and inappropriate, but it's also endangering. *Your life,* that is."

"Whoa, whoa, whoa!" Neil held up both his hands in surrender. The closest he and CJ had ever come to fighting were the arm wrestling matches they used to challenge each other to in their college days. Sometimes Neil would win, and other times CJ would. At this stage of their lives, Neil wasn't sure who would get the victory, but he wasn't curious enough to try to find out, either. He took two steps back. "Hold up, man. You know that's not what I meant. Bad example. Bad example, okay?" He watched CJ's facial muscles relax. "It was just a poor choice of words. All I was saying was that you were doing the laughing, but the sound was coming out of Theresa's mouth. That's all. I wasn't going for any name-calling." As CJ backed away, Neil mumbled, "Good Lord. Just a few weeks ago, y'all were about to turn the church office into a Hampton Inn; now you want to turn your living room into Caesar's Palace. I'ma pray for y'all." He began heading for the front door.

"You don't have to leave, Neil," Theresa said.

"Yes, I do."

"No, you don't. Dinner should be ready now, and you know you love my meatloaf. You should stay and eat with us."

Theresa's meatloaf was good, true enough. And Neil hadn't eaten one morsel of food all day, but he still declined. "I should be getting on home."

"Come on, Neil," CJ chimed in. He pointed at the couch that Neil had been occupying until just a short while ago. "Sit down, bruh. It's cool. I'm fine now."

Neil looked at CJ and scowled. "Man, ain't nobody scared of you. You think I'm leaving 'cause of you? Man, I coulda took you in my sleep."

CJ laughed. "Whatever it takes to make you feel better, bruh."

Neil stretched his body. "I wasn't supposed to be over here this long anyway. When I first got here, I told y'all I was just gonna be here a few minutes." Neil looked at his watch. "It's been almost two hours. I still need to get that work done before I go to bed tonight. I fooled around and let the entire holiday break pass and didn't complete the electronic files that I need to update in the school database. I gave Ms. Dasher half, and I took the other half. She'll never let me live it down if she has hers done when we return on Wednesday and I don't." Neil walked to their front closet and retrieved his coat.

"Man! That sure is sharp," CJ said, admiring the black number that Shaylynn had bought Neil for Christmas.

Neil laughed. "Yeah, I know. You said that when I first got here."

"Did Shay tell you that I helped her pick it out?" Theresa reached over her shoulder and patted herself on the back. "I did good, didn't I?"

"She told me that she picked the coat, but you picked the color."

"That's true." Theresa finally relieved CJ of his duties and managed to sit up straight. "She wanted to buy a brown one; talkin' 'bout, 'But Solomon looks so good in chocolate.' "

Neil laughed at Theresa's pitiful attempt to sound like Shaylynn, but he felt himself blush behind the compliment. "She didn't tell me that part."

"I told her to put that mess back. You already have enough brown in your closet, including a coat."

"I already had a black coat too."

"Yeah, but not like that one."

CJ agreed. "Yeah, bruh. This one is way sharper than that long one you have."

Neil couldn't seem to stop smiling. Shaylynn did, indeed, make a good choice. Both of them had to laugh when they opened their gifts on Christmas Day, because both had bought coats for the other. Shaylynn's peacoat looked good on her too. Not as good as that ring would have looked on her finger, but that was another story. Neil shook the thought from his head.

"You want me to fix you a plate to go?" Theresa offered. "The meatloaf is ready by now. It'll only take a minute."

"It's gonna take you more than a minute just to get up off that couch."

"Shut up." Theresa threw one pillow at Neil for what he said and another at CJ for laughing at it.

"Oh." Neil snapped his fingers after tossing the pillow back on the sofa. "I still need to get that list from you, CJ. I need that in order to complete the updates tonight."

"I'm gonna help Resa in the kitchen. You can go in my office and get it. You can't miss it. It's the red folder in the bottom tray on my desk."

Neil knew the layout of the Loather home almost as well as he knew his own, even though theirs was much larger. Before CJ and Theresa got married, he used to spend a lot more time there than now, but not much about it had changed. Just more flowers and other girlie stuff than before, but the layout virtually remained the same. The baby room was the biggest change, and even that room was already there. Thanks to Shaylynn's genius, it just had a totally different look now.

When Neil reached his pastor's home office, he stood in the doorway for a moment and looked around. CJ had to have about the neatest office he'd ever seen. All of his reading matter, mostly biblical resource material, was neatly lined on the bookshelves. All of his writing instruments were standing upright in a pencil holder. The big framed photo of his parents was hanging on the wall so straight that it looked like it was a permanent part of the structure itself. CJ spent hours in that office during the course of the week, but that couldn't be detected by looking at it. Neil knew that all the credit belonged to Theresa. Before CJ got married, just getting from the doorway to his desk was an Olympic sport.

As Neil approached the desk, he saw the red folder. Like CJ said, he couldn't miss it. It was the only red folder in the bottom tray. No . . . actually, there were two of them. Neil didn't realize it until he began pulling one out and saw that there was another one beneath it. Not knowing which was the right one, he flipped open the cover to inspect the contents. At first he didn't know what he was reading, but it was in CJ's handwriting. The sentences on the page were broken and sketchy. It seemed like the outline for some sort of mystery-thriller that CJ was embarking upon writing. It sure would be a good one. Just the rough draft drew Neil in and kept his eyes scanning the page.

Had interview with sole witness who refused to give his name . . . murdered victim involved in illegal gambling . . . drug laundering . . . prostitution . . . you name it . . . was unfaithful to his wife during entire marriage . . . loved call girls . . . bought women like most men bought suits . . . dirty politics . . . paid by drug lords . . . something happened shortly before murder . . . had a life change and came to Christ . . . conscience kicked in . . . was about to pull the cover off of the operation . . . friends became his enemies . . . price put on his head . . . murder for hire . . . city and state officials probably all involved . . . sole witness to the murder still lives in fear of his own life . . . the shooting was definitely a political cover-up . . . Kris-Cross P.I. conclusion: Mayor Emmett Ford was a dirty politician who was murdered because he got saved . . .

Neil's eyes skimmed over the writings three times. Then they did it a fourth time, just to be sure that they had viewed it right the first, second, and third time. The words hadn't changed. The meaning hadn't changed. Shaylynn's beloved Emmett was a crook. A drug-funded, sleazy-politicking, whore-hiring crook. The shock of the earth-shattering revelation rendered Neil speechless. The best he could do was mouth the words: *Oh. My. God!*

# Twelve

Shaylynn turned over and moaned. It was the middle of the afternoon, but the covers of her comfy temporary bed felt even better now than they had when she lay down about ten hours ago. Every time she visited the city that she'd once called home, Shaylynn lodged at the same bed and breakfast. Lucus and Alice Jessup, the retired white couple who owned the business, repeatedly gave Shaylynn the star treatment during her infrequent visits. The Jessups had once been her neighbors when she was married to the city's new mayor. They were two of the very few true friends she ever felt she had while living in Milwaukee, and whenever Shaylynn came into town, they took her in as if she were family, and never publicized her being at their establishment.

Because of the high-profile individual Emmett was, and the still unsolved status of his murder, even all these many years later it was a sure thing that Shaylynn's privacy would be interrupted by the media if her presence was ever leaked, so she kept as low a profile as possible. Only those she knew she could trust to keep her visit confidential could know that she was in town. Her former parents-in-law certainly weren't going to blab. They wouldn't dare do anything that might give Shaylynn another fifteen minutes of fame, and that was just fine with her. Attention was the last thing she wanted.

It had been her intent to go to her old neighborhood today. Although Shaylynn had made this special return trip to Milwaukee every year for the past six years for Chase to spend some quality time with her estranged former in-laws, Shaylynn hadn't seen the house in which she and Emmett had shared a life, since she and her son made their initial move away from the city when Chase was only nine months old. She'd always avoided that side of town like the plague, but this year, she'd made a mental note to incorporate it as a part of her visit. It was a part of the closure process that she'd set in place for herself, but the snowfall over the past two days had forced her to delay her plans.

Shaylynn sat up in her bed, stretched her arms, and looked around. The walls of her secret quarters were a welcoming shade of powder blue, and they were a perfect match for the white bed linen that was patterned with light pink and baby blue pinstripes. Aside from the white wooden furniture, there was very little to the décor in the room; just a beautiful bouquet of fresh pink and white carnations that sat on a corner stand, and one large framed photo that was mounted on the wall above the entertainment center. The picture showed an endless view of the blue waters of the ocean with sailboats drifting in the distance.

The interior decorator inside of Shaylynn couldn't help envisioning the room looking quite differently. As nice as the space was, to Shaylynn's professionally trained eyes it looked more like something for an adolescent, rather than an adult. If the room was placed in her capable hands, she would replace the enlarged mounted photograph with a framed oil painting of some kind. Maybe a family of deer grazing by a brook in a forest. The only existing décor she would keep was the bearskin rug that lay on the wooden floor at the foot of the bed. Beige walls, mahogany furniture, burgundy and cream floral curtains, and a solid burgundy bed comforter with matching throw pillows in assorted block patterns of burgundy and beige would replace everything else. In Shaylynn's opinion, her ideas would mature the room and give it a cozier feel . . . like the warm colors did in her Solomon's home.

*Solomon.* The random thought of him briefly took her to Atlanta, Georgia, and recent memories curled the corners of her lips upward. She still couldn't believe the irony of them both gifting each other with new coats on Christmas. The one Neil bought for her wasn't built for Wisconsin's winters, but she loved it so much that she'd packed it and brought it along for the ride anyway.

A long yawn returned Shaylynn's mind to her current surroundings. Her room was comfortably toasty, but last night's news reports said today's outside temperatures would remain below zero. She kicked off her covers and walked to her window, opening the curtain just wide enough to peer outside. Her prayers had been answered. The snow had stopped falling, but the blanket it left behind appeared to be five inches thicker than it was when she arrived. From her view, Shaylynn could see the trucks at work, once again, clearing the roadways, so that driving would be a safer and easier task for Milwaukeeans who needed to get from point A to point B. There were very few things that Shaylynn missed about the city that had elected her husband as its first African American mayor some years ago, but the mounds of snow was one of them. As a young bride, she used to enjoy watching, from the window of her sitting room, as the white stuff accumulated on the ground like fallen blown kisses from heaven. Something about being in love had the tendency to put a romantic spin on everything.

Winter expectations were only one of many differences between Milwaukee and Atlanta. It tickled Shaylynn when she heard her new Atlanta friends talk about how cold it was down there. Compared to Wisconsin's brutal temperatures, an average winter day in Atlanta was like beach weather. Just last month, in mid-December, shortly before the Christmas break, nearly all the schools, churches, and even some of the businesses in metropolitan Atlanta had shut their doors for two entire days because two inches of snow had fallen overnight. *Two inches!* She guessed if they ever got even half of what Milwaukee had on its ground right now, those in political power would urge the president of the United States to declare the entire city a disaster area.

The ringing of the telephone drew Shaylynn's eyes away from the goings-on outside her window. Only two people, Lucas and Alice Jessup, knew how to telephone her on the landline of her room, and she knew that only one of them would actually do it. "Good morning, Mrs. Jessup," she said immediately as she placed the phone to her ear.

A soft laugh preceded the response of, "Morning has long come and gone, Shaylynn. It's afternoon now. You had me worried. I just wanted to check to be sure you were okay."

"Yes, ma'am. I'm fine. I didn't mean to worry you." Shaylynn looked at the clock beside her bed. She knew she'd slept late, but she didn't realize it was already after one. She released another yawn. "This is what happens when you give me such a comfortable bed." The truth of the matter was that she'd been up so late last night talking with Neil on the telephone that it was nearly three o'clock this morning by the time she got to bed. And then one of her favorite Julia Roberts movies came on, and even as she lay in bed, she watched it in its entirety before finally drifting off to sleep around five.

Alice laughed again. "Well, I'm glad you

like it. You know it's always our pleasure to have you here. Have you eaten? The staff told me that you never picked up your breakfast tray this morning. They said when they came by your room, the food they set out for you at nine was still there. You must be starving by now. Lucas and I are having lunch in our private dining chambers, and we'd be glad to have you join us."

Shaylynn mindlessly rubbed her stomach. For its clientele, Jessup's Bed & Breakfast only offered one meal a day: breakfast. And that was provided in one dining area where all of their guests were served at once by the hired staff. Most of the guests checked out shortly after eating and continued on their merry way. That was the normal run of things. Shaylynn's extended stay was very out of the ordinary. Each day, she had taken advantage of her VIP option to have her breakfast delivered and set outside the door for her to pick up and bring inside her room to eat in private. When she was done, she would place the tray outside the door, and a staff member would come by at an assigned time and pick it up.

Today, Shaylynn would gladly embrace a change, especially since she'd slept through her morning meal. Alice was an exceptional cook; not as good as Ella Mae, but she definitely knew her way around a kitchen. Since being in Atlanta, Shaylynn had heard some of the black residents there say ignorant things like, "White people can't cook," but she knew better. A person couldn't get much whiter than Alice Jessup, but she held her own, and could out-cook and out-bake plenty of the black people Shaylynn knew; herself included.

"I have Cornish game hen." Alice sang out the words as if she had tied the baked bird at the end of a string and was dangling it in Shaylynn's face.

Shaylynn imagined the perfectly seasoned entrée being fresh out of the oven, lying in a roasting pan and surrounded by a colorful sea of yellow onions, red potatoes, and green peppers. It was one of Alice's signature dishes, and just the vision of it made Shaylynn lick her lips. "Thank you. I'd love to join you," she finally said. "I need to talk to you and Mr. Jessup anyway. I want to get your thoughts on something."

"Splendid." Shaylynn didn't know if Alice was referring to her joining them for lunch, or her request to use them as sounding boards. "Lucas is running an errand, but he'll be back any minute. Can we expect you in about half an hour?"

"Yes, ma'am. I'll be there."

"Okay, dear. We'll see you in a little bit."

Shaylynn headed to her private restroom as soon as she hung up the telephone. It was another perk that all of the guests didn't get. Jessup's Bed & Breakfast was a ten-bedroom estate that Lucas and Alice had purchased with their life's savings, and then they immediately began making a lucrative return on their investment by providing posh accommodations for strangers who were passing through town, or locals who just wanted an overnight getaway. Most guests only stayed for one night, but a few were known to linger a little longer. Two of the ten bedrooms were executive suites. One was the permanent living quarters where Lucas and Alice stayed. The other was extended to any other guest who was fortunate enough to have the deep pockets to afford it. Thanks to the small fortune that Emmett had left her, Shaylynn was one of those people, but thanks to her relationship with the Jessups, even if she weren't, she'd still be allowed to stay there. Shaylynn's executive suite came with a private bath, but the other guests shared four public unisex facilities.

Refreshed from her hot shower, Shaylynn stepped out of the bathroom with a towel wrapped around her freshly moisturized body. The mirror inside was so fogged with steam that she couldn't see how her braids looked pulled back in the high ponytail that she'd created. She finished preparing, using the mirror that was attached to her dresser. It only took a few minutes for her to pull on her blue jeans and the pink turtleneck sweater that Ella had bought her for Christmas. Pink was one of Shaylynn's least favorite colors, but she certainly wasn't going to take back or exchange a gift that Neil's mother had given her. Besides, Shaylynn had to admit it looked great with the pink snow boots that she had bought just so she had shoes to complement the sweater. Her smooth chocolate skin needed no makeup, but she applied eyeliner and lipstick before closing her eyes and saying a silent prayer.

A lot was depending on what happened in the next hour or so, and Shaylynn's stomach fluttered in anticipation. She hoped . . . *prayed* to get something more than just lunch from the Jessups.

## Thirteen

"Shaylynn . . . Come in, my dear." When she made it to the part of the house where the owners lived, it was Lucas that greeted her. His arms were stretched wide as he spoke. Lucas Jessup, a man in his late sixties, was an average height, around five feet nine, and he had an odd, square-shaped physique. Nothing on his body seemed to be defined. His waist seemed to blend right into his hips, and his back did the same with his behind. He was almost completely bald, but there was hair at the base of his scalp, right above his neck, that seemed to want to hold on for dear life. He reminded Shaylynn of Frank Barone, the father of Ray Barone on *Everybody Loves Raymond,* only Lucas was nowhere near as insensitive and nauseating.

"Hi, Mr. Jessup." She smelled Old Spice, Brut, Skin Bracer, or one of those classic older-men fragrances as she received his hug. "Thank you all for inviting me to lunch."

"It's our pleasure." He swept his arm in the direction of their private dining area. "Right this way. Alice has everything all ready for us."

When they walked into the dining area, Alice was just placing the last serving dish on the table. They had gone all out; even had candles lit as though Shaylynn was truly a special guest. Alice removed her apron, grinned, and walked toward her. She wasn't any taller than Shaylynn, but she was wider. Alice had a pudgy frame, and though she was somewhat attractive, she wore a tad too much makeup in her effort to minimize the appearance of her fifty-eight years. Oddly enough, she resembled Marie Barone, wife of Frank Barone on *Everybody Loves Raymond,* but she was nowhere near as meddlesome and annoying.

"Don't you look beautiful," Alice remarked just before they embraced. "I believe pink is your color."

Shaylynn totally disagreed, but she smiled and accepted the compliment graciously. "Thank you." She looked at the spread of food. "The table looks great, and something on it smells heavenly."

"I hope it tastes the same," Alice remarked

with a laugh. "Come on in, dear, and choose a chair."

There weren't a lot of chairs from which to choose. They all took their seats at the table for four, and after Lucas graced the food, the serving dishes began making their rounds. Small talk and chuckles were passed between them throughout the meal, but it was obvious to Shaylynn that her hosts were purposefully avoiding the mention of Emmett. They'd been doing it ever since she arrived. In every visit that she'd made to Wisconsin and stayed at their bed and breakfast, Emmett was never spoken of unless she initiated the topic. And eventually, she always did.

"So are we going to get to see Chase this time around?" Lucas asked after downing the last of his fresh-squeezed orange juice.

Shaylynn nodded. Her hunger pangs were completely satisfied. The meal had hit the spot. "Yes, but only for a little while. I'll pick him up tomorrow and bring him back here for you to see him before we head to the airport. You won't believe how tall he's gotten since last year."

"Oh, I'd believe it," Alice said as she began busying herself with clearing the table. "I'd be more shocked if he weren't shooting up like a weed."

Shaylynn knew that in the woman's mind she was picturing how tall Emmett was, and it only made sense that his son would grow to rival that. But as much as Shaylynn knew it was what Alice was thinking, she also knew it was something Alice wouldn't say. So she did it for her.

"Well, Emmett was over six feet, so I guess he's going to take after his dad and not me."

"I'm sure." Lucas seemed not certain if he should take it any further.

"Do you remember how much Emmett used to love sports?" Shaylynn was determined to break the ice. She needed them to get comfortable with the subject so that she could introduce the other topic of conversation that she wanted to share with them.

Alice nodded where she stood. "Oh yes. *That* one" — she threw her eyes in Lucas's direction — "always had somebody he knew he could depend on if he wanted to go to a game or watch one on television."

Lucas agreed. "Yep. And I don't know why on earth we watched sports together because we hardly ever rooted for the same team."

Grinning, Shaylynn knew she'd gotten a breakthrough. "Except when it came to hockey. I think both of you were fans of the Milwaukee Admirals."

"True. True." Lucas wiped his mouth with a napkin. "But the camaraderie ended there. When it came to baseball, football, or basketball, we were archrivals. And Emmett drew the line at golf. He enjoyed playing it, but watching it on television was another story. Whenever I'd call him up and say, 'Hey, Emmett, the first round of the Masters kicks off today,' he'd respond by saying, 'Mr. Jessup, you're on your own, buddy.' " Lucas chuckled at the memories.

"I think Chase is going to want to play football," Shaylynn injected. She didn't want to lose control of the conversation. Lucas could get lost in the topic of sports.

"Oh, really?" Alice frowned across the room from the kitchen counter. She'd gone there to retrieve the pot of fresh coffee. She poured a cup for herself and one for her husband. She didn't pour one for Shaylynn, probably because she knew she would decline. "I'd hate to see that baby get hurt. Football is such a violent sport."

"It's not violent," Lucas defended. "It's a contact sport, so it's physical."

"Well, all I know is people get hurt." Alice placed fresh slices of blueberry crumb cake on saucers and placed one in front of each of them. She refilled Shaylynn's glass with orange juice before taking her seat. "Do you know I saw a special on television not long ago where a player got paralyzed from the neck down because of how he fell when he got tackled? That poor man is no good for anything or anybody anymore. Paralyzed from the neck down means you can't move anything but your head. I'll bet he wishes he'd never been introduced to a football, let alone played the game."

The last thing Shaylynn needed seared in her mind was the image of Chase Ford as a quadriplegic. She didn't know what she'd do if her baby got seriously injured while playing a sport that she'd encouraged and supported, but at the same time, she didn't want to keep him from doing something that he loved. Shaylynn tried to blink away the imagery. Maybe this wasn't the route down which to take the conversation after all. "He likes to play football now, but he might outgrow it." Saying that pacified her, although she knew full well that it probably wouldn't happen. "He likes to toss the ball around with one of his school administrators."

"His coach, you mean?" Lucas asked, blowing into his hot coffee.

Shaylynn took in a forkful of cake and savored the flavor as the delicious dessert literally dissolved on her tongue. This was

223

the topic she had been trying to work her way toward, but now that the moment had arrived, she felt nervous. "Chase is not on a team or anything, so no, the man is not his coach. He's the director at the Christian academy that Chase attends. He's very interactive with the students there, and Chase likes to play football with him."

The table was quiet for a few seconds that felt like forever. Shaylynn could feel two sets of inquisitive eyes targeted at her, but she kept focus on her plate and pretended to be totally involved with eating her dessert.

"The school's director plays football with the kids?" Lucas probed. "I mean, is he playing with *all* the kids or just Chase?"

Shaylynn suddenly felt as though she was sitting at the table with her parents, and they were scrutinizing her every word, watching her every move. She looked up and found that her earlier feel of their eyes was justified. It was time for her to make them the sounding boards that she had been looking for. "Well, actually, he does interact with all the children, but he has a certain fondness for Chase . . . and for me."

"You're dating again?" Alice approached the question with caution.

When Shaylynn nodded her answer, Alice's eyebrows rose, and that was accompanied by the sound of a soft gasp. The woman's already pale skin became ghostlike. For a moment, Shaylynn wondered whether Alice was still breathing. The sudden inhale of breath that she'd taken moments earlier seemed to have gotten lodged somewhere. Shaylynn never saw it release. Was she happy? Sad? Petrified? Shaylynn couldn't read her face well enough to determine.

"How long has this been going on?" Lucas's voice drew her eyes in his direction. "How well do you know this fella?"

Shaylynn glanced back at Alice, just to be sure the woman wasn't slipping away, then she returned her attention to Lucas. "I met Solomon shortly after moving to Atlanta. Like I said, he's the director at the school that Chase attends. I know him very well." Shaylynn smiled, and then sipped from her juice to moisten her throat. "He's strong, ambitious, smart, protective, kind, and thoughtful. He's romantic, spontaneous, funny . . . he makes me laugh all the time. He has a close-knit, wonderful family who I've had the pleasure of meeting. I really like his family, and they embraced me from the very beginning. Most of all, Solomon is a great role model. Chase loves him, and he loves Chase . . . and he loves the Lord." Lucas and Alice weren't the most dedicated churchgoers, so she didn't know whether that last part meant much to them, but it meant the world to her. None of Neil's other attributes would have won her over if they had come void of his love for God.

"He sounds a lot like Emmett." Alice had finally found her voice.

Shaylynn quickly shook her head in disagreement. There were numerous differences between the two men. The family thing alone was one of the most obvious ones. Emmett's family had never welcomed her. If it weren't for Chase, they wouldn't have anything to do with her even now. Shaylynn purposefully avoided pointing that out though. There were plenty of other dissimilarities she could site that wouldn't test her gag reflexes. "I guess some of their core values are the same, but they are very different men." She knew what Alice was likely thinking: that she was trying to find a substitute for Emmett, someone just like him who'd be able to fill the lingering void. But nothing could be further from the truth. There was only one Emmett Ford. Outside of them both being handsome, God-fearing men who appreciated sports, there was very little likeness between the two.

"Emmett was much taller and leaner. Solomon has a more solid, muscular build, and he's not even quite as tall as Mr. Jessup." She pointed at Lucas when she made the comparison. "And their upbringings were entirely different. Solomon was brought up in the church, and Emmett wasn't. And from what I've been told, there probably were no silver spoons anywhere in Solomon's entire childhood home, but, as you know, Emmett was born with one in his mouth. Emmett loved politics. Solomon hates it." She took a breath before adding. "And Emmett couldn't hold a tune if you stapled it to the palm of his hand, but when Solomon sings . . ." She smiled and closed her eyes. "When Solomon sings . . . something amazing happens. When he opens his mouth and lets the melodies come out, somehow everything becomes right with the world." Shaylynn opened her eyes to see Lucas and Alice looking at her in awe. To them, she probably sounded like a lovesick teenager. She felt like one too. In closing, she said, "Emmett grew up in the big city as an only child. Solomon grew up on a farm with nine siblings. And while Emmett was a few years older than me, Solomon . . . well, Solomon is —"

"Younger?" Alice's eyebrows were up

again. "How much younger? I don't have anything against these so-called *cougar* relationships, but I don't care what anybody says, men take longer to mature. You're barely in your thirties, and you have a young son. A man too much younger than you won't be much more than a child himself."

"I agree." Lucas nodded for added effect. "Sometimes the younger men may seem mature on the surface, but you get them in a marriage, and it's a different thing. Ed and Patsy's daughter married a younger man. There aren't but five years between them, and she didn't think that was anything to be concerned about. But Ed told me the other day that Suzanna called them crying, saying she felt like she had three sons now: the twin boys she gave birth to and the one she's married to. You don't want to wake up one day feeling like you have two sons."

"Patsy told me the same thing over tea." Alice shook her head from side to side, like she felt sorry for their friends.

Shaylynn held up her hand to shush them both. First of all, she had no earthly idea who Ed and Patsy were, let alone their poor, disappointed daughter, Suzanna. All she knew was that the Jessups had drawn the wrong conclusion and were running away with it. "Solomon's not younger than I am.

He's older. A few years older."

Lucas's voice broke through the cloud of silence that hovered over them for several moments. "What's your definition of *a few years*?"

"Almost fifteen."

The amplified clank of Alice's fork as it slipped from her hand and hit her saucer resonated in the dining space, but her voice that followed was barely more than a whisper. "Fifteen?"

"Yes, ma'am. Almost. He's about fourteen and a half years older."

Lucas scratched his chin. "So he's what, forty-six? Forty-seven?"

"Forty-six."

Another uncomfortable silence followed. It was broken by a comment from Lucas that took Shaylynn by surprise.

"That's not so bad."

Shaylynn looked at him and opened her mouth to speak, but Alice's voice beat hers to the punch.

"It's not?"

"No." He reclaimed his fork as though he was satisfied now and ready to resume eating. He picked up a big chunk of cake and said, "I'd rather he be fifteen years older, than five years younger."

"But he's old enough to be her father,"

Alice debated.

Lucas chewed his dessert until it was broken down enough for him to speak clearly. "Not any father I'd ever want to meet. I'm not saying that there aren't fourteen- and fifteen-year-old kids out there with kids of their own, but it's not the norm. Besides, isn't Archibald about that much older than Beth?"

Alice gave it some thought, and then nodded. "Yeah. Actually Archie is seventeen or eighteen years older than Mary Beth. She's a year younger than me, and he's got to be near seventy-five."

"See? And it works fine for them. They've been married for thirty-plus years, got four children and probably seven grands."

Here they were again; comparing her to people she was clueless about. A laugh rose in Shaylynn's throat, but she washed it back down with a few swallows of orange juice, and then reached for the pitcher in the middle of the table to pour herself a refill.

"You seem happy. Do you love him?"

Shaylynn almost lost her grip on the heavy glass container at Alice's unexpected question. She finished her task, and then placed the pitcher back on the table before answering. "Yes. Very much." The expression on Alice's face prompted Shaylynn to make an

observation of her own. "You look surprised."

"How can I not be? I mean, I'm happy for
you, dear, but I can't help but remember a
time, not so long ago, when you swore that
you'd never fall in love again. And now, not
only are you obviously in love, but this
sounds serious. Are you planning to marry
this Solomon? Is that why you wanted to
talk to us . . . to see how we felt about your
decision to remarry?"

Quite honestly, Shaylynn didn't know why
she felt the need to talk to the Jessups. It
was probably because they were about the
closest things to parents that she'd ever had.
Prior to moving to Atlanta and spending so
much time around Ella Mae, Alice had been
the only mother figure Shaylynn had known
since the death of her grandmother when
she was just eighteen. And since she'd never
had a decent father figure in her life, Lucas
had been the only man to even come close
to playing the role. If she coupled that with
the fact that they also knew Emmett and
her relationship with him, it just seemed
natural for her to look to the two of them
for parental-type advice.

"I haven't made a decision to remarry,"
she replied quietly. "Not yet anyway. I can't

really make that decision without first being asked."

"But you think he's going to ask?" Luke's question sounded more like a statement.

Shaylynn nodded. "At least, I hope he does."

"Wow," Alice whispered.

"He must be some kind of man," Lucas commented. "How does the love you have for Solomon compare to the love you had for Emmett?"

Shaylynn wanted to correct him. Her love for Emmett wasn't a thing of the past. "Had" was the wrong word to use. She still loved her former husband and always would. The devotion she now had for Neil in no way erased or replaced it. Shaylynn couldn't explain it, but it was as though God had enlarged her heart so that it could make room for Neil in a major way without having to eliminate Emmett. Shaylynn wanted to say all of that to Lucas, but she knew he wouldn't understand. She didn't quite understand it herself, but she knew it was so.

Instead, she indirectly answered Lucas's question by saying, "You know, all of my saved life, I've heard preachers talk about Boaz in the Bible. And every time I hear a single Christian woman make mention of her desire to marry, she always uses Boaz as the model. She says, 'I'm waiting for God to send my Boaz.' " Shaylynn looked at Alice, and then at Lucas. "I guess Boaz is supposed to be the biblical figure with all the qualities that a woman would want in a man. But that's not the biblical name that makes my heart race, so all of those sisters . . . they can have their Boaz. I'd rather that God gives me my Solomon."

"Wow." Alice stretched the word out longer this time.

Lucas sat back in his chair and crossed his arms in front of his chest. "Emmett was one of the most tenacious young men I'd ever known. He was bold and driven. He was fearless and selfless. He had a giving heart and a kind spirit. All of those different attributes brought about major changes to the city of Milwaukee and to the state of Wisconsin. Most of the issues he pushed during his time in government here are still in place today. There were people who loved him and people who hated him. But even those that hated him to death, *literally,* didn't hate him out of simple hatred; they hated him out of fear. They feared what a person with Emmett Ford's passion, drive, and influence might accomplish. They weren't ready for it, and the only way they knew to stop it was to snuff out his life." In one quick motion, so as not to burn his hand, Lucas used his index finger and thumb to extinguish the flame of the candle nearest him. It was the perfect visual example.

Shaylynn used her thumb to wipe a tear that fell from her eye, and when she looked at Alice, she saw her using a napkin to do the same. Shaylynn turned back to Lucas. He smiled, and then handed her a handkerchief that he fished from his pocket. As if asking permission to continue, he held Shaylynn's hand for a moment as the handkerchief was being passed. Her returned smile granted him silent authorization.

"I still think about my young friend quite often. Emmett's father was rich. Attorney William Ford is still one of the most recognized names in this city. With all that Emmett's family had, he could have taken the easy road in life. He didn't need any of us, but we needed him. The city of Milwaukee needed him, and he answered the call. To this day, I don't think I've ever crossed paths with a man — especially one of his young years — who has done as much for people of all races or made as big a difference in their lives as Emmett. And even eight years later, people speak well of him. They remember him for the mover and shaker that he was."

Lucas rubbed his hand over his clean-shaven chin. "I hope this doesn't sound sacrilegious or anything, but when I think of him, I think of Jesus. Jesus' Father was rich too, so He could have chosen the easy way out. He didn't have to fool with us. He didn't need any of us, but we needed Him, so He sacrificed it all for our needs. He, too, changed lives and reached across ethnic and social lines and did a lot of good for a lot of people, only to have His life snatched away at an early age . . . all because of fear. Neither people nor other political leaders could find a way to control Emmett, so they killed him. Neither people nor other religious leaders could find a way to control Jesus, so they killed Him." Lucas shook his head and finished with, "Fear is a dangerous thing."

Shaylynn looked at Lucas in a new light. He wasn't one to occupy a church pew every Sunday morning, but it was clear that he did, in fact, know something about the Lord. As far as his analogy was concerned, Shaylynn had never thought of it like that, and probably never would have even shaped her mind to compare her husband to her Savior. Everything Lucas said was true, but there was one big difference that just wouldn't let her fully agree with his correlation. Jesus was faultless. Emmett was flawed. As wonderful as he was, Emmett wasn't even close to being the perfect vessel that Jesus was when He walked the earth in human form.

"I guess I'm saying all that to simply say this," Lucas added. "If you can have a man in your life as dynamic as Emmett was, and still somehow, even this many years later, find another who you not only love as you loved Emmett, but possibly even more than you loved Emmett; I say you should go for it." He raised his coffee cup in the air as if making a toast. "Alice and I were witnesses to your life with Emmett. We saw how much you loved him and how much he loved you. Most people only get one chance at that kind of love, Shaylynn. If you're one of the few who gets a second chance, you'd better not let it pass. Not for anything in the world. I've never met Solomon, but I just saw the look on your face when you spoke your heart, and after seeing that, I don't even feel like I have to meet him. If my blessing is what you're looking for, you've got it."

"Mine too, dear," Alice said, raising her cup as well.

Fresh tears rolled down Shaylynn's face, and her vision was cloudy as she picked up

236

her own glass and raised it toward the center of the table to meet with theirs. "Thank you," she whispered.

Now there was just one more person Shaylynn needed to share her heart with if she was going to move forward with Neil, and she was going to need Lucas and Alice's help with getting that done too.

# FOURTEEN

Two weeks had passed since Neil had discovered the jaw-dropping paperwork in CJ's office, and every day since the find, he had stared at the shabbily scribbled words, trying to make a decision on what to do next. Neil felt like a common thief, and rightfully so. He had left his best friend's home with the unauthorized note tucked away in the back of the folder that he had actually gone there to pick up. Every time his phone rang and he saw CJ's name on the caller ID, he wondered if his crime had been uncovered. When CJ asked him to stop by his office before leaving church last Sunday, Neil was sweating bullets. All CJ wanted to do was invite him and Shaylynn to dinner. The guilt he felt wouldn't even allow Neil to accept the kind gesture, but as overwhelming as the guilt was, it wasn't enough to make Neil return the stolen evidence.

"Borrowed . . . not stolen." Neil had been saying that aloud almost every time the thought entered his head. "It's not stealing as long as I take it back. Which I will. Once I'm done doing . . . whatever I'm gonna do with it. I'm just borrowing it." If he said it enough, maybe he'd be able to convince himself. After all, it couldn't be all bad. God had led him to this paperwork. He *must* have. There was just no other explanation. It was only after Neil had prayed for a way to break Emmett's spell on Shaylynn that this information virtually fell into his lap. It was too much to be coincidental. God's hands were all over this.

*Drug laundering . . . prostitution . . . you name it . . . was unfaithful to his wife during entire marriage . . . loved call girls . . . bought women like most men bought suits . . . dirty politics . . . paid by drug lords . . .*

The words that Neil stared at were haunting him. "Emmett was scandalous. A liar, a cheat, and a common criminal." In his dreams, saying such words was a lot more satisfying than doing so in real life. Neil had longed for this chance; the chance to shatter Shaylynn's image of a perfect man; a man who was the only barrier to her giving him her entire heart. But now that he had all the ammunition that he needed in order to smash the image into smithereens, Neil felt caught between a rock and a hard place. He pulled a peppermint from the dish on his desk, opened the wrapper, and popped the candy in his mouth without once breaking his thoughts.

Whether he outright revealed this new-found information to Shaylynn, or somehow figured out a cunning way to feed it to her without her knowing it was coming from him, the woman he loved would be devastated. And as badly as Neil wanted to put Emmett Ford to rest once and for all, the last thing he wanted was to break Shaylynn's heart. He just wanted to break the attachment her heart had to this man. There had to be a way to do one without doing the other. *But how?*

Neil drummed his fingers against the surface of his desk as he thought back to over a year ago. He recalled the day that he'd asked CJ to use his connections as a former law enforcement officer to do some kind of background check on Emmett Ford. Neil knew of the two Jamaican-born men who made up the partnership of Kris-Cross P.I., the name that was scribbled near the bottom of the sketchy notes that CJ had jotted. He was sure that it was Cross — Victor Cross — who CJ had gotten to dig up the information that his eyes had been staring at for days. Victor and CJ were DeKalb County police officers at the same time, and to this day they remained friends. A couple of years after CJ put down his police badge to pick up his clergy collar, Victor had left his public servant's position as well, and had joined his cousin, Kristoff Nain, in a private detective agency that they called Kris-Cross P.I. And Neil knew that if CJ asked Victor to do a little personal snooping for him, he would have done it, and all the barely legible scribbles on the paper were proof that he'd sniffed out a mile-long trail of stench.

Neil also remembered the day that CJ called to inform him that he had, in fact, discovered some not-so-pleasant essentials about the former Mayor Emmett Ford, but by then CJ's conscience had kicked in, and he'd told Neil that he wasn't going to help him destroy Shaylynn's loving memories just to satisfy his insecurities. CJ said God wouldn't be pleased with Neil's self-serving, merciless mission. He'd said if Neil and Shaylynn's relationship was truly God-ordained, it would blossom righteously and without the mudslinging. "God is not the author of confusion," he'd said more than once. And, as was usual in most cases like these, CJ had been right, and once Neil won Shaylynn's heart on his own merit, he'd forgotten about CJ's confession to finding fault in the man Shaylynn thought was so ideal.

Neil had remained confident and sure of himself until recent months. Until lately, hearing Emmett's name slip into a conversation every now and then was no big issue, but now, every single mention of him was like claw-length fingernails against a chalkboard, and the demons Neil thought he'd conquered had returned, and with them they seemed to have brought reinforcements. He hated what this was doing to him. Neil wished that he could just be the bigger man and overlook it like the rest of the world seemed to think he should so easily be able to do, but he couldn't. This eternal love that Shaylynn had for her former husband was one of the most frustrating things Neil had ever dealt with in all his life, and it was impossible to pretend that all was well. Emmett had to go. Plain and simple.

A sudden knocking noise was accompanied by the words, "Knock-knock. Are you busy? Can I come in?"

Neil choked on the remains of the peppermint in his mouth when he heard Shaylynn's voice, which seemed to come out of nowhere. He looked up to see her standing in the doorway of his office, knocking on the doorframe. Neil couldn't speak. The sounds of several hard coughs echoed off the walls of his office as his body attempted to clear his windpipe. Gaining some level of control, he inconspicuously turned the unauthorized document facedown on his desk.

"Are you okay?" Shalylynn's voice amplified her concern. She rushed inside, tossed her handbag on his credenza, and headed to the water cooler alongside the wall, where she filled a small cup and delivered it to him. "Here. Drink some of this."

Neil's brown skin had turned a shade of red. It was more from shame than the lack of oxygen. He took several swallows from the cup, and then managed to croak out a "Thank you," before downing the remaining fluid. Even in his near-strangling state, Neil took note of how nice Shaylynn looked in her charcoal grey scoop-neck sweater, black wool wide-leg capri pants, and long, high-heeled grey boots. She topped it off with the coat he'd bought her for Christmas, and the ensemble looked like something straight out of a fashion catalogue. The only thing that kept it from being a flawless image was the all-too-familiar silver chain around her neck. Although it hung too low inside her sweater for him to see the ring that was suspended on the end of it, he knew it was there.

Shaylynn took the cup from his hand and quickly refilled it. "Did I startle you? I'm sorry." She handed the full cup back to him.

Neil shook his head in a silent lie, and then made the untruth verbal. "You didn't. I was eating." At least that part was true. He cleared his throat and pointed at the glass dish where he stored his favorite candy. "It went down the wrong way, that's all."

"Well, you were certainly engrossed in whatever you were looking at when I first arrived. I stood at the door and watched you for a minute before I said anything. You were looking so intense that I started to just back away and leave. What are you working on?" Shaylynn reached for the single sheet of paper, but Neil's hand became a bullet. When he slammed his palm against the paper to prevent her from turning it, Shaylynn was clearly taken aback.

"Sorry. . . ." Neil's mind searched for words to justify his desperate reaction. "It's confidential." When she looked like she wasn't quite convinced, he cleared his throat and added, "This is information that CJ found out about . . . a parent of one of the children here. The father of one of our students has . . . a criminal history, and it's something that has to be kept private."

The doubt that was once on Shaylynn's face was quickly replaced by alarm. "Criminal history? So what does that mean? Does that put the children here at risk?"

Neil knew that the bulk of her worry was directed at only one of the children at Kingdom Builders Academy. Shaylynn had to be one of the most overly protective parents he'd ever met. "No, suga." Neil smiled, partially because he was glad that the explanation that his racing brain had to come up with on such short notice was actually an honest one. "The children are in no danger. For one, the crime he committed is something that happened a long time ago, and secondly, the child's father is . . . well, he doesn't live anywhere near here. It's just some old news that was brought to our attention that has to be kept confidential." When Neil saw Shaylynn nod her understanding, he stepped closer to her and used his hands to brush back her braids. "You know that I'd never let anything happen to Chase, right?"

She smiled up at him, and Neil felt every

muscle in his body tighten when she gently ran her hands up, and then down his arms. He'd determined a long time ago that his arms were two of her favorite things on his body to touch. His defined biceps were inherited blessings that had been passed along by his father. The natural shape of Neil's arms was deceiving. He seldom did any weight training during his gym visits.

"I know." Her soft reply did nothing to calm his rampant emotions.

By the way she looked at him, Neil knew that she wanted him to kiss her, and he was all too happy to deliver. His lips were another part of his body that he'd concluded were among her favorites. Every time Neil kissed Shaylynn, he literally felt as if he had to hold her up under the pressure. Her body almost became limp upon impact. Knowing he had that effect on her made him feel seven feet tall. He pulled her closer as his lips continued to explore hers, so close that Neil felt like their two bodies were becoming one; like a passionate rapture had taken place and wherever they now were, there was no one else within miles.

"A-hem!"

The exaggerated throat clearing noise proved that Neil's far-away fantasy had been just that — a fantasy. Neil was far more annoyed than embarrassed at being caught in the act. He grudgingly released Shaylynn and took a few steps backward before looking in the direction of his door. Neil's disdain for Margaret's bad timing was obvious. "Yes, Ms. Dasher?"

"Well hello, Ms. Ford." Margaret walked into the office space holding a message pad in her hand. She temporarily ignored both Neil and his look of annoyance. "I didn't realize you were in here."

"Hi, Ms. Dasher." Shaylynn looked embarrassed enough for both of them. She used her fingers to wipe away the moisture that Neil's kiss had left on her lips. "You weren't at your desk when I arrived, so I just let myself in. I did sign the visitor sheet that was on the counter, though."

"You didn't have to sign in," Neil told her. He lifted her chin with his index finger, forcing her to look at him. "And you don't have to be embarrassed, either. At least you knocked, which is more than I can say for some people." He darted a glance toward Margaret after saying that part.

"Well, *some people* work here," Margaret replied with more than a little sarcasm. "And every day, ten minutes before the dismissal bell, *some people* come in to check with you to see if there are any last-minute tasks that she needs to do before leaving for the day. *Some people* don't usually have to knock, so she didn't think she had to knock today either."

Shaylynn fidgeted, and then said, "I'm going to go and —"

"No." Neil caught her by the arm. "You don't have to leave, Shay."

"Of course you don't," Margaret said. "It's a workplace, but we don't *have* to work if we don't want to. And by all means, please don't leave on account of me, because if Dr. Taylor doesn't have anything for me to do, I just need to give him a couple of phone messages, and I can get out of your way. Y'all can go right on back to doing . . . *whatever.*"

Neil balled his hand into a fist and squeezed hard. Where was that stress ball when he needed it?

"No, it's not that." Shaylynn gathered her purse from Neil's credenza. "I didn't realize it was so close to the dismissal bell. I need to get to Chase's class and sign him out before all of the students are released and the halls get congested." She looked at Neil, and he was sure that he saw tears in her eyes. That angered him even more. "I'll see you later," she concluded.

"Okay." Neil leaned forward and brushed

his lips against her cheek. He wanted to say more; so much more. Not to Shaylynn, but to Margaret. He had to remind himself of where he was, and who Shaylynn was. She wasn't just his lady; she was the mother of one of Kingdom Builders Academy's students. Neil couldn't act out of emotion. Not in front of a parent, anyway. "I'll call you later this evening," he whispered. "I love you."

Shaylynn struggled to smile. "I love you too." As she walked away from his desk and out the door, she avoided eye contact with Margaret.

Margaret looked at the door that Shaylynn closed behind her exit. "Well, you have a nice day too, Ms. Ford."

Neil didn't know whether Shaylynn had chosen to close the door because she figured whatever business he and Margaret were about to discuss should be kept private, or because she'd picked up on Neil's enormous displeasure and knew that he would probably lay into his assistant as soon as he knew she was out of listening range. Either way, she was right.

"Ms. Dasher —"

"Dr. Taylor, I know what you're thinking, but before you speak, let me just say —"

"No." Neil's finger was as stiff as his tone

when he pointed to the only chair in his office that was exiled in a corner near the door. "You sit, and I'll do the talking." The iron folding chair was in an area by itself for a reason. Because of its red color, it was commonly called the hot seat, and that wasn't a compliment. The chair didn't get used very often, but when it did, it always meant someone was in trouble. The only time it was ever occupied was on the rare occasion when a student's disruptive behavior got to be too much for the teacher, and the child had to be sent to Neil for reinforcement. Children were known to cry at the very mention of having to sit in that chair. Sitting in the hot seat generally meant that a sentence of detention was about to be handed down.

When parents or administrators were called to Neil's office for whatever reason, they had the privilege of sitting in one or both of the comfortable, black leather chairs that were positioned directly in front of his desk. Today was a historic day. Margaret had just set a record that no other administrator would dare want to break.

With some hesitation, she obeyed Neil's order and eased in the chair. She squirmed a bit, like she was trying to find a comfortable position for her full behind on the modest-sized, hard surface. "Can I just say something?" She raised her finger like a child in a classroom setting.

"No." Neil was unyielding. "I've listened to what you've had to say about Shay and the things you've had to say about us as a couple. I know you don't agree with it, but guess what, Ms. Dasher? You don't have to." Neil was standing just a few feet from her as he spoke. He was giving her the same menacing stare that he had given all the unruly children who had sat there before her. "This is my life, and she's the woman I love. Now you can take it or leave it. I can't make you like Shay, but you *will* respect her. That's something that I demand."

Margaret's eyes shot up at him as if to say, "You *demand*?"

And as if he'd heard her eyes, Neil said, "That's right."

A level of deep concern etched its way on to Margaret's face. "What are you saying? Are you telling me that my job is in jeopardy?"

Neil's brows furrowed. "Of course not. I wouldn't fire you because you don't like Shay. That would be unethical. Your job isn't in any danger, but that's a heck of a lot more than I can say for our friendship."

"What?" Margaret stood.

"Sit!"

Margaret sat.

"We've known each other for a long time." Neil tried to soften his tone, but his insides were still raging. "And I value our friendship and our work relationship. I admit that I'm guilty of entertaining your opinions and even allowing you to make judgment calls on a lot of things that, quite frankly, aren't your business. But here and now, I'm drawing the line at Shaylynn Ford. Do you understand me? That means you don't get to talk to or about her in any cynical or snide manner. What you just said to her was out of order, and it was your last time doing it. If you want to continue any kind of cordial relationship with me outside of an employer/employee one, then that's the way it's gonna have to be from this point forward. Period."

"I have on my hearing aid today. You don't have to yell."

It was an exaggeration. Neil knew he wasn't yelling, but he also knew that the edge in his voice was sharper than normal. "She's in my life to stay, Ms. Dasher. I'm not saying your opinion doesn't matter to me; I'm just saying it doesn't matter when it comes to Shay. And I don't ever plan to have this conversation with you again."

The dismissal bell rang, and it seemed to serve as the end of their fight; or at least the end of round one.

A few moments of silence passed before Margaret cleared her throat and asked, "Can I please get out of this chair? It's not made for butts like mine."

Neil rolled his eyes, and then turned to walk back to his desk. Stand up . . . sit down . . . he didn't care what she did, but he'd meant every word he'd said, so a lot was riding on the words that would come out of her mouth. Neil stood behind his desk and slipped the paper with all of CJ's scribbles back in the red folder he'd taken it out of, and then placed the folder in his briefcase. As he began clicking on the icons to shut down his computer, he could hear Margaret's heels clicking against the floor as she approached his desk with caution.

"I'm sorry if I have offended you, Dr. Taylor. That wasn't my intent." She sounded genuine. "I just need you to understand that my reaction to Ms. Ford isn't without basis. She seems nice enough, as a person she's probably a delight. I just believe she's not the person for you, and as your friend, I think it would be wrong for me to feel that way and not tell you."

Neil stood as straight and as tall as he

could. "What the . . ." He bit his tongue and started again. "How do you know what's right for me? Who do you think you are to draw that kind of conclusion?"

Margaret released a soft sigh. "I didn't pull that out of thin air, Dr. Taylor. I'm drawing that conclusion as a direct result of what she's doing to you. I told you before that it pains me to see what dating her has done to you. You're so unhappy."

Anger was rising in Neil once more. "That's not true! I've never been more in love with any woman than I am with Shay. And whether you believe it or not, she makes me *very* happy."

"Yeah . . . *today.*" Margaret flung her arms in the air, and then allowed them to drop back by her sides. "You're happy today, and you've been happy for the past couple of weeks; I'll give you that. But what about tomorrow? What about next week? You're talking more and more like you might eventually settle down with her. Marriage is supposed to be forever, Dr. Taylor. So, what about the rest of your life? Huh? Does she make you the kind of happy that will last for the rest of your life?"

"Yes!" Neil slammed his fist against his desk, an action he immediately regretted when the aftermath of severe pain radiated through his wrist and up to his elbow. "Ugh!" He shook his arm in an attempt to fling away the pain. "Sit down, Ms. Dasher. Just sit down and listen to me for a minute, okay?" It was a directive that was far less harsh than the one that had banished her to the hot seat. Neil thought hard for a way to try to explain himself to his motherly assistant once and for all.

Margaret sat in one of the chairs situated in front of Neil's desk. She looked at the watch on her wrist, but didn't seem to be in any real hurry to leave. "I didn't mean to make you hurt your hand," she mumbled.

"See, that's it," Neil said. "That's a good way to clarify it to you right there." Margaret looked confused, but he kept talking. "Don't you see? You didn't *make* me hurt my hand. I hurt my hand because of the way I reacted to what you said. You said something that annoyed me, and my knee-jerk reaction was to hit the desk, and because I made that choice, I hurt my hand. It isn't your fault, and nobody should blame you for that."

"Okay . . ." She still looked puzzled.

"That's the way it is with Shay," Neil explained. "You're blaming her for how I'm reacting to stuff, and that's not fair." He massaged his arm, from his wrist to his elbow, as he sat in his chair. "You were right the other week when you implied that I've been on an emotional rollercoaster ever since I've been dating her, but that's not her fault. On the days when my rollercoaster is on the downward slope, it's because of the way I'm reacting to a situation that she probably has no clue about. How I act is my way of dealing with the issue, and you can't rightfully blame her for that. I've never loved a woman more than I love Shaylynn Ford, and I don't think a woman has ever loved me as much as she does. There are just some . . . *things* . . . that I'm struggling to work though."

"Things that involve her?"

"Yes. They involve her, but they're not her fault."

Margaret scooted forward in her chair. "Then why don't you talk to her?"

*Talk to her.* There it was again. If Neil didn't know any better, he'd think that at some point, on one of Homer Burgess's good days, the old deacon had gotten together with CJ, Theresa, and Margaret, and they'd all agreed to throw that line at him at the first available opportunity.

"Talk to her about what?" Neil heard himself ask. "This isn't her problem; it's mine."

"If whatever it is involves her in any way whatsoever, then it's both your problem," Margaret said. "You see that, don't you?"

Neil looked at his watch. "Why don't you go on home," he told her. "I've already kept you past your time."

"Is this your way of avoiding any further conversation about this?"

Neil nodded truthfully. "Pretty much."

Margaret stood. "Fine." She turned to walk away, and then turned back to Neil. "Are we still friends?"

"That's up to you."

"Then the answer is yes. I'll apologize to Ms. Ford first chance I get."

Neil was impressed by her willingness. "I'd appreciate that, and I'm sure Shay would as well."

"Yeah. Now that you've explained everything, I'll stop taking it out on her and start taking it out on you. How's that?"

Neil couldn't help but laugh. She wouldn't be Margaret if she decided to stay out of it all together. "Deal."

"Oh." Margaret looked down at the notepad she was still holding in her hand. "You had two calls that I came in here to tell you about. One was from Sister Teena. She said she needs you to call her, but she said that it wasn't an emergency, so there's no need for alarm."

"Okay." Neil had planned to call Teena today anyway. He hadn't spoken to her or Deacon Burgess since he'd seen them both in church last Sunday. "What's the other message?"

"No message, but you had a call from a man named Sean Thomas."

Neil tilted his head to the side. "Sean Thomas?"

"Don't waste your brain cells, he said you didn't know him. He didn't leave a phone number or anything; said he just wanted to be sure that he had called the right place of employment for you. He said he'd connect with you at a later time."

"He didn't say what he wanted?"

"No. Just that he'd catch up with you later."

Neil stood up from his chair and reached for his hat that sat on the credenza. "Well, I guess it couldn't have been too important."

"You're headed out too?"

"Yeah. Nothing else here that can't wait 'til tomorrow. I'll call Ms. Teena en route. That way, if she needs me to stop by or anything, I can just swing by Deac's place before going home."

Margaret began walking away. "Okay. Well, I'll see you tomorrow."

"Bright and early," Neil replied.

She opened his office door, but stopped short of walking out. Turning to face him again, Margaret said, "Remember what I said. Talk to Ms. Ford. You can't expect to get the closure or the results you want if you're not willing to talk about it."

Neil didn't reply as she made her exit. As he slipped into his coat, he thought about the red folder that he'd shoved in his briefcase. He had to disagree with Margaret on that one. What he wanted was to end Shaylynn's love affair with Emmett Ford, and as the old saying went, there was more than one way to skin a cat.

# FIFTEEN

"Sweetie? Sweetie . . ."

In the middle of what had been a peaceful sleep, CJ smiled at the soft sound of his wife's voice, and he moaned pleasurably at the feel of her hand stroking his back. There was only one reason that Theresa ever woke him up in the middle of the night. Those "wakeup calls" of hers had been coming fewer and farther between over the last four weeks. As their baby grew and her stomach continued to swell as she got further into the final month of her pregnancy, lovemaking had become uncomfortable for her. CJ understood, and didn't press her, even when he was in the mood, but he definitely wasn't going to turn away any opportunities.

"Sweetie, wake up."

CJ turned over in the bed to face her. "I'm woke, baby. I'm woke." He kissed her nose, and then her lips. When she pulled away, he apologized. "I'm sorry. Let me go rinse my mouth. I'll be right back."

"No, sweetie, it's not that." Theresa grabbed his arm. "Don't get crazy on me, because I'm not one hundred percent sure, but I think I'm in labor."

"What?" CJ shot up into a seated position and turned on the lamp beside the bed. He looked down at his wife and watched her squint from the sudden brightness of the room. "Why do you think you're in labor? Are you hurting? Did your water break?" He snatched the covers from both of them and began inspecting the fitted sheet for signs of moisture. "What's going on? What do you need me to do? Should I call the doctor?" Then, answering his own question, he said, "Of course you should call the doctor, you big, dumb idiot. Who else would you call, the Orkin Man?" CJ jumped out of the bed and picked up the cordless phone from the nightstand.

"Sweetie, put the phone down," Theresa instructed.

"What?" For her to say she was in labor and then turn around and tell him not to make the necessary phone call didn't make sense to CJ. "Why am I putting the phone down?"

"Just put it down," she urged while sitting up in the bed. After CJ hesitantly complied, she added, "The first thing I said was for you not to get crazy on me." She patted the mattress beside her. "Come sit with me."

CJ searched her face as he climbed back on the bed. She didn't seem to be in any pain or discomfort. Labor was supposed to hurt. Lamaze classes had warned them of the pain involved in the child birthing process. There would likely be long hours of it, they'd said. And other fathers had told CJ things that even took it a step further. Theresa was supposed to be screaming and calling him everything but a child of God. She was supposed to be making those "hee-hee-hoo-hoo" breathing sounds. She was supposed to be telling him she loved him one minute and growling at him in satanic-sounding voices the next. Theresa wasn't doing any of that. "Your due date is still two weeks away," he said, trying to match her calm. "Why do you think you're in labor?"

"Because a pain woke me up about fifty-three minutes ago, and I've been timing them ever since. They're coming about fifteen minutes apart."

CJ reached out and touched her stomach. "Are you hurting right now?"

"No. The last one was about eight minutes ago."

"And you don't want me to call the doctor?"

"Not yet." Theresa scooted out of the bed and stepped into her slippers. "It hasn't been a full hour yet. I want to be able to time them for an hour. That way, I'll be more certain that they're not Braxton Hicks contractions. I'm going to go and take a shower. If I have another one, then we'll call. My bag is already packed, so we should pretty much be set to go, if needed." Before disappearing in the restroom, she turned to look at him. "You should probably get dressed just in case."

"Yeah. Okay." CJ's heart was pounding as he watched her coolly waddle into the master bathroom. He didn't understand how Theresa could be so composed. He was so unraveled that when he got out of the bed, he had to stop and think for a moment before he remembered which door led to the closet and which led to the hallway of their home.

"Okay, CJ . . . get it together," he whispered as he slipped on a pair of denim pants and a blue pullover sweater that he pulled from hangers in the closet. He'd read all the books and online Web sites that he could in order to ready himself for this moment, but now that it was here, CJ felt more than a little ill-prepared. He stood in front of the bedroom mirror and picked up the brush in preparation of grooming his hair. "No," he said. Going back into the closet, he pulled off everything he'd put on, dropped it on the floor, and started over. When he emerged this time, he had one of his best clergy suits in his hand.

"Having another one, sweetie," Theresa called from the bathroom shower. "Go ahead and call the doctor."

With a face full of perplexity, CJ looked toward the bathroom door. His wife actually sounded like she was singing the words as she made the announcement. What kind of labor was she in? After putting on his shirt, socks, and pants, CJ dialed the emergency number for Theresa's OB/GYN, and gave the message of her status to the answering service. Two minutes later, just as Theresa shut off the shower, he answered a return call with doctor's orders for them to head to DeKalb Medical Center. *This is really happening. I'm about to be a father.* The thought filtered through his head as he placed the phone back on its base charger.

An outburst of laughter from behind CJ caused him to turn and face his wife, who had emerged from the bathroom draped in a towel. "What's so funny?" First singing;

now laughing. Nothing in any of the pamphlets for expecting parents had warned him that delirium was a part of the early labor process, but he was beginning to think Theresa was going cuckoo.

"You, that's what," she said as she headed to their closet. "Why are you dressed like that? We're going to the hospital, not the church. You plan to preach the baby out of me or something?"

CJ looked at his reflection in the mirror. He supposed it did look odd, but there was a method to his madness. "No, but if there's any chance that being dressed like a clergyman will get you seen faster, I want to take advantage of that."

She came out of the closet with a purple and white jogging suit draped over her arm and tossed it on the bed before beginning the slow task of dressing herself. "Thanks, honey, but I don't think that's gonna win us any favors. When it comes to birthing, I'm pretty sure the woman who's dilated the most will get called before the woman with the husband who's most dressed like Father Flannigan." She laughed again.

"You never know." CJ finished brushing his hair, and then slipped on a pair of dress shoes.

"Did Dr. Daniels say what time we were

to meet her?"

CJ looked at the clock for the first time. It was almost three in the morning. Babies sure had strange schedules. "No. She just gave the word for us to head to the hospital." Theresa was having a hard time putting on her socks and shoes, so CJ knelt beside her and took over. "I didn't even talk directly to her, so she may already be there. I'm sure she's got other patients that may have checked in overnight."

"Thanks," Theresa said when he finished tying her tennis shoes. "While I get my coat and purse, you can get the suitcase. It's tucked in the closet in the nursery."

"Oh, yeah. The suitcase." CJ was trying to shake off the nervousness that he felt, but his stomach was insisting on doing backward handsprings. If the woman who would actually have to go through the process could be calm, then he certainly should be able to do the same. When he flipped on the light switch in the baby room, a new dose of reality set in. It wasn't just about him being a father; it was about him being a daddy. A new life, for which God had allowed him to plant the seed, was about to be birthed into the world, and this was the room where he . . . or she would spend their earliest days, months, and years. As a daddy,

CJ would be responsible to provide for and protect his child. The thought was so overwhelming that he found himself fighting back tears.

Using cautious steps, CJ walked inside the room that his son or daughter would soon be occupying. The walls, the bed, the dresser, the rocking chair, the stuffed toys, the framed poster of Dominique Wilkins . . . everything was perfect. All that was missing was his baby, and the mere acknowledgement of that placed a level of fear inside of CJ that glued his feet to the floor. What if something went wrong? What if they had done all of this preparing and something tragic happened during delivery? What if the crib was left empty even after the childbirth process was over?

"The devil is a liar." CJ closed his eyes, willed away the fear, and found his faith. "In the name of Jesus." With those five words, he opened his eyes and rediscovered the strength to put one foot in front of the other. As he walked the floor, he began touching the railings of the crib, the mattress, the walls, the furniture, the toys; all the while, praying in tongues. He didn't know why he was suddenly bombarded with thoughts of the possibility of his child's death, but he refused to accept it. He had waited too long and prayed too hard not to fight for the life of his child. "In the name of Jesus. In the name of Jesus," he repeated over and over.

"I just had another contraction, and it wasn't quite fifteen minutes from the last one." Theresa had a peculiar look on her face, having caught CJ with his hand on the head of Elmo, praying out loud. "We . . . we probably need to be heading out now."

CJ saw his wife and heard every word she'd said, but he didn't readily move.

Theresa looked at his empty hands. More confusion filled her eyes when she asked, "What's the matter? You couldn't find the suitcase?"

Without answering her questions, he walked toward her, knelt on the hardwood floor, placed both his hands on her stomach, and continued his earnest prayer.

# SIXTEEN

Shaylynn thought she was dreaming when her cell phone stirred her at a godforsaken hour of the early morning. She pulled her covers tighter around her neck, and while her mind wrapped itself around reality, her eyes slowly opened and were greeted by total darkness. Shaylynn typically went to bed with her television on, but the automatic shut-off timer on it was set for 2:00 A.M., so even the light that the TV would have provided was nowhere to be found. Sitting up in the bed, she fumbled for the lamp. By the time she found the switch and turned on the light, her cell had gone silent. Shaylynn reached to retrieve it from the shelf over her headboard, but just as her hand could make contact, the telephone on her nightstand began ringing. This had to be something serious. She answered without bothering to look at the caller ID.

"Hello?"

"Shay . . . Sweetheart, I'm so sorry to wake you at this hour, but —"

"Solomon?" Shaylynn looked at the illuminated numbers on her clock, and her mind immediately began imagining the worst. Had something happened to Deacon Burgess? Neil had been keeping her abreast of his steady decline. Or maybe it was Neil's mom. Ella was an aging woman with limited mobility, living in a home all by herself. That was a recipe for disaster. Any number of things could go wrong at a moment's notice. "Oh my God." Shaylynn breathed hard into the phone. "What's wrong, Solomon? What's wrong?"

"Calm down, suga. Everything is okay." He sounded like he was telling the truth, but maybe he was just trying to keep her from getting more upset.

"It's four-thirteen in the morning," Shaylynn pointed out. "Everything can't be fine. Where are you?"

"I'm on my way to DeKalb Medical, because —"

"Oh my God!" Shaylynn jumped out of her bed and began searching through her dresser drawers for the first halfway decent outfit that she could find and put on.

"Shay, Shay, please," Neil said. "I need you to calm down, baby."

All the heavy breathing was beginning to make Shaylynn lightheaded. She had always been a worrywart. That's what her grandmother used to call her. Life had handed her an abundance of reasons to be that way, so it didn't come without warrant. Shaylynn held on to the corner of her dresser and braced herself for whatever. "Tell me what's wrong. What's the matter? Why do you need hospital care?"

"I don't need hospital care. I'm telling you the truth, suga. Everything is fine. I'm on the way to the hospital to meet up with CJ. Theresa's in labor, that's all."

Shaylynn eased into a seated position on the edge of her bed. "Labor? What? No. She can't be. The baby shower is Saturday. She's not due until February eighth. That's two weeks away."

"Well, *I* know that, and *you* know that, but apparently the baby hadn't learned to read calendars yet." Neil laughed, and the sound of it calmed Shaylynn. He wouldn't be laughing if both mother and baby weren't okay. She remained quiet while Neil gave her the rest of the report. "CJ said that Theresa woke up around two this morning, having contractions. When he took her to the hospital to get checked, they kept her once it was determined that she was in active labor. He says she wants to have a natural labor with no meds, but the pains are getting stronger, and they're coming more frequently now. CJ doesn't think she's going to be able to go all the way without getting something for the pain."

As she listened to Neil, Shaylynn's mind traveled back to an early morning, eight years ago, when she was housed on the labor and delivery floor at Aurora Sinai Medical Center, with her doctor at the foot of the bed, telling her to push, and Alice Jessup standing on the side, holding her hand and telling her that everything was going to be okay. That moment to which Shaylynn had looked forward for so long had turned out to be the absolute worst experience of her life. The labor was extensive and hard, but none of that had anything to do with her misery. She would have welcomed a delivery that was twice as long and three times as painful if it had come with Emmett being by her side.

"CJ sounded like he was on the verge of a meltdown when I spoke with him earlier." Neil laughed again, snapping Shaylynn from her travel back in time. "I know there's not a whole lot I can do, but I figured being there might help a little bit."

Aside from Ella, Theresa was the closest

female connection Shaylynn had. She wished she could put on some clothes and be at the hospital for some kind of moral support too, but she couldn't. "If it weren't so late, and if Chase weren't asleep, I'd come and join you," she told Neil.

"I was just about to ask if you want me to swing by and get you. I'm not that far away. I can turn around and pick you guys up. Chase can continue his sleep in the hospital's waiting room."

Shaylynn was surprised by Neil's suggestion. It was impossible. "Chase has school tomorrow . . . well, in just a few hours, actually. He can't lie around at a hospital all night and be properly prepared for school."

"Missing one day won't hurt him. It's Friday, and KBA has a standard policy not to assign homework on a Friday. He wouldn't miss anything major."

Shaylynn had never kept Chase out of school for any reason other than illness. "Thanks, but I don't think I want to do that." She wiped crust from her eyes. "What about you? Are you missing work tomorrow?"

"I will if I have to, but I don't think it'll come to that. I might run a little late, but Theresa has already been in labor for a couple of hours. I have a change of clothes here in my truck. If necessary, I'll get dressed at the hospital and head straight to work. I'm thinking that she will have given birth in plenty of time for me to be punctual."

Shaylynn shook her head. He was talking just like a man who'd had no children. She was in labor for nine hours with Chase, and without Emmett there with her, it felt more like nineteen. She had done it without meds, and although there was some pain, it was no match for the anguish of burying her husband just a few weeks earlier. Losing Emmett must have served as some strange sort of epidural. Shaylynn was still hurting so much from his death that giving birth paled in comparison. Putting away a 180-pound man was a lot more excruciating than pushing out an eight-pound boy.

Admittedly, nine hours was a long time to deal with the multiple physical traumas of childbirth, but by far, it was no record-setting feat. Shaylynn knew women who had attested to suffering through twenty hours or more before all was said and done. Theresa could fall anywhere in between, but Shaylynn didn't want to dash Neil's hopes, so she didn't tell him that. Instead, she said, "I'm sorry I'm gonna miss all the excite-

ment, but will you at least keep me up-
dated?"

"Of course," Neil replied. "And maybe we
can talk more about the new baby over dinner tonight?"

Shaylynn grinned at the way he had posed
his invitation. "I'd like that."

"Good. When I call you with an update
on Theresa, we can set up a time and place."

"Sounds like a plan."

"Okay. Go ahead and try to get some
more sleep before you have to get up to take
Chase to school. I won't call and disturb
you between now and then unless I have a
birth announcement to make. I'll talk to
you later."

"Okay."

"I love you," he concluded.

"I love you too." Shaylynn couldn't stop
smiling. She hung up the phone, turned out
the light, and nestled back into her comfortable space, but slumber escaped her. Going
right to sleep after talking to Neil was next
to impossible. There was just something
about his voice that awakened her in more
ways than one. If he didn't soon ask for her
hand in marriage, she was going to get down
on one knee and ask for his. Shaylynn
giggled as she mulled over her own random
thought. Wouldn't that be a proposal to

remember? Well, unless he rejected it; then it would be a proposal to forget.

Shaylynn turned from her side to her back and stared up at nothing. It was too dark to see the ceiling, but she knew it was there. Neil had changed her over the last year, and all the changes had been for the better. She still loved Emmett; no doubt about it. There was absolutely nothing anyone could say or do to change that. But even though Shaylynn's love for her former husband remained as steady and sturdy as ever, her thoughts weren't consumed with him like they used to be before Neil came into her life.

When she thought about Emmett now, it was mostly when she was out of Neil's presence. Whenever Neil was physically around and looked at her with those captivating brown eyes of his, Shaylynn could barely think of anything else. Sometimes she felt guilty about that. She'd vowed to never forget Emmett, and because of that she sometimes brought up his name just to keep herself reminded. Even with Neil there, she didn't want her memories of Emmett to fade, not even whenever . . . *if* ever . . . she and Neil got married.

"Mrs. Shaylynn Ford-Taylor." She said it aloud and sat up in the bed to get a clearer sense of how it sounded. It was okay, but mixing the two men's last names just didn't seem like the right thing to do. "Mrs. Shaylynn McKinley-Taylor." That wouldn't work either. Emmett and Neil deserved their own space. That was why meshing Ford and Taylor together didn't seem to give either one of them proper justice. But Johnny McKinley . . . well, no part of his name deserved to follow Shaylynn's first or precede Neil's last. One of the earliest perks of marrying Emmett was the ability to finally rid herself of the last name she'd carried for nineteen years. It was about the only thing in life that her father had ever given her, and even that was worthless. It would make no sense for her to go back and pick it up again just for the sake of having a hyphenated last name. "Mrs. Shaylynn Brooke Taylor." There was a time when Shaylynn was ashamed of the middle name that her grandmother had chosen. Not that she didn't like Brooke. She did, but children at her ghetto elementary school used to laugh at it, labeling it as a "white girl's name," and the heartless teasing managed to strip Shaylynn of what little self-confidence she still had at that age. Now that she'd grown beyond fretting over what people thought of her, maybe she'd pick it back up.

"Shaylynn Brooke Taylor." As the name rolled off her tongue, Shaylynn lay back down, satisfied with her choice and hopeful that one day soon she'd have the chance to use it. She was almost sure that Neil wanted to make her his wife, but the more time that passed without him making *the,* doubt was beginning to creep in.

Comfortably under her covers once again, Shaylynn picked up the remote control from her nightstand. Old habits die hard. If there was any hope that she'd get back to sleep before having to get up for good and get her day started, she'd need the help of her television. But as it turned out, Shaylynn must have been sleepier than she realized. One of her favorite romantic dramas, *P.S. I Love You,* starring Hilary Swank and Gerald Butler, had barely gotten past its opening credits before Shaylynn was back in an unconscious state. Her eyes didn't open again until her alarm clock reminded her that she had a son who needed to get prepared for a day of learning.

Getting Chase off to school was never a chore. During the week, he was in bed by nine, which gave him about ten hours to get all the sleep he needed. Kingdom Builders' strict uniform policy simplified the decision-making process of what he would wear each day, and with the school being less than six miles from her home, Shaylynn didn't have to be overly concerned with the woes of Atlanta's morning rush-hour traffic. On average, driving from their home to his school each day took fifteen minutes max. Today, it only took ten.

"Well, kind sir, we have arrived at your destination." Shaylynn teased Chase with her chauffeur voice when she brought the car to a stop in front of the main entrance doors. When her son first began attending Kingdom Builders as a six-year-old, Shaylynn would park in the visitor's parking lot and walk him all the way to his classroom, holding his hand the entire time. She missed those days. Chase didn't want her to walk him inside now that he was eight. For Shaylynn, her little boy was growing up too fast. "Have a good day," she told him. "I'll be by to pick you up at the regular time." She cringed to think that the day might soon come when he would be asking to ride the bus, and she wouldn't even have this experience to hold on to.

"Thanks." Chase smiled over at her as he grabbed his backpack and opened his door. "See you later."

"Okay. I love you." At least he hadn't asked her to stop saying that every time she dropped him off. And even if he did, she wouldn't.

"I love you too, Mama."

Shaylynn watched him until he was inside the building, and then she began driving away. Neil hadn't called her since the wee hours of the morning, so it was safe to assume that Theresa still hadn't delivered. Shaylynn had designs that she needed to be working on today, but if she didn't make time now to go and check on her friend, she was sure that work would bog her down so much that breaking away later would be out of the question. Plus, she wanted to see Neil.

The drive to DeKalb Medical took nearly an hour. Had Shaylynn not been competing with the traffic that was synonymous with Atlanta's morning commute, and had she not stopped by Chick-fil-A for two breakfast chicken biscuits and tea, she could have made it in half the time. Before getting out of the car, she checked her reflection in her rearview mirror. When she initially left home, her only intent was to take Chase to school; therefore, Shaylynn hadn't bothered to put on any makeup. Today was a day to be especially grateful for virtually flawless skin. She fluffed out her braids, and then used her fingers as a wide-tooth comb to tame them to her satisfaction. Thankfully, she had her coat; otherwise, the black short-sleeved T-shirt that she paired with her blue jeans would have left her unarmed against the cold temperatures.

Shaylynn had never been inside DeKalb Medical before, but finding her way around wasn't a challenge. Once she knew where the labor and delivery area was, locating the waiting room was a cinch. There weren't many people gathered there, and Neil must have been a magnet for her eyes, because as soon as she walked in the space, they focused in on him. He was occupying a chair in the back corner with his head resting against the wall, like he was either already in sleep land or well on his way to getting there. The closer Shaylynn got to him, her question was answered. Soft snoring sounds gave him away.

She smiled as she placed the food on an empty chair and removed her coat. She sat beside him, picked up his arm, and carefully draped it around her shoulder before laying her head on his chest. The snoring stopped, and at first he made a subtle movement, but then he jerked into an upright position and slid his entire body as close to the wall and away from her as possible. Shaylynn laughed out loud as he wiped his eyes and recognition set in.

"Woman, don't be doing that." He was clearly embarrassed, but he was a good sport.

"I'm sorry. I couldn't resist. You looked so peaceful."

Neil yawned and stretched his arms. "What are you doing here? What time is it?" He was wearing a watch, but didn't bother to look at it.

"Eight-thirty." When he draped his arm back around her, Shaylynn leaned into his chest again. The sound of his heartbeat was music to her ear. "No word on Theresa?"

"No, and I'm actually surprised. Last time CJ came to give me an update was around six-fifteen." Neil pulled her closer and kissed her temple. Shaylynn's insides moaned. "At that time, he said she was eight centimeters dilated, and her water had broken. When he came by to give me the update, he said, 'I can't stay, bruh. I'm just coming to let you know that the next time you see me, I'ma be somebody's daddy.'" Neil chuckled and said, "*Somebody's daddy.* He's a mess."

"She was eight centimeters dilated at six-fifteen? That was over two hours ago," Shaylynn observed.

"I know. She's probably delivered by now,

but I'm sure they wanted some intimate family time before bringing anybody else in on the celebration." He stopped talking and sniffed the air. "I smell something good. Do you smell that?"

"Oh." Shaylynn didn't want to move from being nestled so close to Neil, but she had to in order to give him his food. "I stopped and picked up some breakfast for you." She handed him his bag. "I figured you hadn't eaten yet. You hungry?"

"Thank you. Yes, I'm starved." The grace he quietly said was the quickest Shaylynn had ever seen. When Neil closed his eyes, it was like an extended blink. Two seconds later, they were open again, and he was tearing into the sandwich wrapper like he hadn't eaten in days. "What?" he asked with a jaw full of chicken biscuit when he caught her staring at him.

"Nothing." Shaylynn giggled and held up her bag. "I bought one for me too, but maybe I should let you have both."

"No, suga. You eat yours. I'll be fine after this one." He washed down the first mouthful with several swallows of the sweet tea, and then immediately took another bite.

Shaylynn bit into her sandwich too, but her bite was much smaller. "Did Pastor Loather say whether she had broken down and accepted the meds yet?" Shaylynn had a feeling that she already knew the answer. If anybody could tough it out, Theresa could.

Neil wiped his mouth with a napkin. "I don't know about now, but as of two hours ago, she hadn't." He released a grunt. "Poor CJ was a mess. He was happy and stressed at the same time. I think when he came out here it was largely just to get a brief break from seeing Theresa in so much pain. He said he had been begging her to get the epidural ever since she was five centimeters, but she wouldn't." Neil looked toward the door. "I expect he'll be coming with the good news any time now. I've already called Ms. Dasher because it looks like I might miss a day of work after all. When he came down to tell me that the doctors said she'd be ready to start pushing anytime, I figured by now she would have had the baby, and I would have seen it, held it, and been on my way to work."

"Childbirth is something else," Shaylynn told him. "It can take a while sometimes. You all get to experience the fun part." When Neil's eyes questioned her, Shaylynn broke it down. "Making the baby is a lot of fun, but not a whole lot of fun stuff happens between that and this." She pointed toward the opening that led into the hospital hall as if the room wherein Theresa was giving birth was just beyond the door. "But it's well worth it," she added as she thought about Chase. "There's nothing like the rewards of motherhood."

Neil shifted in his seat a little, and then in a guarded tone, he asked, "Do you want more children?"

Shaylynn enjoyed talking to Neil about anything that sounded like family planning. This kind of talk fueled her hope. "When I was a little girl, I was adamant about my desire to have two children, but now it's just about what God desires for my life. I definitely wouldn't mind more." She looked at him. "Why do you ask?"

Neil shrugged. "I just remember you saying a while back that you were glad that I didn't have any children, so I was wondering if that meant you didn't want any more."

Shaking her head, Shaylynn replied, "No; I was just happy that being with you didn't mean I'd also have to deal with another woman and your responsibilities to her and the child or children you'd had with her."

Something was bothering Neil. Shaylynn could tell. He finished his sandwich quietly, and then stuffed his trash in the bag his food had come out of before walking it all to the garbage can across the room. Shaylynn rewrapped what was left of her sandwich and placed it in the bag on the vacant chair beside her along with her drink. When Neil returned to his chair, she looked up at him, and he looked down at her and smiled. She didn't want to pry, but there was definitely more on his mind.

He sighed and draped his right arm back across Shaylynn's shoulders, pulling her back into his chest. Then Neil slid his left hand under her left hand and linked their fingers. "So . . . would it be a big problem for you if you didn't have more?"

Shaylynn felt like Neil's questionnaire was more than just a conversation to kill time. She was glad that there were no other people sitting close by to overhear their personal discussion. "Well, I was an only child, and that was a lonely existence for me. That was the biggest reason that I'd made up in my mind all those years ago that I wanted two. I didn't want any child of mine to feel the same sense of isolation and abandonment that I experienced."

"But unlike your parents, you've been and will always be very active in Chase's life," Neil pointed out. "He's a much happier, healthier kid than you ever were, I'm sure. I don't think he's ever felt a day of loneliness.

With a mother like you, how could he?"

Shaylynn looked at their linked hands and smiled. "I know, and I'd never let him feel abandoned or like I didn't care. But still . . . if I married the right guy, I think I'd want to give him a child of his own." When he became silent, she sat up and looked at him. "Do you want children of your own?"

Before he answered, Neil took in a deep breath and slowly released it. It wasn't a heavy sigh, just a long one. "I love kids, always have," he began, "and there was a time when I badly wanted children. Not just one or two, but lots of them like my parents had. I think that's why I'm so good at my job. I get to be around hundreds of children every day who I can play around with, help nurture, and be a role model for. Those are all the things that I wanted to do with my own, but now . . ."

Shaylynn was sure that she knew what he was thinking. He was a man of forty-six years. Having one baby at his age probably wasn't so appealing, let alone having ten like his parents. She'd never considered that Neil wouldn't want to have children if he remarried, but that was certainly what it sounded like he was saying. "Go on." She squeezed his hand, hoping that he would feel her support and know that there was nothing he couldn't share with her. If they were headed toward a lifetime relationship, she had to be willing to listen and be considerate of his feelings on any matter.

"Audrey and I were married for a long time, you know that."

"Yes."

"We never had any children, but it wasn't because we didn't want any. She just never got pregnant. We tried, but nothing ever happened. She couldn't . . ." He paused and seemed to regroup his thoughts. "I couldn't . . . I can't . . . I don't think I'm able to have children." It was an obvious struggle, but Neil had finally gotten through the confession.

Shaylynn squeezed his hand tighter. Neil had never shared this with her before, but hearing it didn't make her feel any stress or distress. If she and Neil got married, she was ready and willing to give him all the children he wanted, but if he didn't want them, or wasn't able to have them, then so be it. She had Chase, and she was happy. This was actually something she could live with, but before she could voice that, Neil spoke again.

"If I ever remarried, the woman would need to be okay with not having any children." His eyes cast down to his lap, and his voice dropped to a whisper when he added, "At least not with me."

There was so much sadness on his face that it broke Shaylynn's heart. Did he feel less of a man because of this? Was his sterility the reason he hadn't proposed? She had to build him back up, and Shaylynn was sure that she knew just what to say to do it, but if she did, it might easily turn into another one of those situations like the night they had the romantic candlelight dinner at Neil's home. She didn't want to go through another four or five days of the silent treatment, but desperate times called for desperate measures.

She allowed a slight grin to crease her cheeks. "Well . . . you're able to go through the motions, right?"

That brought his eyes up to the level of hers, and his brows furrowed in confusion. "What?"

Shaylynn's heart pounded two beats at a time. She couldn't believe she was about to release the words that dangled at the end of her tongue. "I mean, you *can* do . . . what is usually done to make babies, right?"

Neil's eyes brightened and his skin blushed. He looked like a little boy who had just been kissed on the cheek by the schoolteacher on whom he harbored a secret crush. The smile that started at his lips eventually overtook his entire face. "Yes. I'm very well capable of doing . . . what is done."

"Well, that's the fun part I was talking about earlier, so I think if another woman is ever blessed to be called your wife, she'll be quite satisfied just having fun with you." She leaned her head back in his chest and added, "Lots and lots and lots of fun."

Neil released a quiet laugh, and squeezed her tight before pulling his hand from hers. Shaylynn complied with the pressure of his fingers as he used them to lift her chin so that she looked up at him. "Thank you."

"For what?" Shaylynn tried to look innocently clueless.

"For being you," Neil answered. "You're one of a kind, you know that? I love you."

Shaylynn could stare in those eyes of his forever. "I love you too."

Neil's lips immediately covered hers when she finished the sentence, and Shaylynn complied with that too. Neil had told her once, early in their relationship, that she was a good kisser. But to her, he was the one who deserved a blue ribbon. She'd kissed a few men in her lifetime, but none compared to Neil.

"It's a girl."

Pulling apart, both Shaylynn and Neil turned to see CJ standing in front of them, breathing like he'd run all the way from wherever the delivery room was located.

Shaylynn gasped and excitement had her bouncing in her seat. "She had the baby?"

CJ's eyes were red. Probably from crying. Even the toughest of men had the tendency to showcase their tender side at the birth of their child. "Yes. It's a girl," he repeated.

Neil stood, grinning wide. "Man, you mean to tell me you somebody's daddy now?"

"Yeah." CJ's voice broke, and then his eyes did the same, flooding his cheeks with tears. "It's a girl," he said for the third time before collapsing in Neil's arms.

The sight of it made Shaylynn stand up too. These weren't happy tears. Something was wrong.

# Seventeen

What a difference a day made. And the difference made by a span of one week was seven times more flabbergasting. Neil stood at the door of ICU 14 and took a deep breath. Over the past week, this had become a common ritual, and he hated every minute of it. It was hard to believe that at this time last week, he was sitting in the waiting room with the love of his life, counting down the minutes to when they'd hear the news of CJ and Theresa's baby's birth. Theresa had indeed brought a new life into the world, but now, she was fighting for her own.

Neil said a silent prayer before pushing open the door. What he saw when he entered the room was the same bleak picture he'd seen every single day at this same time. There in the bed lay Theresa, with one tube going down her throat, another running up her nose, and yet another that was connected to her arm, feeding her body whatever it was that was in the bag hanging on the pole behind her bed. With her sat CJ. He had been a fixture in the chair beside his wife's bed from day one. Today he had an open Bible on the mattress beside Theresa's lifeless body, and he held one of her hands in his, with the back of it pressed against his lips. CJ didn't even look away from her when Neil entered.

With quiet movements, Neil picked up the only other chair in the room and moved it beside CJ's. "How's it going, man?" It was a dumb question, but Neil didn't know what else to say.

CJ lowered Theresa's hand from his face. "I'm losing her." His voice trembled, but if there were any tears, he successfully held them back. "I've been asking God why, but He's not answering." He finally pulled his eyes away from his wife's swollen face and looked at Neil. "How's our baby?"

True enough, Neil's daily schedule had been shuffled because of Theresa's hospitalization. He always came straight to DeKalb Medical after work instead of being able to go home and unwind, and he'd had to alert Adam that he probably wouldn't be joining him at the gym for a while. But those were changes that didn't seem to deserve mentioning when he compared them to what his sweetheart had done. Ever since the child was released from the hospital as a two-day-old, Shaylynn had put the normal flow of her entire life on hold to become the infant's full-time caretaker.

Everyone could see that CJ was in no condition to care for his daughter, so at Neil's suggestion, Shaylynn had readily stepped up to the plate. The still nameless baby was eight pounds, healthy, and beautiful. Her almond-shaped eyes, caramel skin, and thick thighs made her the spitting image of Theresa. As a child, growing up in farm country, Neil would hear the old folks say that when a child looked too much like the mother, it meant they were taking her place. The mother had to die so that the child could live. Neil had never believed it, and despite the strong resemblance between Theresa and her daughter, he still didn't. His mother had ten children, and in Neil's opinion, all three of his sisters looked like Ella, but birthing neither of them had cost her life.

In answering CJ's inquiry, Neil said, "I spoke to Shay on the drive here, and she told me to be sure to let you know that the little miss is doing fine."

Instead of CJ perking up at the news as Neil hoped he would, his posture slumped.

"I'm sorry to have disrupted your lives like this. I know that having the baby at Shaylynn's house has thrown a big wrench in your normal dating schedule, and if I'd had any other reasonable options, I —"

"Man, don't even go there," Neil interjected. "You know we don't mind at all. Shay and I have adjusted our schedules, and it's not a problem. This is way more important."

CJ acted as though he hadn't heard one word of Neil's interruption. "Other people in the church were willing, but Theresa thinks the world of Shaylynn, and I think I trust you more than I could ever trust a blood brother." That last part of CJ's statement hit hard when Neil thought about the paper in the red folder that was still stuffed in his briefcase. He swallowed the onset of shame as he continued to listen to CJ speak. "Sending the baby so far away from us to live with other family members was just not something I wanted to do. I can't care for her right now, but I want to at least be close to her and be able to see her as much as —"

"Why are you explaining yourself to me, CJ? Shay and I wouldn't have wanted this any other way." Neil thought of their week-old conversation. "She likes babies. Yours couldn't be in better hands. And none of this is an inconvenience for us, so put that out of your mind."

CJ looked back at Theresa. "I hope she's not disappointed in me for not being there for our daughter. I haven't even named her." CJ shook his head, almost like he was ashamed of himself. "I'm a man of the cloth. I should be handling this better, but I can't even think straight right now."

"Your position as a preacher or pastor doesn't stop you from being a human being, man. Any guy who loves his wife the way you love Theresa would feel the same way. Whether he was the pastor of a church or the president of the United States, he would feel the same way you're feeling right now."

CJ's head did a slow nod. "I guess you're right. That's similar to what Reverend Tides said when he was here this morning."

He was speaking of the pastor of one of Atlanta's largest congregations. Reverend B.T. Tides was a famed and revered preacher. He was pastor of New Hope Church and the overseer of the Hope fellowship of churches, of which Kingdom Builders Christian Center was a part. The mention of Reverend Tides made Neil sit up straight. Having a man of his stature take out time to personally come and visit and pray with Theresa spoke volumes about the respect Reverend Tides had for CJ. There were ministers under Reverend Tides who were set in place for things like this, so for the top man in the church fellowship to do the honors himself . . . this was major.

"Reverend Tides was right," Neil said, trying not to look as impressed as he actually was. "Nobody expects you to act like this isn't tearing you apart. This is your wife."

"Yes, she is." CJ was once again having trouble steadying his voice. "Our baby is my daughter, and God knows I love her too, but I can't be in two places at once. Resa needs me more. I can't leave her. Not now. If I weren't here when she took her last breath, I . . . I . . ." He never finished the sentence, opting to shake his head once more.

Listening to CJ's heartbreak was breaking Neil's heart, and he found himself fighting his own tears. This couldn't have happened to two nicer people. It just didn't seem fair. Why CJ? Why Theresa? Why now? He reached over and squeezed CJ's shoulder. "She understands, man. And both of you can rest assured that your little girl is getting the best care possible."

"I know." CJ tried to smile.

Neil looked around the small room. There was nothing but white walls and medical machinery. It looked drab, colorless, lifeless. It was cold, too. The morgue-like setting did nothing to increase the hope of anyone with the misfortune of having to visit a relative or friend there. Neil broke into the lingering silence with, "Have the doctors been by today? Have they given any updates?"

"They're always stopping in. Doctors, nurses, orderlies . . . all of them. They come to take vitals, change tubing, clean her up, and document the numbers on the machines, but they haven't really told me anything new. She's still not expected to make it. Her brain activity continues to decrease. Any day now, they're going to ask permission to disconnect all this." CJ pointed at the medical connections, and then looked at Neil. "What am I gonna do, bruh?" A tear rolled down CJ's cheek, and he wiped it away with the sleeve of his sweater. "I just don't understand it. Resa has always had good health. Women have babies every day of the week. Why would she stroke out like this when it's her turn?"

The news of the massive stroke had taken everyone by surprise. Friends, family, the church members. Nobody could believe it.

Neil's eyes averted CJ's. He couldn't stand to see what this was doing to his friend. When Neil replied, he did so while looking down at his hands. "I was talking to Shaylynn last night while I was visiting her, and she was telling me that childbirth is about as close to death as a woman can get. She said that anything could go wrong just because of how haywire a laboring mother's vitals go during that time."

"I had never seen anything like it in my life." CJ sniffed. "One minute, I was coaching her through pushing and breathing techniques, and the next, she was convulsing with her eyes rolling back in her head. I didn't know what was happening. The nurses got frantic, and Dr. Daniels started calling for medical backup. I knew it was more than something as simple as her passing out, or even something as serious as a seizure. Next thing I knew, they were ordering me out of the room and carrying out an emergency cesarean. How on earth did we go from there to here; from expecting a life to expecting a death?"

Neil knew the story. CJ had told it to him almost every day over the past week, and each time he told it, it was as if it were the first. Neil just about knew the entire story word for word, but he always allowed his friend to unload the details with no interruptions. If CJ needed to keep talking about it, Neil wasn't going to stop him. He wished he had an answer for CJ's question, but he didn't.

"I think this is why I got an urgency to pray right before leaving home to bring Resa here."

This was a part of CJ's story that Neil hadn't heard before. His ears perked into full attention. "You got an urgency to pray?"

"Yeah, but I think I misinterpreted the unction. When I felt the Holy Spirit's urging, I focused on the baby; praying that God wouldn't let anything happen to her that wouldn't allow us to bring her home. I prayed away the spirit of death from our child, but now, I wonder if it was Resa I should have been praying for. Maybe if I had prayed for her, she wouldn't —"

"Don't do that to yourself, CJ." Neil's voice was stern. "Don't start looking for reasons to blame yourself for this. This ain't your fault, and you know it. Don't go there."

"I know, bruh. I know." CJ's tears were constant now. "I just don't know what I'm gonna do without her. I love her. I need her. I'm not ready for this. A piece of me is dying with her."

Neil wiped tears from his own eyes. He

knew the feeling. He'd felt the same way when his brother passed away, but he imagined that it was worse for CJ. After all, this was his wife. All he could think to say in response was the same thing that CJ had told him all those years ago. "God will never leave you or forsake you, man. He made your heart and He's the only one who can mend it. It's gonna take a while, but eventually today becomes yesterday, and then it'll be last week, last month, and last year. You'll get through it a day at a time, and I'm gonna be right here to help you. I got you, man. You hear me? I got you. Anything you need me to do, just let me know."

With his face glistening with tears, CJ looked Neil square in the eyes. "You know what I need you to do? I need you to ask Shay to marry you."

"What?" Neil wasn't sure what he was expecting CJ to say, but that wasn't it.

"Life is too short not to take chances, Neil. Tomorrow ain't promised to nobody. You love Shaylynn, and she loves you. Emmett Ford is dead, okay? He's dead." CJ's teeth were clinched, like he was angry to even be addressing this subject again at all, let alone at a time like this. "You keep harboring all of these stupid feelings of inadequacies when you compare yourself to him. You hear Shay talk about him, and it makes you feel like you can't measure up to his greatness, and that she'll never love you the way she loves him." CJ wiped tears from his face. "Look at Resa." Neil did as he was ordered, but only for a fleeting moment before looking back at CJ and allowing him to continue making his point. "Tomorrow ain't promised to nobody. Contrary to popular belief, Emmett wasn't perfect. He wasn't without some shortcomings, but I believe he truly loved his wife. Even so, you don't have no reason to feel like you don't measure up. That man had a lot of flaws, but I think he did all he could to make up for them and be a righteous, honest man before it was over. Don't ask me how I know all of that; I just do."

CJ turned his eyes toward his motionless wife, and in a quivering voice added, "I don't want to lose her, but if I do, I don't have any regrets. I love her more than I have ever loved any other woman in my life, and I was able to show her that in every way. Her parents had more than I had when I met her. Resa had more than I had when I married her. By anybody's definition, when she married me, she married down. I could have let that intimidate me and scare me into second thoughts and hesitations, but I didn't, because I knew God said she was mine.

"No couple has a perfect marriage. But with me and Resa, whatever we've endured, we've endured together, and in the end, our commitment to each other paid off. God gave me all I needed in order to give her the life she deserved; a life, I must add, that she couldn't have had without me. Resa's better off for having met and married me, and I'm better for doing the same with her. When you put an almighty God and unconditional love together, there's nothing you can't overcome. You and Shay have all the ingredients." CJ's look turned pleading. "Don't put off making the decision until the decision is no longer yours to make. Don't live with regret, Neil. Don't live with regret."

# EIGHTEEN

The first Sunday in February marked the second Sunday in a row that Kingdom Builders Christian Center was forced to carry out morning worship without its pastor. KBCC had a capable staff of ministers, so there was more than one qualified replacement, yet on a first Sunday — the one Sunday per month that carried the title of "pastoral Sunday" — the absence of the church's heartbroken leader and his dying first lady was even more painfully obvious than normal. KBCC members had been charged to go on and keep the faith, but doing it wasn't as simple as saying it. And while CJ sat at Theresa's bedside trying to hold on to what little hope he had left, Shaylynn played surrogate mother to the baby she simply called Li'l Miss, and tried her best not to become too attached.

"They ought to just name her Theresa," Ella remarked. She was sitting on the loveseat, folding laundry and watching as Shaylynn changed the baby's diaper on the sofa.

"She does look just like her, doesn't she?" Shaylynn unfastened the adhesive strips that held the diaper in place and silently thanked God that what she'd smelled earlier was nothing more than gas. The diaper still needed to be changed though.

Shaylynn, Chase, and Neil had accepted the invitation to join Ella for dinner at her house after church. They had shared a full spread, where the main course was chicken and dumplings, and the dessert was fresh-baked apple pie. Chicken and dumplings was another one of those things that Shaylynn had never been introduced to before moving to Georgia. Her favorite part was the dumplings, but on a day like today, even the delicious meal lacked something. They'd tried to have regular conversation during their Sunday meal, but every time the infant known as Li'l Miss made any noise from the baby carrier where she lay, reality would hit them all over again.

Shortly after dinner, while Shaylynn helped Ella clean the kitchen, Neil said he had an errand to run, and Chase had asked to ride with him. Shaylynn didn't ask where he was going, but since Deacon Burgess was at church today, she could rule out the possibility that he was going to check up on his favorite Alzheimer's patient. The only other option was CJ. Neil was likely visiting the hospital to lend support to his best friend. Shaylynn wasn't thrilled at the thought of Neil leaving Chase in a waiting room full of strangers while he went into Theresa's restricted ICU room, but she had grown to trust Neil, and she knew he'd do whatever it took to ensure her son's safety. He wouldn't put Chase in harm's way.

"I guess we'll need to go out and get more Pampers soon," Ella mentioned. "She goes through them like nobody's business."

Shaylynn cleaned the baby's bottom with a powder fragrant wipe, and at the same time, wondered if Theresa had a birthmark on the cheek of her right buttock too. "No, she won't need any for a while. All the sisters at the church who were set to attend the baby shower went ahead and gave all their gifts in light of the fact that the shower had to be canceled. Li'l Miss has plenty of assorted packs of diapers in her nursery at home. Pampers, Luvs, Huggies . . . She even has some of those comparable store brands." Before zipping the baby bag shut, Shaylynn stuffed the folded soiled diaper and the resealable pack of baby wipes inside. "There you go," she said to the baby after pulling up the ruffled bottom to the peach-colored outfit that she wore. Then she picked her up and cradled her in her arms.

"You look real comfortable doing that," Ella observed. Then after a fleeting silence, she added, "You want more?"

Shaylynn looked across the room at Ella. Was that a trick question? Why would she ask her such a thing when she knew her son couldn't have children? Sudden reality prompted Shaylynn to sit forward in her seat. *Oh . . . she doesn't know.* Ella's face was too relaxed, too sincere for there to be hidden motives behind her inquiry. Obviously Neil had never divulged that information to his mother. She probably thought that his childless marriage with Audrey had been a matter of choice. Not being able to plant the seed for a child didn't exactly give a man bragging rights, and Shaylynn could understand why that might be something that Neil wouldn't want to be common knowledge. And as far as Shaylynn was concerned, if he hadn't told Ella, she certainly wasn't going to be the one to do it.

"I wouldn't mind having more, but if I don't, I'll be okay with that too. It's not like I haven't had the experience of being a mother. Chase probably would welcome a little brother or sister, but if he doesn't have one, I don't think he'd miss it. He has a lot of friends at the school that he spends his days with." Shaylynn looked around the room for something else to talk about, but her eyes weren't fast enough.

"He sure did have fun playing with Ty and Kee-Kee when they were here last summer." Ella was speaking of her youngest daughter, Val's, two children, Tyrese and Keisha, who had spent a portion of their summer break with her before the new school year began last fall. Chase and Tyrese were only a few months apart and had quickly bonded upon their initial introduction, a few months before Neil and Shaylynn began dating. Ella folded a bath towel, and then added, "By the time you have another child, Chase might be too big to really want to play with his little brother or sister, but I still think you should do it. If this little one right here is any indication" — she nodded her head toward Theresa's cooing infant — "you sho' got the touch. And besides, just 'cause you've had the experience of motherhood don't mean the man you marry done already had the experience of fatherhood. In marriage you have to think of more than yourself, baby. I'm sure the man you marry will love Chase like his own, but still, he might wanna have his own flesh-and-blood child."

*Poor thing.* Shaylynn's heart went out to Ella. Although she hadn't said Neil's name, Shaylynn knew that he was the one she had in mind during her spiel. Ella was actually looking forward to more grandchildren by way of the only son of hers who hadn't yet given her any. Shaylynn looked down at the baby she held in her arms. She'd done it mainly to avoid eye contact with Ella, but the sight of the alert newborn looking back up at her captured her heart . . . again. Shaylynn felt guilty. She shouldn't enjoy caring for the child like this. Not under these circumstances. Not when the reason she was caring for her was because Theresa was standing at death's door with one hand on the knob.

"I'd have more if Solomon wanted more." As soon as the words escaped her mouth, Shaylynn's lips clamped shut and her eyes popped open. She looked up at Ella. *Oh God!* But it was much too late for her thoughts to be calling on the Lord for help. The words had already been spoken.

Ella chuckled until it turned into an all-out, belly-shaking laugh. It was the first time anyone in the house had laughed all day. Shaylynn couldn't determine whether having Neil's mother laugh at her embarrassing blunder made her feel better or worse. For now, all she knew was that it made her feel hot. Very hot. Like she had suddenly been warped into the central point of menopause.

Shaylynn didn't know what to say to get herself out of this one, but she had to say something. "I . . . I . . . What I meant was —"

"Oh, baby, don't be 'shamed." Ella used one of the washcloths from the basket of freshly cleaned laundry to dab the water from her eyes. Shaylynn wished she had one to wipe the beads of sweat from her brow. "I wouldn't want it no other way," Ella continued. "You and Sol would make me some mighty pretty grandbabies." Her face turned serious, and she scooted to the edge of her seat and leaned forward like she was about to share a secret. In a low voice tone, Ella asked, "Y'all been talkin' 'bout getting married?"

Shaylynn wished she had a different answer, but all she had was the truth. "No, ma'am. Not yet." She had her eyes locked on the baby again. It was like staring at Theresa. CJ would never forget his wife as long as he had his daughter.

"I don't know what y'all waiting on." Ella folded a towel and plopped it on the pile with the others like she was frustrated.

Shaylynn wanted to say, "I'm waiting on your son; I don't know what *he's* waiting on," but she didn't. "Everything happens in God's own time."

Ella shook her head. "Some things God ain't got nothing to do with. He gave you Sol, and He gave Sol you. He done did His part. The rest is up to y'all."

"If it's meant to happen, it'll happen." Shaylynn placed Li'l Miss back in her carrier, all the while wishing that believing her own words was as easy as saying them.

Taking a break from her laundry duties, Ella said, "Wonder where that young'un of mine run off to anyway? Did he say?"

"No, ma'am." Shaylynn looked down at the watch on her wrist. Two hours had passed since Neil said he'd be back "shortly." She could only hope that by the time he rejoined them, Ella would have forgotten about her slip of the tongue.

"Just have a seat over there; I'll be right back." While Neil peeled off his jacket, he watched Chase obediently walk toward the king-sized bed. The television was already on, but before dismissing himself from the master bedroom, Neil hung his jacket on the knob of the front door and used the remote control to find the Disney Channel.

"Just watch a little bit of this until I come back." Some cartoon was on that showcased a weird-looking character with a flat nose and green hair. Neil was sure that Chase had no interest in it, but this was only going to take a few minutes, so it shouldn't have been too tortuous for him.

"Whoa . . . *Phineas & Ferb*. Cool!" Chase jumped up with excitement and made a perfect landing in a seated position on the mattress.

Neil laughed as he placed the remote control back on its stand. It really took so little to make Chase happy. He looked a lot like his father, but the boy shared many of his mother's personality traits, including this one. Shaylynn wasn't hard to please either. Neil glanced over his shoulder at the boy one last time before strolling out of the room and into the long hallway that would eventually deliver him to CJ's private office. With his elbows propped on his knees and his chin resting in his hands, Chase was already engrossed. Neil knew the sight of that oversized, wall-mounted flat screen would hook Chase; that's why'd he'd taken him in CJ and Theresa's bedroom versus sitting him on the couch in the den. Neil needed Chase to be thoroughly occupied while he did what he did. If the boy wasn't absorbed in television, he might wander into the area where Neil was headed, and in a way, that would make Chase an accomplice. Neil felt bad enough as it was. The last thing he needed to do was drag Chase in on it.

The Loathers' home was at least twice the size of Neil's. Kingdom Builders paid CJ well, and their house, with its original, signed artwork and genuine African artifacts, reflected that. He used to tease CJ and Theresa for having such a large house when there were only two of them living there. CJ would tell him that they were living for the future. It wouldn't always be just two, he'd say. Someday they were going to have a family, and the extra space would be put to good use. Now here CJ was, finally having the family he'd been anxiously awaiting, and at the rate things were going, when all was said and done, there would still be only two people living there. The thought made Neil shake his head. He found himself constantly praying for CJ. They all loved Theresa, but no doubt about it, CJ's love reached much higher and dove much deeper than anyone else's. Neil had never seen his best friend so despondent. And it was going to get a whole lot worse before it got any better.

Knowing that was a harsh reality. It was

difficult to believe that it could get any worse than today. When Neil left his mother's home to go to the hospital to see CJ, he'd used his cell phone to coax his friend to leave Theresa's ICU room long enough to come and meet him in the waiting room so they could talk. He couldn't take Chase in the room, and although Neil believed the eight-year-old would be fine if he left him alone in the waiting area for a little while, he didn't want to chance it.

Maybe he shouldn't have watched that special last night on the Biography Channel about Adam Walsh, the six-year-old son of John Walsh, creator of the television show *America's Most Wanted.* That poor kid's mom had walked away from him in a Sears store for only seven minutes, and the next time the Walshes saw their child, it was two weeks later, and even then, all they saw was his head, which had been found floating in some river. Just that fast . . . in seven minutes . . . some crazy fool had taken that boy and changed his parents' lives forever. If a fraction of something that horrendous happened to Chase while in Neil's care, he would never forgive himself . . . and Shaylynn would never forgive him either. He didn't know which of those thoughts was more chilling.

He wasn't able to talk to his preacher/ friend for too long, because CJ was too afraid to be away from Theresa's side for any extended period of time. When Neil looked at his friend, he appeared to be carrying around at least forty-eight hours of sleep deprivation. CJ didn't look ragged, but he looked thinner, tired, older. The two-week ordeal was taking a toll on him, and as CJ was telling Neil that the doctors were beginning to hint that he should consider disconnecting his wife from life support, CJ struggled not to fall apart. Had Chase not been sitting in view of them, he probably would have. Even with all of the other strangers who were sitting in the waiting area, Neil was certain that Chase's presence was the only reason CJ held his tears. Seeing what his best friend was dealing with made all of Neil's problems and insecurities seem futile; including this whole stupid thing with Emmett.

He paused at the closed door of CJ's study. The possibility that it might be locked didn't faze Neil. For years now, he had been entrusted with a key to CJ's home and the code to disarm the security system. The key ring he carried held three keys: one for the front door, one for the back door, and one for the study. Rarely did Neil use any of

them, and today was his first time ever using them without CJ's permission. The
folder in his hand felt heavy as he turned
the doorknob to enter CJ's office. It was
unlocked, so it opened with ease. He hesitated in the doorway for a moment, scoping
out the space before entering. It felt like he
was being watched. Those were probably
God's eyes, and Neil was sure that they
were filled with disappointment. He never
should have taken the paper in the first
place.

Neil wasn't quite sure what had driven
him to bring back the evidence without
presenting it to Shaylynn. That paper was
his winning hand, yet he was folding like his
playing cards were losers. Either the overwhelming guilt that had haunted him ever
since he'd removed the private notes was
what led him to return them, or it was that
inexplicable look in CJ's eyes the other night
when he told him to stop wasting the time
that he could be spending with Shaylynn
worrying about her memories of Emmett.
But then again, maybe what had given him
the courage to believe he didn't need the
leverage of the proof of Emmett's sins was
how perfect things had been between him
and Shaylynn lately. Although there were
days when he could still see the chain

around her neck that bore the "charm" that was always conveniently tucked behind the top of whatever outfit she was wearing, Shaylynn hadn't said a mumbling word about Emmett in Neil's presence for over a month. That was a record for her. If it weren't for Theresa's horrific plight, Neil would feel like his world was perfect.

In a matter of seconds, he had slipped the paper with all of the handwritten scribble on it from the folder he currently had it in and placed it back in the original red folder from which he'd taken it. Then he put both folders back in the stack, being careful to put the one he had permission to take on the very top. The one with CJ's handwritten notes was placed near the bottom of the stack, where it was when Neil first lifted it. The entire exchange took less than a minute, but sweat was dripping from every pore of Neil's body by the time he exited the office and closed the door behind him.

He stood with his back against the door for several moments, trying to steady his racing heart; then he escaped into the closest of three restrooms where he splashed his face with cool water and used several sheets of paper towel to absorb the moisture. When Neil finished drying his face, he pulled the tail of his dress shirt from his pants, lifted it as high as necessary, and dried his armpits as well. He would make a pitiful criminal. If taking and returning a sheet of paper without permission made him react like this, then stealing anything worth over a buck and a quarter would probably give him a massive heart attack.

"Ready to go?" Neil set his face and hoped his innocent act could at least fool a child as he returned to the master bedroom.

"Can I finish watching this?" Chase pointed at the television screen.

Neil couldn't stay in the house another moment. "Sorry, kiddo, we have to get going. We need to get back to the house with Ms. Ella Mae and your mom."

"Aw, man." Chase's dismount from the bed was far less enthusiastic than his mount. "It was way better watching cartoons on this big screen than it is to watch them on the TV in my bedroom. I gotta tell Pastor Loather how cool that was."

"Come on. Put your coat back on and let's go." Neil wiped his brow with the paper towel he still held in his hand. At the sound of Chase's words, his sweat glands reactivated. Now he had to figure out a way to make the child forget his plans to share the joys of his television-watching experience. That wouldn't be so *cool* after all, considering the fact that they never should have been in the house in the first place . . . and definitely not in the master bedroom.

# NINETEEN

The days were passing slowly for Neil. Today was Wednesday, but it felt like Friday. He hadn't slept well this week, but he wasn't exactly sure why. It couldn't have anything to do with the notes he'd taken from CJ's place. He'd returned those and felt good about doing the right thing. Something else was causing this. Neil was growing increasingly worried about CJ and Theresa's plight, but it didn't feel like that was the reason that his nights were becoming so restless, either.

The sleep deprivation was making him cranky, too. The sounds of Li'l Miss's cries last night worked his nerves as he sat up at Shaylynn's house, watching movies with her. Then today, Margaret chose not to wear her hearing aid, and as accustomed to that as Neil was, today he was fed up with having to raise his voice every time he said something to her. Now, on his lunch break, when his intent was to sit in his car and catch a nap, he was headed down Wesley Chapel Road — a street on which he hated to travel during any high traffic time — on his way to see Deacon Burgess. Today of all days, the old man had decided to behave so badly that his caretaker had to call for backup.

Neil desperately needed to have a few minutes of quiet time to calm himself before getting out of his SUV and entering the home, but that grace wasn't extended. Teena must have been watching through the window for his arrival. She opened the front door as soon as he pulled into the driveway, so Neil had no choice but to get out.

"Thanks for coming, Deacon Taylor. I know you're busy in the middle of the week like this, but I didn't know what else to do." She said all of that before Neil even reached the front door.

Her big Erykah Badu/Macy Gray/Tina Turner hair assaulted Neil's face as he accepted her embrace. "That's okay, Ms. Teena. I told you to call me anytime it was necessary, so it's fine." He'd said that in part to remind himself that he couldn't rightfully be annoyed with her. "Where's Deac?" Neil looked around the living room as he followed Teena inside.

"He's in his bedroom right now. He done calmed down some, 'cause just a little while ago, he was banging on the door."

Neil looked at her, knowing the answer before he asked the question. "Why was he banging on the door?"

Teena handed him a single copper-colored key. "Because I locked him inside." She shook her head. "I'm sorry, Deacon Taylor, but I can't do the stuff I needed to do if I have to keep running after him when he wanders outside. I know locking him in the room sounds cruel, but it ain't crueler than him walking out the door and getting too far away before I realize he's gone. Anything can happen to him if he gets lost out there, and if he becomes a Channel 2 News feature, I'll never be able to find work again."

"I understand." Neil took the key from her hand. Imprisoning Deacon Burgess in his room wasn't what Neil wanted Teena to do, but he couldn't exactly blame her under the circumstances. "I'll go talk to him."

"Thank you." Relief washed over Teena's face like Neil was some sort of miracle worker, but he knew that if the old man was as far off his rocker as was explained to him in their earlier phone conversation, his talking to Deacon Burgess wouldn't do much good.

"I'm coming in, Deac." After Neil unlocked the bedroom door, he eased it open while simultaneously knocking and making the announcement of his entrance. "Deac?" He spoke with a little more caution after finding the room empty and hearing a rustling in the adjoining bathroom.

"Who dat?" It sounded somewhat weak, but it was definitely Deacon Burgess's scratchy voice.

"It's me, Deac. Neil Taylor."

"You by yourself, Deacon Taylor?"

That question took Neil aback for a couple of reasons. One, he hoped Homer Burgess wasn't about to walk out of the restroom naked. It was true that the old man was almost like a father to him, but Neil wouldn't have wanted to see his daddy without clothes on either. Seeing Deacon Burgess in his birthday suit just wasn't something he wanted to experience, and definitely not after he had just wolfed down a sandwich he picked up from the drive-thru window at Arby's. He didn't need his lunch to come up the same way it had gone down. The second reason the question thwarted Neil was because Homer had called him Deacon Taylor. On days when Alzheimer's had the best of him, Homer never called him Deacon Taylor. As a matter of fact, he didn't call him anything at all. On those days, *if* he communicated with Neil at all, he just talked. It was rarely a personal or sensible conversation; just babble, mostly.

"Yes, I'm alone. Is everything okay in there?" *Please don't come out naked. Please don't come out naked.* Neil hoped all the stuff he'd heard about telepathic messages was true.

The sound of the flushing toilet deepened Neil's confusion. *What on earth?* Homer had been wearing adult diapers for at least six months. Even on his good days he wore them in case of an accident, but on days like the one Teena had described to Neil less than an hour ago, Homer would have absolutely no reason to flush a commode. Seconds later, the faucet came on, and moments after that, Neil saw the deacon's head peek around the doorframe before he finally shuffled his way out into the bedroom, using his cane for assistance. Deacon Burgess walked at the speed of a three-legged turtle, so it took him forever to cover even the shortest distances. Neil watched him make his way to the bed, then slowly climb on the mattress into a seated position, cover his legs with the bedspread, and use the headboard as a back rest.

"Hey, Deacon Taylor. How you?" The short but difficult walk to the bed had rendered him winded, but other than that, Deacon Burgess seemed perfectly fine. Boy. That Alzheimer's was something else; here one minute, gone the next.

"Hey, Deac." Neil eased closer to the bed, but chose to sit on a chair beside it. "You look well."

"You look shocked," the deacon replied. "Ain't you happy I look like I'm doin' well?"

Neil relaxed in the chair, crossing his right leg over his left knee. "Yeah, I'm happy, I'm just surprised. Ms. Teena called me a little while ago and said —"

"That I was ova' here cuttin' the monkey?"

Neil tilted his head and thoroughly searched Homer's face. This was getting weirder by the minute. When Deacon Burgess snapped out of his Alzheimer's episodes, he never recalled the way he had misbehaved during the episodes; at least not verbally. Neil didn't think the man was even aware of his actions during those times. "Yes." Neil's reply was guarded.

Homer waved a carefree hand at him. "I'm sorry, Deacon. I didn't mean to get her so revved that she'd call you over here. I know you have a lot to do at work."

With narrowed eyes, Neil blurted, "Are you telling me you were faking it?"

"Shh! Boy, hush yo' big, fat mouth 'fo' she hear you. Go lock the door." When Neil didn't move immediately, Homer added, "Go on. Lock it."

After obeying, Neil stood in front of the door and looked at who could possibly be the greatest actor on the face of the earth. This time he spoke softly when he said, "If you tell me that you don't have Alzheimer's —"

"Of course I got it," Deacon Burgess said. "Can't nobody fool a doctor into thinkin' they got that mess. Them pills I'm on woulda been done killed me by now if I didn't have it." He pointed to an area of the mattress beside him like he wanted Neil to sit there. When Neil complied, Deacon Burgess continued. "The truth is, I got it, but I ain't got it as bad as everybody thinks."

Neil could hardly believe his ears. For a while now, he'd been thinking the progression of the disease was moving too fast, but he had no idea that Homer was putting on. Neil was trying not to get angry, but he had been paying good money for a service that now seemed unwarranted. He needed some answers, and he needed them now. "I don't understand, Deac. Why would you do this?"

Deacon Burgess ran his palms over his full head of silver, wavy hair, then he clasped his hands together and looked down at them as he placed them in his lap. "I don't be pretendin' all the time, just some of the time. I have days that I don't know where I am or who the people 'round me are, but some days I know and just act like I don't." He unlatched his hands and picked non-existent lint from the sheet draped over his lap. "Two or three Sundays ago, Pastor Loather preached so good up in that church that the Holy Ghost started rising up in me. Do you know how hard it is to quench the Spirit? Well, I had to do it that day. I couldn't go to hollerin', 'Thank you, Jesus' and 'Glory to God' when Alzheimer's was s'posed to have me."

Neil shook his head. "So how much of it is real and how much of it is made up?"

" 'Bout fifty-fifty." Homer looked up at Neil. "I ain't got long to be here, Deacon Taylor. I know you say I look good, but there's a plenty of folk who look better dead than they did when they was alive by the time the undertaker get through making 'em up. I don't know when the good Lord gonna call my number, but I know I ain't got long, and well . . . I don't want to die by myself."

The sincerity in Homer's eyes softened

Neil's heart. "People live a long time with Alzheimer's, Deac. Look at Ronald Reagan. He lived with it for at least ten years."

"Ronald Reagan also had hair that looked like it had been colored with black shoe polish, but I don't want that either. I don't wanna live wit' this for no ten years. I don't wanna hang around 'til I don't even recognize my own chil'ren. And Lawd knows I'd rather be dead than to live so long that I lose my memories of Odette." When the old man's eyes began to glisten, Neil had to look away. But he could still hear the pain in Homer's voice as he continued. "I done asked God to take me 'fo' then. I been serving Him for a long time, and I ain't never asked for a whole heap, so I know He gonna honor my prayers."

Neil sighed. There was just too much dying going on and not enough living. Deacon Burgess, Theresa . . . It was getting to be too much. Neil felt roughness when Deacon Burgess reached over and placed his hand on top of his. That tough skin came from years of hard labor, working with his hands as a construction worker and brick mason to provide for both his wives and all his children . . . children who now repaid the sacrifices their father made by unanimously voting to put him in a nursing home rather than adjust their lives so they could care for him. Homer had earned those calluses. He'd also earned the right not to die alone.

Turning back to face the deacon, Neil asked, "What do you want me to do?"

A smile tugged at Homer's lips. "I just want you to keep doin' what you been doin' all this time. You been a good boy, Deacon Taylor; a good boy. You been here for me when I didn't have nobody else, and I thank you." He patted Neil's hand a few times, and then put his hands back in his own lap. Homer dropped the volume of his voice even lower when he said, "I like that woman out there." He looked toward the closed door. The confession didn't exactly shock Neil. Deacon Burgess had hinted at it, although jokingly, in an earlier conversation. "Teena been the next best thing to a wife," he continued. "The only reason I won't ask her to marry me is 'cause I know she wouldn't, and I don't blame her one bit. She'd be crazy to marry me. I'm a old man, and there ain't nothin' I can do for a woman that young. But I like havin' her around, and I know as long as she think my mind ain't good, she'll be here."

As twisted as the rationale of that story was, Neil knew that he was in no place to pass judgment. The last year of his life with

Shaylynn had taught him that a man would do just about anything for love. But there was something that Homer didn't know. His plans were about to backfire on him. "Deac, Ms. Teena sounded like she was at her wit's end when she called me today. You're so busy trying to keep her here that you're about to run her away. All before noon today, you almost caused a grease fire, you broke a lamp, and you tried to wander off three times. You're taking it too far."

"I had to. It was the only way I could make her stay home."

Neil was confused. "What do you mean?"

"That drummer — the high-yella one — at the church been sniffin' 'round Teena lately. Last Sunday, I sat in the car for thirty minutes waiting on her while that rascal held her up outside talking. That was the second Sunday in a row that he done that. I let my window down a little so I could hear, and I heard him ask her if he could buy dinner and bring it ova' here and eat with her Friday night. She told him that it depended on how I was doing. So I figured if I start cuttin' up now, by Friday, she'll be too wore out to even think about sittin' 'round with that jackleg."

Neil struggled not to laugh at the deep scowl on Homer's face. Apparently jealousy had no age limit. "But aren't you the one who told me that I shouldn't be worried about Shaylynn's former husband?"

"That man's buried under the earth; it ain't the same thing. Plus you a young man, and even the Five Blind Boys of Alabama can see that that pretty girl loves you. Ol' drummer boy ain't dead, I ain't young, and Teena don't come nowhere near lovin' me. You ain't got nothing to be worried about. I do. You still got a full life ahead of you. I ain't got long, and I don't want to die by myself."

Neil sighed. "Stop saying that. You're not about to die."

"No . . . not today, and not tomorrow either, but I wanna go before it gets bad. I admit that I been puttin' on some of the time, but I have more bad days now than I used to, so I got a feelin' that the time will come more sooner than later. I ain't scared. Whenever the good Lord is ready, I'm ready too. And when I go, I want you to sing at the funeral."

"Oh come on, Deac. Let's not talk about this right now."

"Shh! Listen at me, boy." Homer's hand was back on top of Neil's. "I ain't plannin' to go nowhere yet, but I want you to know some things just in case God sees fit to take me whether I'm plannin' to go or not." Neil's back slumped against the headboard as he allowed Homer to continue. "I know wit' all that's in me that you anointed. In the Bible, God had prophets who He anointed to speak and a man would live, or they could speak and a man would lie down and die. I believe He done gave you that same anointing in your voice. You don't use it enough, Deacon.

"You seen how all those young folks came to the Lord the other Sunday while you was up there singing?" Neil nodded. He remembered, but he didn't think Deacon Burgess would. That must have been one of his acting days. "When I leave here, I want you to sing; you hear?" Homer had a look on his face that said he meant business. "I want you to sing like you givin' me the best send-off to heaven that there ever was. I ain't gonna tell you what to sing, 'cause God might give you a brand new song, one you made up just for that day."

Neil didn't know about all that. It had been a while since he'd actually written any original lyrics. It hadn't been anything he'd been inspired to do . . . not since Dwayne died.

"Don't you shortchange God none." Homer said it like he was in Neil's head and had heard his thoughts. "I told you long time ago that you ain't even scratched the surface of what God's gonna do wit' that voice of yours. He gon' give you some new songs, and them songs gonna do some amazin' things. The one you sing at my funeral might make me wanna rise up out that box and cut one last step before going to glory for good."

Homer laughed, but Neil didn't see the humor. "Deac —"

"I ain't heard you promise me my song yet."

Neil conceded because he knew he had no choice. "Promise."

"Something else you need to know is that I got a life insurance policy. It ain't a whole heap, but they'll be plenty left after my burial is paid for. When I go, I want you to have the leftovers."

That made Neil sit up straight, and then lean forward. "But what about your children?"

"What chil'ren?"

Neil searched Homer's face to see if Alzheimer's was sneaking up on him. "*Your* children, Deacon Burgess. You still have living children — five of them, all sons — and they would expect you to give them, *not me,* your money during that time."

"And they got a livin' daddy. It ain't but one of me, and I expected them, *not you,* to be the ones here wit' me during this time." He picked up his glasses from the nightstand and put them on his face before dramatically looking around the room for added effect. "I don't see a single one of 'em sittin' in this here room wit' me. Do you?"

Neil thought the question was rhetorical, but when Homer looked at him and said nothing further, it was apparent that he wanted an answer. "No, sir. Not today, but —"

"You seen any of 'em come by and visit me yesterday?"

"No, sir."

"What about the day 'fo' that?"

"No, sir." This could go on forever, and Neil's answer wouldn't change. As he thought about it, he realized that he hadn't seen any of Homer's sons since the old man had to be put in the hospital almost year ago. And it seemed that the only reason they'd gotten together then was to break the news to Homer that they had made the decision to place him in a nursing facility.

"Well, all right then." Deacon Burgess took off his glasses and placed them back where he'd gotten them. "Like I said, I want you to have it, and just so my hardheaded boys don't give you no legal trouble, I already got it in my will, and my lawyer got a recorded message of me talking that he'll play at that time, too. It won't be no mistaking that I was in my right mind when I changed the will. The money is all yours. Just give me an honorable burying, pay tithe to the church off what's left, and then do what you want with the rest."

Neil was about to say something, but Homer spoke up again. "And this here house, I'm leavin' that to you, too, but I want you to give it to Teena. She gave up her place to move in here to take care of me, and I think she really likes my house. I wanna be sure she still got a nice, stable place to stay when I'm gone. In the will, the house is left to you. It don't say nothin' 'bout you givin' it to Teena, so I need you to promise me you'll see to it that she gets it at no cost. I paid this house off years ago. It ain't costing me nothing to live here. It won't cost you nothing when it's passed on to you, and I don't want it to cost her nothing to get it from you. You hear?"

Neil nodded. "Sure, Deac." He needed to lighten the mood. "But what if she marries that drummer at the church? Is it gonna be okay for him to stay here too?"

Homer took a moment to ponder before saying, "Ol' sorry rascal. He ought to have a house of his own to move his wife in. It ought not to be the other way. But if it comes down to it, then yeah, he can stay here too, I reckon. I want that girl to be happy." He looked at Neil and pointed an arthritic finger. "But not 'til I'm gone."

Neil couldn't help but chuckle. "Right. No happiness for Ms. Teena 'til you're gone."

Homer nodded. "Thank you, son. Now I just got one mo' thing that I want you to promise me you'll do, but I want this one done in my lifetime."

"Anything."

"I want you to marry that pretty gal of yours. Before I leave here, I wanna see you get married, and I wanna dance wit' yo' bride at the wedding. Promise?"

Neil nodded, and he meant it. He wasn't changing his mind anymore. His planned proposal was just days away, and Homer Burgess would be dancing sooner than he thought. "I promise."

Homer smiled like he was satisfied. "Good. 'Cause if that first husband of hers is up there" — he pointed upward — "one of the first things I wanna be able to do when I get there is find the man who been givin' you all this grief from the grave and tell him you down here doin' the *bow-chicka-wow-wow* wit' his wife."

# TWENTY

"Her brain activity has ceased, Reverend."

CJ's mother used to say that bad news sounded worse when it was heard at night. It was nearing eight o'clock on Saturday evening, but Dr. Hale could have said those same words at eight o'clock in the morning, and CJ couldn't imagine the time of day making them sound any better. He had clearly heard the doctor's pronouncement, but his ears were desperately trying to redefine the words and make them mean something different. Something less devastating. Something that didn't tell him that his life was over. If it weren't for the strong arm of CJ's father in the ministry, which was wrapped solidly around his waist, CJ was sure his buckling knees would have sent him tumbling to the floor.

The Hawaiian-born physician obviously recognized CJ's instability, because he made haste to grab a chair and pull it behind him.

338

CJ's bishop, the Reverend B.T. Tides, helped guide him to a seated position. "We talked about this several times, Reverend Loather. Remember?" An island accent was only barely detectible in the doctor's kind voice.

CJ nodded the word that his mouth couldn't speak. Of course he remembered, but there was just no preparing for this. No amount of forewarning could take away the massive sting of the words that told him that no natural life was left in Theresa's body. The only reason her chest was rising and falling now was because a pump was feeding her oxygen. Oxygen that was doing her no good. Her brain was dead. She was dead.

"We aren't trying to rush you to make any decisions, Reverend," Dr. Hale said, "but when your wife was first admitted, you asked for my honesty in every step of this process, and that is what I'm giving. We did all that we could do for her, but even the best of modern medicine sometimes fails. Our concern is now for you, and the truth of the matter is, the only reason to keep these machines running is to make you feel better. It's no longer for her." Dr. Hale's voice was saturated with compassion. "I'm sorry, sir."

CJ was so numb he felt paralyzed. When

he remained unable to form the words of an intelligent reply, Reverend Tides stepped forward and spoke. "Thank you for your candor, Doctor." Reverend Tides was known for his slow, almost rhythmic dialect. It was that tone that many black theologians seemed to master. That Martin Luther King connotation that made listeners sit up and take notice. "We'll need to consult privately as well as contact the rest of the family before any final decisions are made."

"I understand." Dr. Hale accepted Reverend Tides's handshake, and then after one last concerned glance at CJ, he left the room.

"Charles." The door had barely closed behind the doctor's exit when Reverend Tides called CJ's name. The bishop was one of only a few people in CJ's closest circle who still opted to address him by his proper given name.

The summon had been heard, but CJ's body felt so weak that he didn't even have the strength to lift his head, let alone answer. In his peripheral vision, he saw Reverend Tides grab the only other chair in the room and place it right beside his.

"I know this is a devastating time for you, Charles, but I don't need you to sink into a place of darkness. How your church and your in-laws take any news about Theresa's well-being will largely depend on what they see from you. And regardless of what happens, you must remain lucid for the sake of your child; even if God decides to take Theresa home."

"*If* He decides to take her?" CJ's tongue had broken free. "What do you mean, *if?*" Tears welled in his eyes and wasted no time lining his cheeks. "You heard what the doctor said. She's already gone."

"Yes, I heard the doctor, and if you think Theresa is ready to give up the fight, and if you yourself are ready as well, I'll do the same, and we'll accept the doctor's report."

CJ wiped away the excessive water that obstructed his vision and looked at Reverend Tides. There wasn't a preacher on earth, his late father included, whose prayers CJ had ever had more confidence in than those of Reverend B.T. Tides. This was the same man who, after missing for months, an entire city — an entire *country* — had given up for dead just a few years ago, yet prayers had helped him be found alive. This was the same man whose youngest son had stopped breathing during a Sunday morning service, and when the bishop stretched his body on top of his son's and prayed, like the prophet Elisha did to the dead boy in the Bible, God gave Reverend Tides's son back his life.

CJ wasn't 100 percent certain, but he was almost sure that he'd just detected residual hope in the bishop's voice. But still . . . "It's not about whether I'm ready to give up. I'd hold out for a lifetime if I thought it might bring Resa back. But it's not up to me. Dr. Hale just said —"

"But it's not up to Dr. Hale either." Reverend Tides placed a comforting arm around CJ's shoulder. "I'm not trying to give you false hope, Charles. Theresa may very well be gone. It's a very real possibility that all we're looking at is the shell she once occupied. There may be no reason to keep her on the machines, and her brain might no longer be functioning. I heard every single word the doctor said, but now I'm listening for the voice of God. The doctor said it's all over, and I'm not saying it isn't. All I'm saying is that God hasn't given me the release to leave this room yet, and until He does, I'm prepared to stay right here and keep praying."

With new tears streaming down his cheeks, CJ reached for Theresa's hand and gave it a gentle squeeze. He'd give anything, even his own life, to feel her squeeze back, but she didn't. Her hand was limp and cold . . . just as any dead person's hand would be.

"What do you want me to do, son?"

CJ looked at Reverend Tides, and then slowly set his eyes on Theresa's swollen face. She looked so pale and pasty that his heart broke all over again. He knew his wife wouldn't want to be kept on machines like this. To keep her on it, just like Dr. Hale had all but said, would just be a selfish move on his part. CJ felt his bishop's arm tighten around his shoulders, and he knew the man was waiting for his reply, but the heavy gasps caused by his increased tears were choking back any words that he could say. He thought he'd gone through the hardest thing in life when he buried both his parents within months of each other, but he was wrong. Just the *thought* of burying Theresa was more tormenting than had been the actual act of burying his parents. In the midst of his continuing sobs, CJ felt Reverend Tides's hand press against the top of his head, and although he heard no words, he knew his bishop was praying, and right now, he needed all the prayers he could get.

# TWENTY-ONE

Sunday morning, Neil was uncommonly sluggish, and as a result, he was moving at the speed of a much older man. There were few things that aggravated him more than being late for church, but since he was only partially dressed, still had to pick up Shaylynn, Chase, and Li'l Miss, and morning worship was to begin in less than half an hour, today would likely be one of those days. Saturday had brought on another night of tossing and turning for Neil, but this time it was different. Instead of simple restlessness keeping him from a sound sleep, last night it was music. Loud music. And it wasn't coming from a neighbor's house, but from inside his own head. The sounds of an unfamiliar tune and the letters of lyrics swarmed through his head, ultimately combining to form a song he'd never heard before. A song so loud and persistent that it hindered him from finding peaceful sleep. It wouldn't stop playing in Neil's head until he gave up the fight for slumber and got up, grabbed a pen and notepad, and wrote down the words.

Neil didn't know why it was so pressing, but the first thing that came to mind was Deacon Burgess's request. Neil couldn't remember the last time a song had weighed so heavily on him, and it was just too ironic that three days earlier, Deacon Burgess had planted the seed in his head of writing an original song for his funeral. The song had Neil wondering if the Lord was preparing him for the death of his old friend. He had his doubts though. The words weren't quite fitting for a burial, but what else could it be? Even as Neil finished shaving the overnight stubble from his face, he subconsciously hummed the relentless tune.

As he put the final touches on his wardrobe, Neil splashed on the cologne that had twice caused Shaylynn to press her nose into his chest and inhale deeply. She said Issey Miyake was her favorite, and as long as it was her scent of choice and drew the kinds of reactions from her that it currently did, Neil was going to stick with it. When he opened his jewelry box to retrieve his watch, the case that had been holding Shaylynn's engagement ring for nearly two months captured his attention. The box always caught Neil's eye when he opened the wooden drawer that held his watches, cufflinks, and the signet ring that his brother was wearing on the day he collapsed and died.

With more time ticking away on the clock, Neil picked up the box and opened it. He was already running late. Whether he left now or five minutes from now, it wouldn't make a difference. Neil sat on the edge of his bed and opened the casing. Shaylynn's ring was more beautiful now than it was on the day he made the purchase. His planned proposal was now only two days away. No date on the calendar could be more perfect than Valentine's Day, and for the first time in all the time he and Shaylynn had been dating, Neil had no reservations. At least none that were caused by Emmett Ford's ghost. His only apprehension now came from CJ and Theresa's misfortune. It almost seemed cruel for him to propose to Shaylynn at a time like this. CJ had been Neil's best friend ever since Dwayne died, and if Shaylynn accepted Neil's proposal, he would want to share the good news with CJ first. But there was no way CJ could genuinely celebrate the moment with him . . . not with Theresa slipping away.

Neil closed his eyes and released a puff of air. It was still hard to believe Theresa was dying. Going to the hospital to visit her was becoming increasingly difficult, but Neil knew that he couldn't bail out on CJ during the greatest tragedy of his life. The process, by far, had to be more agonizing for CJ than anyone else. Neil made a mental note to go to the hospital after church. It had been a few days since Shaylynn had been able to go due to her surrogate mother duties. Today, Neil figured that they could take Chase and Li'l Miss to Ms. Ella Mae's and let them spend a little time with her while he and Shaylynn spent time with CJ and Theresa.

"Two more days." As much as his heart went out to CJ, Neil couldn't reschedule the proposal. He had an entire evening planned that included a concert and a romantic dinner. And knowing CJ, even with all that he was facing right now, he wouldn't even want Neil to delay it any longer.

Neil's eyes fell to the legal pad that was resting near the foot of his king-sized bed. He wished the words to this new song of his were fit for a wedding. If they were, he could sing them to Shaylynn as she marched up the aisle to meet him at the altar. Neil was certain that she would love to have him do that, but this wasn't a love song. It wasn't a song for a wedding, nor was it a song for a funeral. As Neil placed the engagement ring back into his jewelry case and grabbed his keys and wallet, he figured that when the time was right, God would reveal the reason for the lyrics that had robbed him of his sleep.

"You're late." It was the first thing Shaylynn said when she opened her front door for him to enter.

"I know, suga. I'm sorry." Neil wanted to greet her with a kiss, but Chase was rounding the corner to the living room, lugging Li'l Miss's baby bag on his shoulder.

"You smell good though," Shaylynn whispered.

Neil grinned and gave her a quick wink. He couldn't wait for the day when she would be able to do more than smell him. "I'll take that to mean I'm forgiven." He gave Chase a high five, and then took the baby carrier from Shaylynn's left arm so she could have a better grip on the baby, who was cradled in her right. "Ready to go?"

"Yes. Can you lock the door for me?"

After securing Shaylynn's house, Neil made sure that everyone was loaded and buckled safely into his SUV. Li'l Miss was wrapped so securely in her blankets that there was no way she'd catch a cold. Ella had fussed about them bringing the baby out into the winter elements so soon after her birth, but the doctor had given them permission to do so. She'd said that the advice to stay indoors for those extended weeks after giving birth was actually for the well-being of the mother, not the child. Dr. Daniels had assured them that there was no danger in taking the baby to church as long as she was wrapped well and not being touched and kissed by others who might be carrying a cold virus.

With Li'l Miss being the daughter of the pastor and the church's ailing first lady, the doctor was concerned as to whether Shaylynn would be able to hold back the sympathetic congregants who would surely want to fawn over the firstborn of their church leaders. But apparently, Dr. Daniels didn't know Shaylynn. As overprotective as she was, the church members didn't stand a chance.

Praise and worship had already begun as they entered the sanctuary, but prime seats were still available. Shaylynn and the children were directed to the edge of a row near the front of the edifice, and Neil followed the usher who escorted him to his regular spot in the deacon's corner beside Deacon Homer Burgess.

After Neil placed his Bible and keys on the seat behind him, the first thing he did was look at Homer, who sat, staring straight ahead, as he sang the words of VaShawn Mitchell's "Nobody Greater" along with the praise team. His eyes had that faraway look that Neil had become accustomed to equating to Alzheimer's, but with the old man's recent revelation, Neil wasn't sure whether what he was looking at was authentic or just another Oscar-worthy performance. He was tempted to lean over and say something to the deacon and see what kind of response he got, but decided that this wasn't the right time. Neil would corner him after the benediction.

Although praise and worship was as enjoyable as usual, it ran longer than normal. Most Sundays, unless the Holy Spirit orchestrated a major takeover, the praise leaders were relinquishing their microphones to the assigned service leader at the thirty-minute mark. Today, that wasn't the case, and by the time they had stretched it to fifty minutes, Neil began getting the feeling that the songsters were, for some reason, trying to delay the progression of the service. Only four more minutes would pass before his suspicions were validated.

Loud applause erupted from the sanctuary when CJ, dressed in one of his finest clergy robes, appeared from behind the wall that divided the platform from the hall that led to the pastor's study. Nobody had expected to see him today, Neil included. When Neil visited him yesterday afternoon at the hospital, he could tell that CJ was nearing a breaking point. Not one speck of good news had been given since Theresa's admittance. Her condition was on a steady decline, and although CJ didn't verbally say he was giving up hope, it was beginning to look that way to Neil. And when he looked at Theresa lying in the bed, bearing little or no resemblance to her former self, Neil could understand why. It didn't look good, to say the least.

The CJ who was now approaching the dais was different. His countenance wasn't the usual jubilant one to which the members of Kingdom Builders Christian Center were accustomed, but he was clean shaven, well groomed, and looked a far cry better than he did less than twenty-four hours ago. The applause died down when CJ accepted the microphone from the praise and worship leader, but they immediately increased again — even louder than before — when Reverend B.T. Tides, clad in a burgundy single-breasted suit and his signature silver cross necklace, rounded the corner, preceded by one of his armor bearers, and joined the pulpit staff. Having the bishop in their midst was a very rare treat. On average, he visited KBCC twice annually: once to preach on Founder's Day, the day they celebrated the memory of the church's visionary, Dr. Charles Loather Sr., and again for the closing service of CJ's pastoral anniversary.

At first, Neil thought that Reverend Tides was going to join CJ at the podium, but after he waved out at the congregants in a silent gesture of appreciation for their warm reception, he elected to sit in the pulpit chair beside the one that was reserved for the pastor. The church members continued standing in anticipation of whatever CJ was going to say, but after a brief silence, he gestured for them to take their seats.

Upon sitting, the first thing Neil realized was Deacon Burgess's demeanor. He hadn't stood when the bishop entered, and he didn't even seem to notice that their pastor was in their presence for the first time in three weeks. Homer wasn't faking it today. This was genuinely one of his bad days. Neil patted him on the knee, and Homer looked at him and gave him one of those mechanical smiles.

"In the book of I Thessalonians 5:18, the Word admonishes us to give thanks to God for all things," CJ said while spying out the congregation. "So today, I thank Him." His bottom lip quivered a bit, but he quickly steadied it. As a matter of fact, the pastor somehow mustered a small smile just before saying, "I thank God because I know that if I can't appreciate Him when times are bad, then the appreciation I say I have during the good times really isn't genuine. I'm thankful because I know that even on a bad day, God is good and yet worthy to be praised. I give Him the glory in spite of today, because I know that all the yesterdays I've had, I never would have been blessed to have if it weren't for Him." He stepped from behind the book board and added, "Just because what I'm going through today is breaking my heart doesn't give me the right to forget how good God is."

CJ's voice had gotten stronger, and by now, some of the audience members were on their feet, clapping and offering words of worship to the Lord in agreement. Neil was one of them. He knew how difficult this must be for CJ, and if all he could do was show his support by standing and letting his best friend know he wasn't alone in the struggle, then that was what he was going to do.

CJ cupped the cordless mic in his hands and challenged all the believers in the building. "Have you ever been in a dry place where you didn't realize that God was all you needed until you realized that He was all you had?"

Shouts of "Amen" resonated in the building. More members were now on their feet. CJ hadn't opened a Bible, taken a text, or given them a subject, but he was already preaching whether he realized it or not.

CJ turned to face the bishop. "I thank God for you, Reverend Tides. If it weren't for your prayers and counsel, I wouldn't have had the strength to be standing here in this place today." He turned and faced Neil. "I thank God for you, Deacon Taylor. If it weren't for you, I wouldn't have had a brother, sitting with me at the hospital every single day of this process, telling me that I didn't have to go through this alone." CJ looked out into the audience, quickly finding where Shaylynn sat, holding Li'l Miss, and said, "I thank God for you, Sister Ford. If it weren't for you, I would not have had anybody to give our baby the love and care that she needed while her biological mother fought for her life."

*Fought?* Neil stiffened, wondering if it was over. Had CJ come to church because there was no longer a reason for him to be at the hospital? Neil questioned whether anyone else had caught that past tense reference. There was no indication that they had, because they kept right on clapping and praising God behind their pastor's words.

"But most of all, I thank God for Jesus," CJ continued, "because had it not been for Him, I would have no life. When you're in a desert place, it's hard to see life. If you can't find the water — the life source — then you can't see where your next breath is coming from. You need an inhale in order to exhale, and in my darkest hour, I couldn't find my inhale. I needed Jesus to breathe on me." Amid responses from the audience, CJ found his way back to the book board and stood behind it. He quickly flipped through the pages of his Bible, but even when he'd apparently found the reference he was looking for, he didn't read it.

Looking out at the crowd, he said, "I was reminded, even on this morning, of the words from the book of Romans, chapter eight. I'm paraphrasing it, but somewhere between verses twenty-five and thirty-five, the Bible tells us that if we hope for something that we don't see, then we have to be patient to wait on God to do it. It tells us that when we pray, even when we don't know what to say in our prayers, the Spirit of God serves as an intercessor, and He fills in the blanks when all we can do is groan." CJ wiped his face with a handkerchief that he pulled from the pocket of his robe. "This is the same scripture that later assures us that all things work together for the good of those who love the Lord, and then gives us the promise that as long as God is for us, nothing or nobody can be against us."

CJ's voice dropped and the crowd calmed to hear his next words. "I meditated on these verses of scripture last night. I had to in order to not lose my mind when the doctor came in and told me, in so many words, that it was time to pull the plug because there wasn't anything else he could do." Loud gasps ran around the sanctuary.

Neil felt a tightening in his gut, and at that moment, he wished he was sitting beside Shaylynn instead of Deacon Burgess. CJ could have announced that Martians had just landed on the church rooftop and had demanded that they hand over their eldest church member, and Homer wouldn't have batted an eye. But knowing Shaylynn as he did, Neil knew that she was probably on the verge of a meltdown at hearing the woman she'd come to view as her big sister had run out of time.

CJ kept talking despite everyone's reactions. "I walked out of the hospital this morning for the first time since walking in last month. I left distraught in-laws there who couldn't understand why I would choose today, of all days, to leave." He wiped his face again. CJ's voice sounded steady enough, but Neil wondered if it was only sweat that he was erasing with the handkerchief. He wondered if there were some tears mixed in there as well. "For the first time in three weeks, I walked into my own house, took a shower in my own bathroom, shaved in my own mirror, and sat on the side of my own bed while I slipped on my shoes in preparation to come here today. When I walked out of my bedroom, I found our bishop walking the length of the living room and walking the length of the hallway, and all I could hear him saying was, 'Breathe, Jesus. Breathe, Jesus. Breathe.' " CJ shook his head. "It was like he had been reading my mind."

While others were again clapping and worshipping, Neil sat frozen in his chair with the words, *Breathe, Jesus. Breathe,* ringing in his ears. *Breathe, Jesus. Breathe.* If Reverend Tides had read CJ's mind, then they'd both read his. *Breathe, Jesus. Breathe . . .*

"The bishop and I have to head back to DeKalb Medical," CJ announced. "I just needed to stop by KBCC to let you know that it's gonna be all right. I have to trust in God and lean on His Word, because I don't have no other choice. Somehow, someway, even in our darkest hour, it's working for our good." With those words, CJ placed the mic on the stand, and then turned and walked back toward the dividing wall. Reverend Tides did the same, making quick steps to keep up with CJ's longer strides.

Neil never made it a practice to walk out of church before the altar call and benediction, but today he had to make an exception if he was going to catch his bishop and pastor before they left the premises. He grabbed his Bible and keys and took the long way around the sanctuary to locate Shaylynn so that he wouldn't walk in front of people and disrupt the minister, who was now talking from the podium.

Neil saw the tears in Shaylynn's eyes when he squatted beside the place where she sat. He wanted to hold her and comfort her, but there wasn't time. Not right now. Instead he pressed his keys in her hand. "You drive the truck home; I'm gonna ride with CJ."

Questions swam in the water of her eyes. "But —"

"Please, suga. Do this for me. I'll explain everything when I catch up with you guys later this evening. I promise. But right now I have to go."

"Okay." Shaylynn closed her hands around the keys. "Do what you need to do. I'll take care of the truck and the kids."

As Neil rushed out of the church, he mulled over Shaylynn's words. Besides the fact that they demonstrated how much she trusted and supported him, he thought of how "family like" the words had sounded; how naturally they'd flowed from her lips. When Neil rounded the corner of the church and saw Reverend Tides's armor bearer close one of the passenger doors, and then climb in the driver's seat of the vehicle in which they'd arrived, he pushed the thoughts of Shaylynn aside and broke into a sprint. Right now, he needed to have only one thing on his mind.

# TWENTY-TWO

When Theresa yawned, the truth that God still worked miracles became evident to everyone inside her ICU room, as well as the family members who'd been forced to wait for updates in the family waiting room down the hall. Hardly a dry eye could be found. Even the lady who had been Theresa's primary attending nurse for the duration of her hospitalization had cried. And though no tears manifested from Dr. Hale, the firsthand sight of it all had rendered him speechless. He'd had to sit in the same chair that he'd grabbed for CJ the night before.

En route to the hospital, Neil brought Reverend Tides and CJ up to speed on last night's restlessness and the song he'd been inspired to write in the middle of it. "And when you said the words 'Breathe, Jesus,' " Neil had told CJ, "I finally realized why God had given me this song. It was for you and Theresa."

Reverend Tides had sat silently in the front passenger seat for all of Neil's speech, but soon after he finished talking, the bishop turned to CJ and said, "When we get to the hospital, tell the doctor to pull the plug."

"Sir?" CJ looked terrified.

"God is giving the release," Reverend Tides told him, "and either you're going to trust Him or not. I wouldn't tell you to do this if I didn't know that it was what God is saying. If there's paperwork to sign to authorize the process, sign it. I don't know what His will is, but whatever it is, it will be done." He looked at Neil who sat beside CJ in the backseat of the Cadillac. "And while the doctor is shutting down the machine, you sing."

Neil swallowed hard. The thought that all of this was being done because of a song was unnerving. What if all their uses of the words "Breathe, Jesus" were just coincidental? Doubt was smacking Neil in the face with both hands.

As if the bishop could detect both their lingering apprehensions, he spoke once more before turning back around in his seat. Pointing at each man, he said, "You sign, you sing, and then let's all stand still and see the salvation of the Lord."

Had the miracle not happened, CJ would probably have never found forgiveness from his in-laws. Just like Jesus did when He entered the room of the ruler's dead daughter in Matthew, chapter nine, Reverend Tides put everybody out of the ICU room with the exception of those who needed to be there. Aside from the bishop, only CJ, Neil, Dr. Hale, and the attending nurse remained. Theresa's parents weren't at all happy about the temporary ban that their son-in-law had the audacity to authorize despite their protests, but CJ apparently didn't have the time nor energy to worry himself with their displeasure. They were all on a mission.

Reverend Tides appeared to have no reservations about what was about to take place, but while the doctor began the task of shutting off the equipment, CJ appeared to be holding his breath as he held Theresa's hand and kept the back of it pressed against his lips. The bishop knelt beside Theresa's bed and prayed silently, and when he knew the time was right, he opened his eyes, looked at Neil, and nodded his cue.

The song wasn't complicated, and the lyrics had played loudly in his head for so long that night that by the time Neil got up and wrote them down, he had already memorized the words, but with his nerves now on end, he hoped he remembered what had been written on the paper he'd left on his bed at home.

With two fish and five loaves of bread . . . The five thousand hungry, you fed. And children of Israel were free . . . Because you parted the sea. You are the same, Lord . . . You never change, Lord . . . So please, Jesus, do this for me. I ask you to . . . Breathe, Jesus . . . Breathe, Jesus . . . Breathe, Jesus . . . Breathe. Oh, won't you just breathe, Jesus . . . Breathe, Jesus . . . Breathe, Jesus . . . Breathe. And I'll tell the story . . . Give you the glory . . . I'll testify and . . . shout the victory. And all will know . . . Without a doubt . . . That it was you . . . Who brought me out. I know . . . I'll live . . . indeed . . . if you just breathe . . .

By the time Neil was singing it for the third time, it was evident that God was in the middle of doing something incredible. The machines were no longer attached, but Theresa's chest was still rising and falling; something that would not have continued if she weren't breathing on her own. Reverend Tides had anointed her with so much blessed oil that her entire forehead was glistening.

While Neil made his fifth go-round on the lyrics, the attending nurse was taking vitals and documenting her findings with visibly trembling hands. The seventh time around, others in the room had caught on to the simple but meaningful lyrics, and they sounded like a harmonizing quartet with everyone except Dr. Hale joining in on the chorus of "Breathe, Jesus," and they continued to softly sing the two words even after the rest of the song had stopped being sung.

"Breathe, Jesus . . . Breathe, Jesus . . . Breathe, Jesus . . . Breathe . . ." they sang.

The chant-like vamp seemed to go on forever. It didn't stop until Theresa squirmed in the bed in a manner that almost seemed like she was stretching her body, and then opened her mouth in a lengthy yawn before becoming still again. The sight of it sent CJ to his knees in tearful thanksgiving.

"I have been doing this for twenty-two years," Dr. Hale said once all of the family had been allowed back into the room to witness the aftermath of the miracle, "and I can honestly say that I've never seen anything like this before."

Neil had never seen anything like it before

either, and he was more shaken by it than anyone realized. For more than half of his life he had been told by different ones, including the late Dr. Charles Loather Sr., that his singing carried a special anointing that could produce miraculous results. Neil had seen people give their hearts to God under the sound of his singing, but what he'd just seen was almost too much to digest. Deacon Burgess had told him only a few days ago that his singing could raise the dead, but Neil hadn't taken that literally.

"What does this mean? What's going on with her now? Does this mean she's going to be okay?" Theresa's mom broke into Neil's thoughts. She stood at the head of her daughter's bed, stroking her hair, while Theresa's father sat in a chair, dabbing at his eyes with a monogrammed handkerchief. The phenomenon had overwhelmed him almost as much as it had CJ.

"Well, as you can see, she is still not awake, so it's too soon to declare her as out of the woods," Dr. Hale said, all the while scribbling notes on his clipboard, "but she's not on life support, which is a remarkable improvement. As we speak, I'm preparing to order a series of tests so we can find out where she is right now." He handed the clipboard to the attending nurse, and, without a word, she excused herself with quick footsteps. "Our largest immediate concern is whether any damage was done to the brain in the weeks that she's been unconscious. Very recent tests showed that there was absolutely no brain activity, so we have to find out what short- or long-term concerns that may have created."

Dr. Hale stuck his ink pen in the top pocket of his uniform and crossed his arms. "Judging from the extensive movements she made a moment ago, I predict that there's no damage so serious that it resulted in any paralysis." He looked at CJ. "That is also remarkable, by the way." Dr. Hale turned his eyes back to Theresa's mother and finally gave a more direct answer to her inquiry. "If I were to give an expert conjecture, I would say that she is semi-comatose at this moment. As a part of the battery of analyses we'll be running over the next few hours, we'll be using various forms of stimuli to see if we can rouse her. If she responds to the stimuli, my educated guess will be proven accurate, but until we have the results of those tests, I cannot give you any concrete answers." He paused, and looked around the entire room. "All I can say right now is you should be very thankful to your God for answering your prayers for breath."

Replies of "Amen" seemed to be uttered from everyone simultaneously.

"I understand that everyone is excited about this turn of events," Dr. Hale said, "but please understand that we will need the crowd to thin." He looked at CJ. "Reverend, there are times when we will need even you to leave the room. I hope you understand."

"Yes. Fully." It was good to see a genuine smile on CJ's face.

"We'll be removing her from this area for some of her tests, and my guess is if you sing a few more rounds" — the doctor looked at Neil — "we'll be removing her from this area permanently in the next day or so."

Neil felt his face flush under the pressure of the eyes that turned to look at him. He didn't know how to respond to Dr. Hale's words, so he didn't. At least, not verbally. All Neil offered in return was a slight duck of his head and a smile.

The doctor had more advice, and he looked around at everyone in the room as he offered it. "At this point, although Mrs. Loather is not strong enough or alert enough to open her eyes or respond in words, I do believe she, like many semi-comatose patients, can hear and understand what is being said around her. If you're going to speak to her, say encouraging things. Let her know you're here and that you are wishing her well. Believe it or not, something as simple as that can play heavily into how well and how speedy she recovers."

"Thank you, Dr. Hale." CJ extended his hand.

Upon accepting it, the doctor said, "I wish I could take the credit for this, Reverend. It would look amazing on my résumé. But there comes a time when even we doctors must admit that it was out of our hands, and this is one of those times. Congratulations on getting your wife back," he said as their handshake broke. "And congratulations on being connected to such people as these" — he pointed at Reverend Tides and Neil — "who are connected to your God enough that they can offer such a healing source." He shook his head in wonderment as he walked toward the door, mumbling, "I never would have believed it if I hadn't seen it with my own eyes."

## TWENTY-THREE

"You've been flying high for two days, Dr. Taylor," Margaret said as she entered his office and handed him the stack of folders in her hand. "You hit the lottery and didn't tell me?"

Neil laughed. "You know I don't gamble, Ms. Dasher. And don't act like you're not on the same high that I'm on."

Taking the liberty to sit in the chair across from his desk, Margaret said, "Lord have mercy. I have hardly slept since Sunday evening when I heard the news. Now, I'm not saying I haven't seen any miracles in my day, 'cause truth be told, it was a miracle that I didn't kill my first husband when I found out that he'd been sleeping with our neighbor . . . in the same bed that he and I slept in." Margaret pursed her lips and grabbed the letter opener from Neil's pencil holder, clutching it like it was a switchblade. "That devil didn't know how close he came to getting something cut off him that he needed."

"Whoa . . . whoa. Hold up," Neil said. Margaret always had the tendency to go into some kind of bipolar-like twisted tangent when she referenced her first husband. "Just calmly put that down and back away from my desk."

She put the letter opener back and just as quickly as she'd gotten riled, she shifted back to first gear. "I'm so happy for Pastor and First Lady. And see? I knew you'd learn sooner or later that what everybody's been telling you about your voice is true."

Neil smiled. He knew it was only a matter of time before Margaret would get to her "I told you so" speech. He probably would have gotten it yesterday, but Neil opted to take the day off in preparation for today. He had only stopped by his office briefly, to print some ticket information that he had saved on the hard drive of his computer. Shaylynn knew that he had planned something special for Valentine's Day night, but she had no idea just how special it was going to be.

"There are a few things that became clear to me over the past couple of weeks," Neil admitted, "and my calling to sing is just one of them. I mean, I've always known I had a special gift, but God confirmed some things for me in all of this."

"Yeah. He confirmed just how stupid you've been for doubting it to begin with."

Neil couldn't deny it, so he moved on. "Pastor Loather said that although Theresa hasn't awakened yet, she's been responding well to the tests they've been giving her at the hospital, and all her MRIs and other scans have come out normal. No brain damage has been detected."

Margaret stood. "Well, as big a miracle as that is, to tell the truth, none of it should surprise us. We're always talking and singing about how all-powerful God is, but as soon as something like this happen, we act all shocked, like we didn't even know God had it in Him. We serve a good God, and He doesn't do anything halfway. If He wants to heal a person completely, then that's what He'll do."

Nodding in agreement, Neil said, "So true. When Shaylynn and I went to the hospital last night, Theresa was looking like herself for the first time. She just looks like she's asleep. She even stirs if you nudge her or tickle her feet. Dr. Hale says they expect her to open her eyes any day. Since all her tests are fine, as soon as she wakes up, they are going to move her out of ICU. Her unconsciousness is the only thing keeping her there."

"I hear there's going to be a write-up on it in this weekend's edition of the *Atlanta Weekly Chronicles*."

Margaret had to be the nosiest person Neil knew. How she'd found that out, he didn't know. CJ had just told Neil about it last night while he and Shaylynn were visiting. Hunter Greene, the owner of the highly popular newspaper, was the son-in-law of Reverend Tides, and he had gotten exclusive rights to print the full story. It would be on the front page when the paper was released on Friday.

"Yes, that's true." Neil decided against asking her where she'd heard it. If there was a long "he said, she said" story attached, he didn't want to hear it.

"I sure wish Pastor would let us come out and see First Lady, especially now that she's doing so much better. I don't know why he let some and not others."

"I think there's a good chance that he'll completely lift the restrictions once she's in a regular room." Neil knew when Margaret said "some," she really meant Shaylynn. He and Shaylynn were the only two non-related church members who had been allowed, and by process of elimination, he knew

Margaret wasn't talking about him. There was no one who would not have expected CJ to allow Neil access.

"So do you and Ms. Ford have plans for tonight?" Margaret was looking over her frames at him now. Neil knew that meant only one thing: her nosey nose was about to start sniffing.

"It's Valentine's Day, of course we do." Neil pretended to busy himself with organizing the files she'd brought him. Margaret was good at reading eyes, and he didn't want her to decipher his plans for the evening. This was his and Shaylynn's second Valentine's Day together, so he knew a marriage proposal wouldn't be Margaret's first guess.

"Where are you going? Dinner? Dancing?"

"Maybe a little bit of both." Neil figured the best route was to just tell her the part he didn't mind her knowing. Margaret would stop fishing if he just handed her a nice-sized perch and called it a day. "I'm taking her to dinner at Canoe and to the concert at the civic center."

Margaret's eyes grew large. "The one with Peabo Bryson?"

"That's the one."

She wrapped her arms around herself like Peabo was in front of her. "I love that man!

And isn't James Ingram there too?"

"And Jeffery Osborne." Judging from Margaret's reaction, Neil knew he'd hit a home run with this choice. He could only hope that Shaylynn would feel the same.

"Well, shoot! You could've given me tickets to that show. I didn't have to be a third wheel; I could have driven my own car and sat clear on the other side of the auditorium."

Neil laughed. "There's just no pleasing you. Didn't I present you with a dozen roses this morning?"

"Yes, you did. And they were real pretty up until you told me you had tickets to this concert. The good seats sold out real fast."

"I know," Neil said. "The brokers bought them as soon as they hit the Web so they could jack up the prices and resell at a hundred percent profit. I only know one guy who was idiotic enough to go to them and pay those ridiculous prices rather than settling for seats that were farther back."

"Who was that?"

When Neil raised his left hand, both of them burst out laughing. "Hey, an idiot's gotta do what an idiot's gotta do. Valentine's Day comes only once a year, right?"

"I hope Ms. Ford knows she's got a good

one. I still can't believe my niece let you get away."

"You mean the niece with the bench warrant for assault and battery? The niece the police came and handcuffed *while* we were on our date?" He laughed again. "I don't mean no harm, Ms. Dasher, but she didn't *let* me get away. I was getting away with or without her permission."

Margaret shook her head. "My poor Lawrence . . . God rest his soul. His family is so messed up. Even the ones with good book sense are just a bunch of educated fools."

Neil never knew either of Margaret's husbands, but from all he'd heard, she seemed to really love the second one. That was more than could be said about the first man she'd married. Every time she mentioned him, she did so through clinched teeth. Lawrence was the only one she'd even identify with a proper name. The first guy was always identified by words like *devil* and *beast.* On good days, he was upgraded to *fool* or *scoundrel.* Neil had often wondered what the man's given name was, but he was too afraid for his own life to ask.

"Well, let me get back to my desk and finish things up so I can get out of here on time." Margaret began walking to the door, and then stopped. "Did Sean Thomas call you today?"

"Who?"

"Sean Thomas. That's the same man who called here for you a few weeks ago and said he just wanted to be sure he had the right workplace. He called again yesterday while you were out."

Neil hadn't heard that name since the first message Margaret gave him. At that time he didn't see any need to be concerned, but now that the man was calling again, his curiosity was piqued. "Did he leave a message or a call-back number this time?"

"No." A slight grin tugged on Margaret's face. "This fellow has a young voice. You don't think that maybe Ms. Ford has an ex she never told you about, do you?"

The thought had never crossed Neil's mind, but now, thanks to Margaret, it was sitting front and center. He shook his head despite his doubts. "No. Shay would have told me." He tried to shrug it off like before. "Oh well. As long as he's not leaving a message, it can't be too important."

Neil wished he believed his own words.

# TWENTY-FOUR

If Margaret Dasher thought he was flying high today, she should have seen him tonight. Neil felt like he was floating on cloud nine . . . and that was only because that was the highest-numbered cloud he'd ever heard mentioned. If there was a cloud ten, eleven, twelve, or twenty, then that was the one he was riding.

*She said yes!*

The look in Shaylynn's eyes, the joy in her voice, the tremble of her hand as he slipped on the ring — all of it was etched in Neil's mind forever. He'd sworn that he'd never take this step again, but right now, he gladly called himself a liar. Nothing in the world could be better than this feeling of making Shaylynn his wife, and when he held and kissed her tonight, Neil found an amazing sense of relief in knowing that his days of having to leave the house after saying good night to her were coming to an end.

He shuddered when he thought of how he'd almost changed his mind again. Everything had been going so well. Shaylynn enjoyed the concert more than Neil imagined she would. In fact, she enjoyed it just a little too much. Her reaction to James Ingram had Neil wondering if he should shave his head bald. Not only had the concert gone better than expected, but upon leaving the auditorium, Neil noticed a missed call, and inside the quiet of his truck, he and Shaylynn listened together while CJ tearfully told them that Theresa had opened her eyes. Shaylynn broke into such praise that Neil wondered if she was going to open the door, jump out, and take a lap around the crowded parking lot. To his relief, she didn't.

After all the highs, things took a downward turn at Canoe. After weeks of not hearing Shaylynn mention Emmett's name, she'd worked it into their dinner conversation. Neil had to excuse himself from the table and go into the men's room to regroup. And even after regrouping and rejoining her at the dinner table, doubts continued to plague him. If she rejected his proposal on any day, it would result in major dejection, but if she rejected him after referencing Emmett, it would be emasculating.

When he took her back to her house and

they were saying their good-byes, Neil knew he couldn't let the moment pass. This was their first night out together since Shaylynn had become Li'l Miss's caregiver. They had been fortunate enough to get his mother to keep both children tonight, but Neil was getting tired of enjoying dates with Shaylynn only to have to say good night at the end of it all. He wanted to hear Chase call him something more than Dr. Taylor. He wanted more than hugs and kisses from Shaylynn. He longed for all the . . . *fun* that she'd assured him would satisfy his next wife. And if he was going to be able to get any of the things that he wanted out of this relationship, he was going to have to lay all his insecurities on the line, go for it, and hope to God that she said yes. And he did. And *she* did.

*Thank you, Jesus!* That was the umpteenth time the praise had played in his head. Neil removed his hat and coat, and sat on the sofa. He felt so happy that he could hardly contain himself. He felt *too* happy, and that thought alone made him put the brakes on his overactive heart. If being shot down at the happiest moment could possibly be a genetic trait, he was headed for trouble. His father, his brother . . . both of them had died in the middle of their happiness.

Leaning his head against the back of the sofa, Neil laughed out loud. He wasn't going to allow the devil to steal his joy. He didn't believe in bad luck or family curses. Just because things happened to others in his family certainly didn't mean it was going to happen to him. He had brothers who were happily married and had great families. Death and disaster hadn't run them over, and he wasn't going to allow it to overtake him either. There was no way he'd die before experiencing a life with Shaylynn. He'd kill death before he'd allow death to kill him. The irony of him killing death made Neil laugh even harder, but the humor dried when he heard his doorbell.

Who would be coming to his door at this hour? He sat in the quiet darkness for a moment, wondering if he was hearing things. A second chime verified the obvious, and Neil stood and flicked the wall switch that brought light to his living room. There was no sense in pretending no one was home. Whoever was at his door had surely heard him laughing just moments earlier. Neil looked at the watch on his wrist. The little hand was grazing the edge of the one, and the big hand was on the ten. It was probably CJ. It had to be. He was the one person who knew Neil's Valentine's Day plans, and he probably couldn't wait to hear the results. Neil couldn't wait to tell him either. No doubt, CJ had told Theresa by now, and more likely than not, she was the one who had shooed her husband to Neil's house to get the juicy details.

A smile twisted his lips, and he reached for the doorknob. But just to be sure, he asked, "Yes? Who is it?"

"Sean Thomas."

An automatic reaction snatched Neil's hand away from the door. *Sean Thomas?* One moment, the name sounded vaguely familiar, and the next, it was very familiar. This was the mystery man who had called his office twice over the past two months, but had never left a detailed message with Neil's assistant. Neil knew the name, but he didn't know the man. Whoever this Sean Thomas character was, Neil wasn't about to let him in his house at ten minutes before one in the morning.

"Who are you looking for?" Maybe the gentleman was confused. Neil Taylor was a pretty common name. Maybe it was a different Neil Taylor he was searching for. Maybe —

"Neil Taylor, son of Ernest and Eloise Taylor," the voice replied.

Okay . . . maybe not. Only a few people in

Atlanta knew his mother by her given name of Eloise, and even fewer knew his father by anything other than Pop, so this person must have known Neil from his youthful days in Mississippi. But he still wasn't ready to identify himself as the person being sought. He wasn't exactly fearful, but he could hear his heart pounding in his own ears. Neil had no idea who Sean Thomas was or what he wanted, but for some reason, his gut feeling told him that this wasn't good news.

"What business do you have with Mr. Taylor?"

For a few seconds, it was quiet on the other side of the door. Then . . . "Well, I've been told that you . . . I mean, he . . . made a mistake a few years ago. So I guess you can say that my business with him is that . . . I'm his *oops* baby."

Neil felt his legs become weak. It was worse than he thought. Maybe dying before the wedding wasn't such a bad idea after all.

Shaylynn lay in bed with her left arm raised and her fingers spread out like the feathers of a peacock. She had never had anything so uniquely beautiful in all her life, and every time the overhead light struck the diamond, it made her think of all the fairytales that she used to read about and watch on television as a child. There was always something that sparkled in those fairy tales. A shoe, a crown, a star, a ring . . . *something.* She felt like one of them — a damsel in distress — who had just been saved by her prince. She thought the day would never come that Neil would ask her to be his bride, but now, in this moment, the wait was all worth it. Of course! Why hadn't she thought of it before? Valentine's Day was the perfect time, and while she was fretting for no reason, Neil had probably had it earmarked all the while. Shaylynn was glad that she'd been patient and had never pressured him . . . even though she wanted to . . . *badly.*

She turned over in the bed but kept her hand out where she could see it. Now it lay on the pillow beside her face. Even from this angle the light ricocheted off of it. Sooner or later, if she planned to get any sleep at all, she'd need to turn off her overhead light, but for now sleep was the last thing on her mind. The only sad part about all of her wonderful news was that she had no family to share it with. No parents, no siblings; not even a best friend. The closest friend she had was in the hospital recovering, and having not seen Theresa since she opened her eyes, Shaylynn wasn't sure how coherent she was. But as soon as she thought it was a sensible time to go by the hospital for a visit, she would find out. Since CJ and Neil were so close, Shaylynn figured Neil would probably beat her to the punch, but still, she was going to share her joy with Theresa.

"I wonder if she'll be my matron of honor?" Shaylynn thought aloud. Was it acceptable for the first lady of the church to stand with her as she got married? Shaylynn didn't know what the rule book said, if there was a rule book, but she definitely was going to ask. If Theresa didn't do it, she didn't know who else would. She had no other women in her life who she considered her friends.

"I'll ask Mr. Jessup to escort me down the aisle." Before Shaylynn knew it, she was sitting up in her bed with her laptop powered and planning out her entire wedding. She knew it seemed foolish and premature, but right now, becoming Mrs. Neil Taylor was all that she could think about.

"Matron of honor, Theresa Loather. Bridal escort, Lucas Jessup. Gown color, ivory." She said the words as she typed them, and tradition had everything yet nothing to do with her decision not to wear white.

Tradition said that as a woman who had been married previously, she didn't qualify for a white gown, but had Shaylynn wanted to wear white, she knew she could without raising too many eyebrows. When it came to weddings, most customs that were once mandatory were optional in the twenty-first century. Tradition also said that bridal veils represented innocence and purity. Shaylynn had worn a veil for her first marriage, and she was nowhere near a virgin. She and Emmett were practically living together, and everybody knew it, but nobody challenged her decision to march down the aisle with a covered face.

This time around, Shaylynn wanted to do it right on every level. She and Neil had kept their courtship pure, and she didn't know about him, but for her, it hadn't been easy. There were days when she had to pray against the enemies of her own hands. She loved touching Neil, and knowing that he relished her touches only encouraged her urges. Reaching for him felt like second nature. Withdrawing her hand from him didn't come so easily. She had been celibate ever since Emmett died, and up until she began dating Neil, staying celibate hadn't been a struggle. She now understood the message she'd heard CJ preach when she first began attending KBCC as a habitual visitor almost two years ago. In it, he'd said that there was no testimony in a person's purity if they weren't being tempted. In a case like that, CJ said that person was celibate by default. Only when the opportunity was there, yet the person *chose* to live according to God's will did they have a testimony of victory.

When Shaylynn married Emmett, everything about the wedding was exaggerated. There was a horse-drawn carriage waiting outside to take the bride and groom to their honeymoon suite after the reception, and six limos to transport the thirty-two attendants wherever they needed to go. Shaylynn didn't know a single one of her sixteen attendants. They were all friends and relatives of the Ford family who, if they were anything like Emmett's parents, couldn't have cared less about the girl for whom they were serving as attendants.

But as much as Emmett's parents hated her, they'd picked up the full tab for the celebration. Shaylynn didn't have to pay a dime, which was good, because she didn't have much more than a dime to pay. Had Shaylynn had to foot the bill, she and Emmett would have been getting married at the courthouse, and Melinda Ford would have never tolerated such foolishness. Emmett's mother wanted to make sure that her son's wedding would be the talk of the town. And it was.

The train of Shaylynn's wedding gown was so long and had so many pearls and flowers sewn into it that it made moving uncomfortable. The entire time that she was walking up the aisle, she felt like the details of her train were getting caught in the fibers of the carpet. By the time she made it to the front of the cathedral where they were wed, Shaylynn felt like she had been punished. She was left to wonder if her mother-in-law had purposefully made the walk a chore. And the church was so full of flowers that Shaylynn felt like she was getting married in the middle of somebody's funeral. Now that she thought about it all, she wondered if that was a deliberate move on her in-laws' part too. Emmett's parents probably saw their son's wedding as their funeral. If Shaylynn hadn't loved him so much, in hindsight she would see their stupidity as comical.

This time, she was marrying a man whose family was going to welcome her with open arms. She was about to become a part of a real, loving kinship, and never before in her life — her biological family included — had she ever had that. Taking in the full picture, Shaylynn couldn't be more grateful that heaven had sent her a godly man who never pushed the envelope that left her with a decision of should she or shouldn't she. As attracted as she knew he was to her, Neil had never tried to cross the line; not even that one time when he thought she was opening the door for him to. She was thankful, and she wanted to be the best wife she could be.

To get it all started, Shaylynn desired an elegant, traditional wedding; one that reflected both their personalities. Neil was a country boy, a man who appreciated the best, but enjoyed the simple things in life. And even though Shaylynn had never lived on a farm or worked in the fields gathering crop, she, too, enjoyed simple elegance. For the wedding, neither of them needed the fabulous in order to be happy. They didn't have anything to prove to anyone, so a nice, traditional setting would be perfect. Shaylynn's ivory dress would reflect that. It was the proper color to wear for her status in life, but what made the color most appealing was that it also happened to fall into that category of colors that were Neil's favorites.

What better day to be dressed in one of his favorite colors from head to toe? There was no more perfect occasion to have Neil look at her and desire her than on the day of their wedding. Wrapping herself in his pet colors would only make unwrapping her more sensuous. And their wedding day would mark the first day that doing so would have God's stamp of approval. Shaylynn got chills at the thought of it.

"Okay . . . let's think about decorations." She hit the tab key to advance to the next section. It was definitely time to move on from her previous thoughts.

Shaylynn typed the word "flowers" at the top of the new section, and then stopped and laughed at herself. She had been engaged for less than two hours, and she was already planning the details of a day for which they hadn't even set a date. Intuition told her that their engagement wouldn't be a long one. All the key cards were already in place. His family had accepted her, Chase had accepted Neil, and she had a rock on her finger that made it all official. She could hardly wait to tell her son. She could hardly wait to tell the world. There was absolutely nothing that could stand in their way now.

Or so she thought. . . .

# TWENTY-FIVE

Neil felt like he was on some hidden video show, and at any moment someone was going to jump out and yell, "Psych!" But he knew that wasn't going to happen. As he looked across his living room, staring at the twenty-one-year-old who sat on his sofa, Neil knew without a doubt that Sean was his son.

There wasn't a strong resemblance between the two men. Sean looked more like his mother than he did Neil, but there were enough similarities to erase any doubts. Sean shared his height, his skin complexion, and the shape of his lips. He also wore his watch on his right wrist, which meant that like Neil, Sean, too, was a lefty. But the larger convincing came by way of dialogue. For more than an hour, Sean had been reminding Neil, in intricate details, of a life he thought he'd left behind with no trace. People, places, events; Sean knew them all.

In spite of the pending consequences, a small part of Neil found a reason to rejoice. Sean was living, breathing proof that Neil wasn't sterile, as he'd feared for so long. But the larger part of him found reason to fear.

Sean represented a life that no one other than his brother, Dwayne, knew Neil had. Dwayne had taken the secret of Neil's offense to his grave, and since it was a bygone that Neil never thought would reappear, he'd never bothered to tell anyone else. Not his mother, not his siblings, not his friends, and not Shaylynn. And the last person in that lineup was the one who concerned him the most. Ella would be disappointed, his siblings would be shocked, and his friends would be taken aback, but eventually all of them would get used to the idea, see Neil's sin as a thing of his past, and move on. Neil was sure of that. But Shaylynn had plainly and openly said that she wouldn't have even given him the time of day if he'd had any children. When she found out about Sean, he could lose her forever.

Sean must have detected Neil's dilemma in his demeanor, because the next words he said were, "I didn't come here to start trouble for you."

Neil wanted to yell, "Too late!" But he

remained silent and allowed Sean to explain himself.

"I just wanted to see you in the flesh. See where I came from. See the man who was never a part of my life."

Neil's head was throbbing from the overload. He was finding words hard to come by, but he couldn't let Sean think he'd abandoned him. In his past, he'd had the capability of being a lot of things, but a deadbeat dad wasn't one of them. Even though he and Abigail were never an official couple, he would have never knowingly left her to raise his child on her own. That went against everything he believed in. "I didn't know," Neil told Sean. "I really need you to believe that."

Sean fiddled with the car keys that he held in his hand. "I believe you. Mama used to tell me that my daddy was dead. I believed her 'til I graduated high school."

"What happened to make you start doubting her then?"

"That's when she found out she had stage three breast cancer. When she started getting real sick, she started telling me a lot of stuff because she thought she was gonna die at any time, and I guess she wanted to clear her conscience."

Neil sat forward in his seat. Abigail, or

Gail, as everyone called her back then, was one of the nicest people he'd ever known. Granted, he didn't spend enough time around her to say he knew her well, but she was nice to him. She was pretty too, and she had a smile that had the tendency to brighten even his gloomiest of days, and his gloomy days were plentiful at that time. Neil met Gail during the second of three separations from Audrey before they finally just called it quits and got a divorce. Dwayne decided to take a vacation in Detroit, and as much as he loved music, Neil wasn't letting his big brother go to Motown without him. It was there that he met Gail. She was a waitress at a twenty-four-hour café that he went to one night when he just couldn't sleep. Neil found her attractive on many levels, but he didn't love her. In truth, his heart, at the time, was still with Audrey. But Gail treated him like Audrey wouldn't, and before his two-week visitation was over, the two of them had consummated a relationship that never should have been.

"Are you telling me that your mother is dead?"

Sean shook his head. "No, she's not dead. She had a mastectomy and went through a few rounds of chemo. Lost all her hair at one time, but it eventually grew back. She's in remission now. She's a three-year breast cancer survivor."

Neil sighed. "Thank God." He didn't know why the news relieved him. If she were dead, it would better his chances with Shaylynn. At least then he could assure her that "the other woman" wouldn't at all be a part of his life. But Neil was glad she'd survived the cancer scare. Gail deserved a second chance just like anyone else. And her being alive meant their son hadn't been without both parents for the past three years. At least one of them was doing their job, and from the looks of things, Gail had done it well. Sean was clean-cut, well-mannered, and articulate. Neil cleared his throat. "When she finally told you the truth about me, what all did she say?"

"That you were married and that what happened between the two of you was a one-time mistake."

That wasn't exactly the truth. They'd spent two nights together, but Neil wasn't going to tell Sean that. "I was separated from my wife at the time."

"That's what she told me. She said you were just visiting Detroit when she met you, and she really wasn't sure in what part of Mississippi you lived. She mentioned that you were honest and upfront with her about where your heart was, and when you left you told her that you were going back home to try to work things out with your wife, so she didn't even bother to try to find you even after discovering she was pregnant."

Neil felt bad and thankful at the same time. Gail shouldn't have had to keep Sean a secret, but he was glad that even in his sin, God had mercy on him. Neil realized that as little as he'd known about Abigail Thomas, she could easily have been the type of woman who would have tracked him down and caused him grief for the first eighteen years of Sean's life. "Did she tell you anything else about me?"

"Uh-huh. She told me that I got my ability to sing from you."

Neil's eyebrows arched. "You sing?"

When Sean smiled, Neil saw Abigail. "Yeah. I do a'ight, but I hear that you da man."

Neil would have blushed deeper if the memories hadn't flooded back. It was at church where Gail had heard him sing. Dwayne had run into a pastor when he went to get a haircut at a barbershop in the area, and once finding out that Dwayne was one half of a singing duo, the preacher had invited the brothers to come to his small storefront church and share their ministry.

Neil had invited Gail, and he remembered her being taken with his voice. That was on a Friday night. Saturday night, they slept together for the first time. What a disgrace. Singing for God one night, and sinning for the devil the next.

Neil shook off the shame and addressed Sean's compliment. "Thanks. I wouldn't describe myself as *da man,* but I do sing. Just about everybody in my family sings."

"So tell me more about your family," Sean said. "I think you know just about everything about me and mine. What about you?"

For the next several minutes, Neil told Sean about the family he'd never met. The young man looked blown away when he found out how many uncles and aunts he had by way of his father, and Neil detected a spark of sadness on Sean's face when he heard the stories of his grandfather's death and the passing of his Uncle Dwayne. Neil also told Sean about his job and his church affiliation.

"So, you're not married anymore?" he asked after Neil finished speaking.

"No. It didn't work out. I've been divorced for fifteen years now. I'm engaged to be married though."

"Oh, yeah? When's the wedding?"

"No date has been set yet. I just proposed

a few hours ago."

"Oh . . . For real?"

"Yeah."

"Congratulations. My mama's about to get married too."

Neil smiled. "That's great." He was feeling more comfortable now. "So how long are you gonna be in town?"

"Just 'til the weekend. I gotta get back to the D. I can't miss too many classes, plus I gotta be back at work on Monday."

"Classes?"

"Yeah. I'm an education major at Wayne State. Got one more year to go."

Neil beamed without even knowing it. "I majored in education when I attended college too."

"Yeah. I hear you got your doctorate. I'm not sure I'm gonna take it that far. We'll see."

Neil wanted to press Sean to reach for the highest possible goal, but he didn't feel that it was his place. They'd just met. He hadn't earned the right to push the boy to do anything yet. He watched as Sean stood and stretched his body.

"Thanks for opening the door and letting me in. I know I took you way off guard, but I had been searching for you for two years. When I was finally sure that I had found the right Neil Taylor, I said I'd better go ahead and do this before I lost my nerve. Like I said, I just wanted to meet you. I don't want nothing from you, so you don't have to worry about that." He reached his hands in his pockets and pulled the insides out so that Neil could see them. "I didn't bring no cameras or recording devices, so you don't have to worry about that, either. I won't be uploading stuff on Facebook or calling your family or your fiancée and telling your people that I'm your long-lost son. We can keep on living like we been living. It's good to meet you, and I'm glad to find out that you're a cool brother and all, but you don't owe me anything."

Neil stood too, and he couldn't believe his own words. "So this is it? You're just gonna appear out of nowhere, spend a couple of hours with me, and then just disappear again?"

Sean shrugged his shoulders. "Isn't that what you want? You didn't know anything about me, which means nobody else does either. I was a mistake you had with another woman while you were married."

"I never called you a mistake, and I wish you wouldn't either."

"Well, I wasn't exactly planned," Sean said. "I'm just trying to help you out of something you didn't mean to get into anyway. You just sat here a few minutes ago and told me that you're a lead deacon in your church, and the pastor is your best friend. People look up to you. You can't possibly want them to know about me. That would just be crazy."

Sean was right, and Neil knew it, but now that he had been made aware of his son, he couldn't pretend he didn't exist. That would be even crazier. Even at the risk of losing it all, he couldn't let Sean just walk away.

# TWENTY-SIX

"How's Theresa?"

CJ was glad to hear Neil's voice on the other end of the line. He was just about to call him when he looked at the screen on his ringing cell phone and saw Neil's name. "She's good, bruh. She's sleeping right now, and the temperatures aren't so frigid today, so I thought I'd come outside and get a little fresh air. She ate her breakfast and lunch really well today and guess what?"

"What?"

"She's talking."

"She's talking?" Neil's tone said he was surprised. "Is she saying words or entire sentences?"

CJ could barely contain himself. "God is so good, bruh. The first thing that came out of her mouth was, 'Where's my baby?' She wasn't talking to me. I wasn't even in the room. She just blurted it out to Dr. Hale when he stopped by to check on her. I was in the bathroom at the time, and I almost hurt myself zipping up when that man knocked on the door and told me that my wife was talking."

"Oh, man, that's awesome! I guess that means she's about ready to see Li'l Miss."

"Keola."

"What?"

"We named Li'l Miss this morning. Her name is Keola. K-e-o-l-a." He pronounced it again, slower this time, and enunciating each syllable. "Keh-o-la."

"Okay. That's . . . different. What happened to naming her after you, or giving her a strong, timeless name?"

CJ chuckled and headed toward his car to get out of the wind. That was the same question he'd asked when Theresa immediately latched on to the name when it was presented to her. "Dr. Hale suggested that name," he revealed. "Actually, both you and Dr. Hale named her."

"Me?"

CJ was thoroughly confusing Neil, and it was intentional. He knew that would throw his friend for a loop. "Technically, yes. It's a Hawaiian name, and in Hawaii, Keola means *breath, life, health, and well-being*. Dr. Hale casually mentioned that as we were getting Resa moved out of ICU and into her regular room. We were talking about her finally getting the chance to meet her own baby, and when Dr. Hale found out that we still hadn't given Li'l Miss a name, that's when he said it. And Resa jumped right on it."

"So you told her about the song?"

"Didn't have to. She said she could hear you singing it. She doesn't remember anything between trying to push out the baby and when Dr. Hale was disconnecting her from the machines, but she says she could hear you singing. And to prove it, she hummed the tune. The only words she could remember were 'Breathe, Jesus,' but she had the tune committed to memory." CJ leaned his head back against the headrest in his car. "That song brought her out, bruh. I'll never be able to repay you for letting God use you like that."

"We can call it all even if you can tell me how to get out of the mess I'm in right now. I wish God would give me a song that would bring myself out."

Neil's words reminded CJ of the monumental move his friend had planned to make last night, and the strain in his voice led CJ to draw his own conclusion. "Shay turned you down?"

"No. She accepted."

CJ gasped. "So you're engaged?"

"For the moment, yes."

CJ didn't know what to make of Neil's demeanor. He expected him to be swinging from pillar to post with excitement. "Why don't you sound happy? You're not having second thoughts, are you?"

"I'm pulling into DeKalb Medical's parking lot right now," Neil told him. "Are you still outside?"

"I'm parked in the lot right outside the emergency room entrance doors. I'm sitting inside my car."

"Okay, give me a minute to find you. We'll talk more when I get there."

CJ ended the call and shook his head. He didn't know what he was going to do with Neil. If that boy told him that he was getting cold feet already, CJ didn't know what he was going to say or do. He sat impatiently in his car with the engine running and the heat adjusted just right. CJ was glad that Theresa was sleeping, because this conversation with Neil could take a while. CJ had some things that he needed to talk to Neil about anyway, but he'd let his friend go first. A tap at his passenger side window meant Neil had found him quicker than he'd expected. CJ unlocked the doors.

"I thought you said it wasn't cold out

there," Neil said as he climbed in. "Man, it's freezing."

"It's not as cold as it has been," CJ pointed out.

"If you say so."

CJ waited for Neil to say more, but he sat in silence, staring out the front window. CJ looked at him. "Well, I want to congratulate you, but you're not giving me much to work with here. You were so keyed up about your Valentine's Day proposal, and you said she accepted." CJ reached over and pulled down the sun visor in front of Neil and flipped up the mirror cover so that he could see himself. "This doesn't look like the portrait of a happily engaged man."

Neil closed the mirror and pushed the sun visor back into place. "I found out something, and I'm trying to figure out how to tell Shay."

If this was what CJ thought it was, he was prepared to lay into Neil without showing a drop of mercy. "Why are you trying to sabotage yourself, Neil?"

"What?" Neil turned to face him. "I'm not trying to sabotage anything."

"That's what it looks like to me. You got the girl. She's agreed to marry you, and you're still not satisfied. You're determined to dredge up the past, and I'm telling you right now that if you do that, it's gonna backfire. You're going to lose her if you do this, Neil."

Neil removed his sunglasses and scowled at CJ. "How do you know about this?"

"I have my resources. And first of all, let me make it clear that I'm ticked off that you would be that sneaky and would actually take something that you had no right to *touch,* let alone take. And secondly, for me to find out about it any other way than directly from you makes me even angrier."

"Man, what do you think I came here for?" Neil spat. "I just found out about Sean myself. And you're the first person I'm telling, so I didn't think you'd find out any other way. He told me that he hadn't told anyone and wasn't going to tell anyone. I know I had no authorization to touch or take, but I did, and I can't change that. I usually think you give good, sound advice, but for you to tell me that I shouldn't tell Shay about my son is just wrong. Even if it ruins everything, I have to tell her. Sean's not going away."

CJ blinked hard. "Wait a minute. What?"

Neil stared back. "What?"

"What are you talking about?" CJ felt like they were on two separate planets right now. "You have a son? What son? Who's Sean?"

Neil looked just as lost. "I found out last night I have a son. Isn't that what you were talking about?"

"No, but forget what I was talking about for now. What do you mean you have a baby? Where is he? When did this happen?" There had to be a story behind the story. CJ couldn't imagine Neil sneaking around behind Shaylynn's back.

"I didn't say I had a baby. I said I have a son. He's twenty-one years old, and he's the product of an affair that I had when Audrey and I were separated. He'd been searching for me for two years, and he found me early this morning, just a few hours after Shaylynn accepted my marriage proposal. I never saw it coming."

CJ sat quietly while Neil unburdened himself. He'd known Neil a long time; even at the time all of this had taken place. They weren't as close then though. CJ and Neil hadn't become best friends until after Dwayne passed away. CJ knew that he couldn't possibly take Dwayne's place, but he had definitely filled a slot that Dwayne left vacant.

"I'm a dead man," Neil said as a conclusion to his story. "This is a no-win situation. I can't deny my son, even though he's given me the permission to. I couldn't live with myself if I did that. But knowing that Shaylynn is going to break off the engagement is killing me too. I'm a dead man."

"No, you're not." CJ searched for words to make Neil feel better, but they temporarily escaped him.

"You're right. I'm not dead. Dead men only get buried six feet under. I'm gonna be so far down under that I'm going to be able to see Australia."

"Listen, bruh. All of this happened light years before you ever met Shaylynn. Do you really think she'll hold this against you?"

"You don't understand, CJ. Shaylynn has always been guarded. She has a good life already. She's got a home, a job that she loves, money in the bank from Emmett's life insurance policy that she doesn't even have to touch, a son who adores her . . . everything. She doesn't need me, and she certainly doesn't need my baggage. Sean represents two things: I now have a child, and she's already made it clear that my not having any kids was a big plus for her; and secondly, he means that I have the capability of being unfaithful in a marriage."

"Neil, everybody has the capability for infidelity."

"But I acted on it, and as hard as it was for me to win Shaylynn's trust . . ." He shook his head. "Man, this is gonna blow me out of the water. I'll be back to square one where she'll be comparing me to her perfect Emmett, and I'm gonna be out the door. I can't let that happen; I just don't know what to do to stop it." A soft gasp released from Neil's mouth as soon as he finished the sentence.

CJ saw the light bulb when it popped on in Neil's head, and he knew he had to intercept fast. "You're not showing her that paper, so don't even think about it."

Neil's face snapped toward him. "What?"

"When I was talking about you touching and taking stuff earlier, *that's* what I was talking about." CJ looked into Neil's shocked eyes. "You do know that I have surveillance equipment in my home, right?" The frozen astonishment on Neil's face said he didn't. "I have hidden cameras in certain rooms of my house, and my office is one of them. I saw the footage Monday when I dropped by the house to pick up some fresh clothing."

The revelation clearly embarrassed Neil. He wiped his hands over his face and slumped back in his chair. A lengthy silence lapsed before he finally said, "I'm sorry, man. At the time I was desperate. I wasn't thinking straight. I knew it was wrong; I just needed something . . . *anything* that would show her that Emmett wasn't perfect after all." He sighed. "I'm sorry."

"So you didn't show it to her at all, right?"

"No. I wanted to, but I couldn't figure out how to do it without breaking her heart. I didn't want to hurt Shay; I just wanted to kill Emmett for good. And when I saw those notes, I knew I'd struck gold. But at the end of the day, I couldn't do it, and eventually, I found out that I didn't even need it. But now, here I am again."

"And you still don't need it."

"I don't know about that, CJ."

"Well, I do. Just listen to yourself, Neil. You're sitting here wanting to break back into my office again and steal some of my private papers so that you can prove to Shaylynn what a great guy you are. So you want to do something rotten to show that you're good. What kind of sense does that make? And why do you want to do all of this foolishness? To pull the covers off of a dead man's past. Yeah. Okay. So Emmett was so crooked that he couldn't even walk a straight line. He dealt in drugs, theft, money laundering, prostitution . . . all that. But you know what, Neil? You think Emmett's sins were worse, and by showing them to Shay, it'll make your sin look better. But in

God's eyes, there are no degrees of sin. What Emmett did was in his past. All the markings on that paper you saw represented the old him. That man died a Christian. God had forgiven him for all those horrible transgressions, and you have no right to bring them back up to tarnish his former wife's memories for your own gain.

"And at the end of the day, bringing that up ain't gonna make you look no better, because at least when Emmett carried out all of his sins, he was doing the work of his father. He was a member of the devil's team, wearing the devil's uniform, and his life reflected that. Emmett was a sinner who did what sinners do. He sinned. You, on the other hand, were saved. Twenty-one years ago, you already knew God, but you allowed the devil to take control of your mind and your body. In essence, you were a member of Jesus' team who somehow found himself pinch hitting for the devil. You were the one who was out of place, not Emmett. And now you want to use that against him? How dare you!"

Neil closed his eyes and blew out a lungful of air. CJ saw the pain on his face. He had taken his tongue-lashing like a man, but CJ could tell that his harsh words had cut deeply. Seeing Neil's pain softened CJ.

Maybe he'd come off too strong. This was the man who, three days ago, had sung life back into Theresa. He owed Neil more sympathy than he had given.

"Listen, man; I'm sorry."

"No," Neil whispered. "Don't be sorry. I needed to hear that." He opened his eyes but kept them set straight ahead. "The truth hurts, but it's still the truth, and if there's one thing you got from your daddy, it's the ability to tell it like it is; like it or not. And I must have wanted to hear it straight, or I wouldn't have come to you, right?" He glanced at CJ, and then looked out the front window again. "The world needs more men of God like you and fewer ear-ticklers who say only the stuff that you want to hear. I mean, when it comes right down to it, I can be a pretty funny dude, so I don't need nobody to tickle me. I can make my own self giggle."

CJ leaned back and laughed. Only Neil would think to say something like that.

# TWENTY-SEVEN

Shaylynn peeked through her blinds and smiled. She had been anticipating this moment for the past five hours. When Neil called at one o'clock and filled her in on Theresa's upgraded condition, and then told her that he wanted to come and pick up her and the kids so that they could all go by the hospital for a visit, and then go out to dinner, Shaylynn was ecstatic. Not just because she knew how much joy it was going to bring Theresa to see and hold Keola, but it would be her first time out with Neil since they got engaged.

As soon as Shaylynn heard Neil's shoes hit her top step, she opened the door. "Hi, Solomon." She wrapped her arms around his neck and kissed him before stepping aside so that he could enter.

"Hey, suga. You look beautiful, as usual."

Shaylynn knew he'd like the animal-print top that she'd paired with blue jeans and brown boots. "Thank you." She pointed to the sofa. "Sit down for a second. I'll run up and get the children. Chase calls himself babysitting today."

Neil caught her hand. "Wait, Shay. Can we talk for a minute?"

Shaylynn wasn't sure how she should read the look on his face. He didn't look sad, but he didn't look happy either. Butterflies fluttered in her stomach as she allowed him to pull her to the space on the couch beside him. "What is it? Is something wrong?"

Neil stalled. At first he seemed to struggle with looking her in the eyes. He sandwiched Shaylynn's left hand between both of his and slid his hands back and forth like he was trying to warm her hand with his. When he finally looked up at her, he searched her eyes for a short while, and then brought his lips to hers and kissed her deeply. Neil had never kissed her like that with Chase so close by. Shaylynn had never allowed it in the past, but today she did.

When he pulled away, he said, "I had to get that in now, because after I say what I say, you might not ever let me do it again."

"What?" Now Shaylynn's butterflies felt more like wasps, and they were stinging the insides of her stomach. "You're scaring me," she said. "What's happened?"

Neil squeezed her hand. "I found out something last night after I left here and went home. I had a visitor come by my house, someone I had never met before, but someone I really want to get to know better and make a permanent part of my life. And I really need you to understand this and —"

Shaylynn snatched her hand from his. She couldn't believe her ears. "What? You left my house last night after proposing to me, and then you meet some strange woman and, just like that, you want to be with her?" Shaylynn grabbed her engagement ring and began angrily twisting it from her finger.

"No, suga, wait." Neil placed his hands on top of hers, stopping her feverish motions. "That's not what I'm saying. I love you, and I want to spend the rest of my life with you. This isn't about another woman. That's not what I'm saying at all. Please listen to me, okay?"

Shaylynn stopped her struggle, but her insides were still trembling from her earlier fury. "What are you saying then?" She didn't know what she was bracing herself to hear, but she braced anyway.

"My visitor was a young man. He knew of me, but I didn't know anything about him." Neil tightened his grip on her hands again, like he thought his next words might make her get up and run for the hills. "I found out last night that I have a son."

Shaylynn gasped. "What?"

"His name is Sean Thomas, and he's twenty-one years old."

"Twenty-one?" This wasn't making mathematical sense to Shaylynn. She tried to keep her voice at a lowered level so that the conversation wouldn't be heard upstairs. "How could you have a twenty-one-year-old son and not know it? You were married then. How could Audrey hide a baby from you? That doesn't make sense."

Neil brought her hand up to his lips and kissed it, then he looked her square in the eyes. Shaylynn had never seen him look at her quite like that before. Was that fear that she saw in his eyes? She braced herself again.

"He's not Audrey's child. I . . . I, uh . . . We were separated at the time, and I was on vacation with Dwayne, and I, uh . . ."

"You had an affair?" Shaylynn could barely say the words, but when she did, Neil seemed overcome with relief that he wasn't the one who had to say them.

"Yes," he whispered. Then in a slightly stronger voice, he added, "There was no excuse for it. It was a really bad time in my life, and instead of talking to a counselor or God or even Audrey, I confided in another woman, and it led to a two-night fling that produced a child, who I never knew about until the wee hours of this morning when he came knocking at my door."

"Are you sure he's your child?" Shaylynn had watched enough episodes of Maury Povich's talk show back in the day to know that men shouldn't just take a woman's word, especially if they weren't in a bona fide relationship. Plus there was that question as to whether Neil had the ability to have children.

He must have read her thoughts. "Yes. He's mine. The ten-year drought I had with Audrey was apparently not because of me. Sean suggested a paternity test, and we're going to take one just to erase all doubts, but I already know he's mine."

"Wow." Shaylynn could imagine how having a son appear out of the blue might knock the wind out of a man. "Well, if you're that sure, then I can understand you wanting a relationship with him. I mean, what kind of man would you be if you didn't?"

Neil looked up at her and opened his mouth to speak, but closed it back up. When he opened it again, he said, "What are you feeling, suga? Are you upset with me about this?"

Shaylynn couldn't lie. "I don't know what I'm feeling right now. I'm not angry, but this is a lot to digest without some time."

Nodding, Neil said, "I know. It was a lot for me too. Sean said he wasn't asking me to be his father. He gave me the option to walk away, no strings attached. All he wanted was to meet me after finding out that I wasn't dead, as his mother had told him for years. He searched for me against her will. She and I are kind of in the same situation right now. Abigail . . . Gail — that's her name — is about to get married and didn't want this to cause any trouble for her and her fiancé, and I had just proposed to a woman who had told me that she was glad I had no children, so I was scared about the repercussions too."

Shaylynn wasn't going to admit it out loud, but the fact that Neil's former fling was in love and about to get married served as a source of comfort. "Well, I'm glad you told me. Your honesty means a lot."

Neil looked at her like he needed more. "But what does this mean for us? I need to hear you say it. Whatever *it* is, I need to hear it. You didn't want a man with children. I love you with all my heart, and I can't remember the last time I wanted anything more than I want to make you my wife and Chase my son. There aren't a whole lot of things that I wouldn't give up for you, Shay, but Sean is one of them. I don't know him, and I can't even say that I love him yet in the way a father should, but he's still my son, and I want a chance to get back some of the time that we lost. I can't deny him. Not even for you. So tell me now, suga. Is this the end of us?"

From the expression on his face, Shaylynn knew that her answer meant everything to him, and that meant everything to her. She looked down at her hands in his, and then back at his face. "You know what I did when I went to Milwaukee for the New Year? I went to Emmett's gravesite. I hadn't done that since I buried him. I'd never been able to do it until this year, and I realized that I was able to do it because of you."

"What do you mean?"

"I mean, it was hard enough to watch him be lowered into the ground over eight years ago. Seeing him covered in dirt, grass, and a slab of concrete, like a forgotten piece of history, was just too much for me to consider. But when I was there this year, I asked Luke and Alice Jessup to go with me to the cemetery. I needed to say good-bye to Emmett, to tell him that I was moving on with my life. I needed to feel like he was okay with me living and loving again." She whisked a tear from her cheek. "I'm not crazy. I know the real Emmett wasn't there, but being there made me feel close to him, and I felt like he could hear me, even from heaven. When I left, I felt like he'd given me his blessings; like he approved not only of me moving on, but with me moving on with you.

"I meant it when I said I wouldn't have begun a relationship with you if you'd had kids. But I believe God intended for the two of us to be together, and that's probably why He waited until I was already head over heels before we came to the knowledge of your son. I wouldn't have let you in if I'd known about this at the start, but what I know now is that it would have been my loss. I can't bail out now, Solomon. I love you too much."

"Oh, suga." Neil leaned in and kissed her. "I love you too. I was so afraid of how you'd handle this. You just don't know the lengths I was prepared to go to just to convince you stay. You make me so crazy. I sometimes feel like I'm fighting a losing battle here, and it aggravates me. You're still so attached to Emmett, and I can't lie. That frustrates the heck out of me. For over a year now, I've been trying so hard to beat him at something . . . *anything.* I've tried to be perfect just like him, but every time I turn around, I fall short."

Shaylynn was shocked by what she heard. "Perfect? Solomon, Emmett wasn't perfect. He was just the perfect man for me. He had a lot of flaws. Most of them, he never told me about until he gave his life to Christ, but he wasn't even close to being without faults. Overall, by anybody's standards, you are a much better man." Shaylynn saw the surprise on Neil's face. "He was in *politics,* Solomon. There's no such thing as a perfect politician. Some are worse than others, and for a while, Emmett was among the worst of the worse. I'm not going to go into details, because I don't want to rehash the hurt in my own heart, but I didn't even know my own capacity to forgive until he shared all the things with me that he had once been involved in.

"My love for and continued attachment to Emmett has nothing to do with perfection. I loved him and will always love him in spite of his imperfections. I think I was able to forgive him because I didn't have to find out about his indiscretions from the headlines of the morning paper. Once he got saved, God wouldn't allow him to keep them hidden from me. Many of the things he'd done were ongoing inside of our marriage, so forgiving him wasn't easy, but I did it, and the last year of our marriage was the best ever. I remember the good times, not because that's all there were, but because those are the times I *choose* to remember. There were plenty enough of them to make me have no regrets. And if I can look past the admitted sins of a man who committed them while we were married, I can look over those of a man who made mistakes long before he ever even met me."

When Neil leaned in to kiss her again, this time he went deeper. Shaylynn kissed him back and could taste his love, his appreciation, and his relief.

"Let's get married tomorrow," he whispered upon releasing her.

Shaylynn licked her lips and slid back a little to put some much-needed space between them. "We can't. I sat up last night and planned out the entire wedding. It's not something that can be put together in a day. My matron of honor is still in the hospital."

Neil straightened his posture and laughed. "Fine. Just promise me that you'll look at what you want and factor in the minimum time needed to do it. Then let's set the wedding for the day after that."

"Promise." Shaylynn smiled. He just didn't know. If Neil thought for one minute that he was any more ready to make this thing legal than she was, he had another thought coming. "So all this time you thought you had to compete against Emmett? That's sweet."

Neil shook his head. "No, it's not. It's been nerve-wracking." Shaylynn retracted a little when he reached forward and pulled at the chain around her neck until the jewelry that dangled at the end of it was unearthed. "Do you know how hard it is to compete against a man whose ring you still wear and whose flowers still sit on your mantel? I can't help but wonder what the heck this man did to make you want to hold on to this kind of stuff."

Shaylynn closed her right hand around the ring that now hung in front of her blouse. Out of respect for Neil, she'd only worn the necklace when she had on clothing that could conceal it. She had no idea he knew it was there, but she prayed he wouldn't give her an ultimatum, because just like he wasn't willing to deny Sean for her, she wasn't willing to deny Emmett for him. "He loved me, Solomon. Flaws and all, Emmett loved me."

"I love you more."

That brought another smile to Shaylynn's face. Neil was still competing and probably without even realizing it. She tucked the necklace back into her blouse, and then touched his cheek. "Wait here for a minute." She could feel Neil's eyes watching her as she disappeared behind the door of her bedroom. It only took her a moment to find what she was looking for, and when she did, she returned to the living room, holding the box she'd retrieved. "I've never shown this to anyone," she told him as she lifted the top and began pulling out memorabilia.

"This," she said as she showed him a black napkin, "was on our table that night that I met you at Sambuca for your forty-fifth birthday. We weren't even dating then, but I knew you had the potential to be somebody special, so I kept it just in case." She handed it to Neil and wished she could freeze-frame his expression. Next she pulled out a stack of greeting cards, all bound together by a red ribbon. "These are all the cards you've given me throughout our relationship." He took the pile from her hand, and she reached inside again and pulled out silver paper that was neatly folded into a perfect square. "This was the wrapping that was on the very first gift you bought for me. Do you remember what it was?"

Neil grinned and nodded. "The sterling silver holder that I bought for your new Shay Décor business cards."

"Very good," Shaylynn said before pulling out a small envelope. "These are the stubs from the first circus show, the first concert, and the first movie that we attended together."

"Wow," Neil said as he looked through the envelope's contents.

"Do you want me to go on?" Shaylynn raised her eyebrows. She was really being sarcastic, so she was surprised when Neil had an answer.

"I want a song."

Shaylynn was temporarily puzzled. "You're the singer, Solomon, not me. If either of us needs to be singing to the other, I think —"

"No. That's not what I meant. You have a song with him. That Brian McKnight song that had you crying when that guy performed it that night we were at Sambuca."

" 'Still in Love,' " she recalled.

"Yeah, that one." Neil grimaced. "Well, call me egotistical, but I want one too. I want you to have a song that makes you think of me. I want a song that we can call ours."

Shaylynn shook her head and giggled at the same time. She didn't know why she'd never picked up on how threatened Neil was by Emmett's memory. Though his insecurity was unnecessary, in hindsight she could see that it wasn't unfounded. She pointed at herself, and then at Neil. "*We* have had a song for a long time."

"We have?"

"I made the song 'Still in Love' mine and Emmett's because of something he said. Our song — mine and yours — became our song because of *who you are*. And it doesn't make me want to cry, it makes me want to dance."

"Dance? Really?" Neil's face brightened with approval. "What is it?"

Shaylynn got up and walked to her DVD/CD player and popped in a CD that she pulled from the rack beside the television. Then she used the remote to turn on the TV and changed the setting to play the music. She watched the sequence of Neil's facial expressions while he tried to pick up on the song's identity as he listened to the introductory music, but no recognition ever came on his face. This probably wasn't music that a man like Neil would gravitate toward, but because of its lyrics, Shaylynn loved it, and once he heard them, she hoped he would see the significance and love it too.

"Is that Beyoncé?" Neil asked when the highly recognizable voice resonated from the speakers.

Shaylynn nodded and pressed her index finger against her lips. "Shhh. Listen to the words." One minute into the song, Shaylynn began bobbing her head to the music, and then, taking it a step further, she began Latin dancer-like movements, swaying and dancing around the living room. The four-inch heels of her boots clicked rhythmically against the wooden flooring. She closed her eyes and joined Beyoncé in singing, "Everywhere I'm looking now, I'm surrounded by your embrace. Baby, I can see your halo, you know you're my saving grace . . ." She wasn't the greatest singer, but she could hold a tune nicely.

Shaylynn opened her eyes when the music suddenly got louder, and she saw Neil using the remote to increase the volume. In the next moment, he was standing in the floor, dancing to the music with her. They'd never danced together other than a slow drag to jazz music. Shaylynn giggled at Neil's moves. He wouldn't stand a chance on *Dancing with the Stars,* but if nothing else, he displayed great rhythm as they moved to the pulse of "Halo's" catchy tempo. At around the three-minute mark, they saw a flash of light and looked up to spot Chase standing at the top of the staircase, holding a camera and laughing at their efforts as he snapped away. Knowing they were being captured on film just fueled their arms, hips, and feet, and when the song ended, Neil picked up the remote and ordered a repeat.

Shaylynn wrapped her arms around his waist and held on tight, placing her nose in his chest and breathed in deeply, filling her nostrils and lungs with the familiar, enchanting scent that had become synonymous with the man she called Solomon. In her wildest dreams, she had never fathomed having a stepson who was only eleven years younger than she, but if that was the side order that came with *this* main course, she'd take it.

# EPILOGUE

At two o'clock on a Sunday morning, Neil was staring up at the ceiling of the room that had served as his honeymoon suite. If the walls of this space could talk, they would say things that came with a rating that even his mother wasn't old enough to hear.

Careful not to awaken his sleeping June bride, Neil eased out of the bed, slipped on his boxer shorts, and stepped out onto the balcony of the cabin that would be his and Shaylynn's love nest for the next seven days. The week-long Eastern Caribbean cruise had been a gift from CJ and Theresa. The moon reflected beautifully over the waters beneath them, and the boat sailed with such smoothness that it barely felt like it was moving at all. Neil and Shaylynn hadn't been out of their room since they permanently checked in after the standard safety drill that the cruise ship ordered.

By sunup, they would be docked in the

Bahamas, and before the week was out, they would have also visited the US Virgin Islands, Puerto Rico, and Grand Turk. For the sake of having honeymoon photos for their wedding memory book, maybe they'd come up for air long enough to tour the lands. *Maybe.* Neil had never visited any of those islands before, but he couldn't imagine that any of them had sites any more beautiful than the one he was able to explore just a few hours ago. The island he called Shay had more excursions and adventure than he ever expected. After this week was over, he predicted that he'd need a vacation to recuperate from his vacation.

Neil closed his eyes and allowed the refreshing ocean breeze to brush over his face while he relived the series of events that brought them there. Sixteen hours ago, he was standing at the altar, reciting vows to a woman he knew he'd love forever. Shortly before that, he was in the groom's chamber, allowing CJ to help him fix his tie, while Sean stood off to the side giving him dumb marital advice like, "Make sure you've packed *everything* you need for the honeymoon, old man. There are already too many years between me and Chase, but if you mess around and make another one, by the time he's born, both of y'all gonna be in diapers at the same time." Even Neil had to laugh at that one. The fact that his family and friends had welcomed Sean meant the world to him, because the early evidence already proved that Neil and his son were going to have a close-knit relationship.

The ceremony had been almost as lovely as the bride who had dreamed it all into reality. The church, decorated in an elegant combination of black and ivory, looked like something straight out of a Grimm fairytale. The church was packed with well-wishers, but the wedding party was intimate, consisting only of Neil's younger sister, Val as the bridesmaid, Theresa as the matron of honor, and Val's daughter, Keisha, as the flower girl. With Neil stood Sean as his grooms-man, CJ as his best man, and Chase as the ring bearer. He couldn't have been more honored when Reverend B.T. Tides agreed to officiate. Luke Jessup was elated when Shaylynn asked him to escort her down the aisle, and Neil didn't know who did the most crying between Alice Jessup and Ella Mae. He'd come close to tears himself as he watched Shaylynn draw closer and closer to him during her march. Her laced and layered ivory gown was fit for a princess . . . right up to the tiara she wore on her head. She resembled a black Cinderella, and Neil would have bet any amount of money that it was the look she was going for. Shaylynn was such the hopeless romantic.

The elegant wedding was followed by a reception that was just as noble. Aside from the couple's first dance, Neil's favorite moment was watching Deacon Burgess take his turn with Shaylynn. Without his cane or walker to assist, it was more like watching two people rocking from side to side to the beat of the music, but the old man had gotten his wish, and Neil was glad that he was able to deliver. Homer had danced with Teena too. Neil was the only one privy to the answer to which dance had made his friend happier.

As the groom, Neil had stayed out of the planning of the day. He'd told Shaylynn to do it just like she wanted it done, but if he'd had a say, Neil couldn't think of a thing he would have changed. The designer and decorator in Shaylynn had found a way to make the wedding stylish and modern without ever making it lose its flair of tradition. Everything about it was polished, and the photos were going to make for a sensational scrapbook, but Neil just wanted it all to end so that he could get to the honeymoon phase.

However, just as he thought he was on the

brink of ecstasy, his wonderful best man, along with Shaylynn's wonderful matron of honor, got up to make the long-awaited announcement that the limo was outside, waiting to whisk away the happy couple. But as they made the proclamation, they also held up two tickets and unveiled the surprise that instead of taking them to the undisclosed hotel that Neil had booked, the limo was escorting them directly to the airport to catch a flight to Port Canaveral, where they would be going on a seven-day, six-night cruise to the Eastern Caribbean. The reception hall erupted in thunderous cheers like Neil and Shaylynn had won the grand prize on some Hollywood game show, but Neil just wanted to take the cords from CJ and Theresa's microphones and wrap them as tightly around their necks as they could stand. Thanks to them, he would have to wait the length of a flight and the time it would take them to get through the long, wrapping lines of cruise port security before he would be able to fully enjoy his wife.

It was a true test of patience, but Shaylynn Brooke Taylor had been worth the wait. My, oh my, had she been worth the wait! Neil had been so nervous in the weeks leading to the nuptials that he couldn't get his thoughts together to write a song for her. His plan was to serenade Shaylynn as she was being escorted down the aisle, but he just couldn't get it together. But around five o'clock yesterday afternoon, all kinds of original lyrics began playing through Neil's head as he and Shaylynn were anointing the bathroom of their cabin with the oils of their love.

It all started when Neil decided that it wasn't very gentlemanly to let his new bride shower alone. He had prepared himself, for Shaylynn's sake, to start things slow and let the passion increase in increments, but Neil soon found out that his preparation was in vain. Shaylynn's eager reception of him made Neil wonder which of them had been most waiting for that moment. Soap and water had never been so sensual, and their bodies were barely dry when they took their show to the bed for the grand finale. Their room was rocking, and it had nothing to do with the fact that they were in a cabin that was floating on water. Just the memories of it all stirred a new desire inside of Neil.

"Solomon?"

*Perfect timing.* Neil opened the balcony door and stepped back inside the room that was only lit by a dim lamp in the corner farthest from their bed. Shaylynn was sitting up in the bed wearing nothing but the braids in her hair that cascaded past her shoulders and rested on her chest. This must have been what Adam felt like when he first saw Eve.

"Hey, suga." Neil's stomach growled, and it had little to do with his having not eaten since they boarded the ship. He stepped out of his boxers and slipped under the covers with her. When he lay back against the pillows, Shaylynn did the same, resting her head on his chest.

"Sing to me."

Neil had heard her softly spoken order and was glad that he was prepared to deliver. Admittedly, singing wasn't what he was in the mood to do right now, but he wasn't going to turn her down. Neil knew that once he granted her wish, she would grant his.

If there was one thing that he had learned over the course of the last few months, it was that great things happen . . . when Solomon sings.

# READERS' DISCUSSION QUESTIONS

1. Neil unquestionably loved Shaylynn, and he knew she loved him. Why then was he more than a little insecure in their relationship? Were you able to empathize with him under the circumstances, or did you see it as totally unfounded?

2. After falling for Neil, Shaylynn removed from her finger the wedding ring that her late husband, Emmett Ford, had given her, but she didn't totally abandon it. Do you think she was wrong? Why or why not?

3. Pastor Charles Loather Jr. (CJ), and his wife, Theresa, have a very solid marriage that seems to remain in the honeymoon stage even six years later. Their strong affections almost make them "cross the line" in the pastor's study at church. What are your thoughts on that? The Bible says "marriage is honorable in all," but are

there some places (such as church property) where these type affections are off-limits and deemed sinful?

4. In a day and age when an overwhelming amount of pastor's wives serve in the capacity of co-pastor, there is no mention that Theresa wore any type of ministerial title at all. What are your thoughts on that? Should the wife of a senior pastor automatically serve in a ministerial leadership position?

5. As a way to protect her eight-year-old son from possible heartbreak, Shaylynn set certain rules in place so that Chase wouldn't get too attached to Neil, just in case things didn't work out between them. Was she overly protective or do you believe that more single mothers should use this type of caution when they begin dating?

6. Neil kept two distinct secrets in this story. One that involved Shaylynn, and one that involved his old friend, Deacon Burgess. Do you recall what they were? Was Neil wrong for keeping them? If you were in his shoes, would you have told?

7. What were your overall thoughts about

Deacon Homer Burgess? Did you sympathize/empathize with him after he made his confession? And what did you think about the decisions he made regarding his will?

8. What about the information Neil uncovered regarding Emmett? Do you think he ultimately handled it the right way? What do you believe would have been the outcome if he had carried out his initial plans?

9. Neil felt that God had led him to the information about Emmett because the discovery of it was made very shortly after he'd inwardly hoped for something that could give him an upper hand. Do you believe that the devil can hear the prayers of the righteous and produce counterfeit "blessings" in hopes that God's people will fall prey?

10. CJ became somewhat emotionally unraveled when tragedy struck his household, and he made the comment that as a pastor, he should have been able to handle it better. What are your thoughts? Should a church leader be able to remain strong during times of great trials? Does God expect more of them during trying times

than He does of others?

11. A medical phenomenon took place in this story, and it was performed by way of a song. Do you believe God still works miracles in this day and age? Have you ever witnessed a miracle orchestrated by God?

12. When Sean Thomas's name was first mentioned in this story, did you have any idea who he might be? What did you think once his identity was revealed? Did you think he was right in his decision to seek closure, or should he have honored his mother's wishes and let bygones be bygones?

13. When the sins of Neil's past were uncovered, it was also made clear that no one other than his deceased brother, Dwayne, was privy to it. In light of the fact that the offense came back to haunt Neil, was it something that he should have openly confessed to others on a volunteer basis? Was he in sin by not doing so?

14. In this story, Chase is shown giving his life to Christ and becoming born again. Do you believe that children as young as

he (eight) have reached the age of accountability wherein they are capable of understanding what it means to be saved?

15. What were your thoughts on some of the other secondary and/or minor characters, i.e. Ella Mae Taylor, Margaret Dasher, Reverend B.T. Tides, attorneys William & Melinda Ford, Lucas & Alice Jessup, Teena Marie Mitchell, Audrey Taylor, etc.?

16. On some level, both Shaylynn and Neil struggled with their vows of celibacy and keeping their physical/ sexual attraction for each other at bay, especially when they were alone in each other's presence. Do mature Christians have this problem, or do their struggles represent spiritual weakness on their part?

17. The question of having children remained unanswered. If you were a forty-six-year-old male (or were married to a forty-six-year-old male) would you want children? Do you believe Neil will?

# ABOUT THE AUTHOR

**Kendra Norman-Bellamy** is an award-winning, national bestselling author, as well as the founder of **KNB Publications, LLC.** Beginning her literary career in 2002 as a self-published writer, Kendra has risen, by the grace of God, to become one of the most respected names in Christian fiction and inspirational nonfiction.

She and her titles have been featured in several national print publications, including *Essence,* and *Upscale* magazines, and she has been spotlighted on BET's Christian television broadcast, *Lift Every Voice.* Kendra is an active member of the national organization, American Christian Fiction Writers (*www.ACFW.com*), where she served as a past Georgia Area Coordinator, and she is the current national president of M-PACT Writers (*www.M-PACTWriters .com*), an accountability focus group for African American wordsmiths. She is a founding member of Anointed Authors On Tour (www.AnointedAuthorsOnTour.com).

With a calling that reaches beyond books, Kendra is also a licensed minister and motivational speaker. She serves as the visionary of The I.S.L.A.N.D. Movement (*www.IShallNotDie.org*), a motivational and empowerment ministry, and the founder of Cruisin' For Christ (*www.CruisinForChrist .org*), an at-sea ministry that celebrates Christian writing, gospel music, and other artistries that glorify God. Most recently, she launched Gospel Girls Group, a Facebook-inspired women's empowerment and Bible Study fellowship.

A native of West Palm Beach, Florida and a graduate of Valdosta Technical College, Kendra is an active member of Iota Phi Lambda Sorority, Inc. She resides in metropolitan Atlanta, Georgia with her family.

*When Solomon Sings* is Kendra's nineteenth published work.

Feel free to visit Kendra's official Web home at:
*www.KendraNormanBellamy.com*

Or connect with her via social networking on Facebook at:
*www.facebook.com/KendraNormanbellamy.*